After The End

Book one of Nova Nocte Series

Written and Published by Melissa A. Gibbo

Cover art designed by Melissa A. Gibbo

Copyright 2014 Melissa A. Gibbo

Acknowledgements

I would like to thank my wife, Brenna, for all she's contributed. She has read this story dozens of times, provided me with honest feedback, sacrificed date nights, been awakened by my typing at 4AM, and still loved me enough to allow me to pursue this dream.
I am also thankful to my family and close friends for their patience and indulgence. This story absorbed my attentions for long durations and I'm lucky to have such support. Thank you to my parents, John and Pattie, and sister, Heather, for always being there to reassure me when doubt got the upper hand.
Thanks to the Orange County Library System, particularly Jen and Marianne, for the wealth of assistance they offered. Whether it was a stack of books on writing or kind words of encouragement, it made all the difference.
Thank you to my friends and readers who have put up with my jabbering over the characters and conflict.
Thanks to the numerous teachers who made reading enjoyable and to the many authors whose stories give my life joy and inspiration.

And finally, I would like to dedicate this book to the memory of my Grandma Mary, Grandpa Bob, and Papa Bill. They didn't get to see me publish, but they never doubted that I could do anything I put my mind to. I'm thankful for the time I had with them and the time I continue to have with my family, who believe in me every day.

CHAPTER 1 DECEMBER YEAR 2

I kneel in the darkness, shifting the ashes of our encampment. The vampire watches me intently as I pull destroyed knives and cookware from the rubble, the remnants of our former life. He probably came with me as much to keep Daemon and I apart as to aid me in my recon. The groans of the risen Dead amplified; my burnt journal sits in the skeleton of my cabin.

"Are you ready, Squirrel? It would seem we will not be alone much longer."

I leaf through the pages and find some of the writing intact. The shuffling of a zombie grows nearer. Cal prods some of the ruins, kicking dirt and bullet casings with a frown. Placing the journal in my bag, I stand and rub my cracking hands together.

"Yeah, I think I've got enough info to make the decision."

It was barely a whisper, but I know the Undead Roman can hear me. He nods and moves towards me as the fleshie stumbles into view. Florida weather has not been kind to it. We watch the lone corpse as it lumbers on a broken leg and opens its sagging jaw; three broken teeth inhabit the rotting cavity. The stench of decay and mildew reach me and set my stomach tumbling. It's amazing how much longer they last after the humid summer ends; a little cool dry air and these fleshies get a reprieve from Mother Nature.

My companion steps to put it down and I wave him off. Closing the distance to the creature, I draw my broadsword up on the diagonal, slicing the head from chin to temple. Black blood arcs through the air; the cadaver crumbles to the ground in a moist thump. Wiping my blade on its torn Disney tee, I turn to leave with Cal. The others will be expecting us.

CHAPTER 2
SEPTEMBER/OCTOBER YEAR 1

    I'm rewriting my journal of life since the zombie outbreak, using the one I lost in the fire, my memory, and the calendar I carry. I met Chase and Sunny around a month after this Cadaver Fest started.
    The air had begun to grow dry and cool as I hunted for food in the wild lands beyond the Orlando city limits. I trekked further from the Dead-laced asphalt river in search of game; even with the light breezes, direct sunlight kept my tee glued to me with sweat. The books I'd taken from the library shifted in my backpack and dug into my sore muscles; the camp shovel and broadsword each swung awkwardly from my hips. I froze at the muffled sound of footsteps.
    Peering through the brush, I pulled taut the high-tech slingshot — I wasn't that good with my bow yet. I saw a couple talking: the guy looked like Rob Lowe with a Jim Carrey grin and terrible sunburn, the lady was the girl next door type with a fitted tee and old jeans. After a moment's hesitation, I decided to approach.

Lowering my weapon, I made sure to tread loudly so I wouldn't startle the pair. I felt my heart jumping with my empty stomach; I hadn't dealt with any other survivors in three weeks according to my calendar. That last interaction hadn't ended well...

An ax and makeshift spear both pointed at me.

"Hi. I don't mean any harm; I just thought maybe we could help each other for a bit."

They exchanged glances while I waited and tried to maintain my mellow. The weapons lowered and the guy stepped forward with an outstretched hand.

"Um, hi. I'm Chase and this is my wife Sunny. Sorry about the standoff; crazy days lately. So what do you go by?"

At that moment, I spotted a squirrel digging nearby. On reflex, I shot it and announced "Squirrel". Apparently, they thought I was either touched-in-the-head or that my folks were hippies, cause they just went with it and I've been known as Squirrel ever since.

"Nice to meet you, Squirrel." Sunny forced a smile. "Why don't we all have a seat and eat something. It couldn't hurt to have another human being around."

Sunny brushed her auburn hair out of her face while Chase began pulling cans of vegetables from a bag. I cleaned my quarry and we ate a sparse meal. The moans from the swarms of fleshies on the defunct roadway drifted to us sporadically. I tried to push down the memories that rose with each guttural utterance. I decided to leave behind that life and become the survivor known as Squirrel.

Over the next few weeks, the three of us became a team and we learned more about one another. Each time talk brought us to our losses, we would focus instead on practicing hunting or fighting the zombies who'd driven us together.

When this chaos started: Chase worked in a call center, Sunny was a server at Denny's, and I was a minimum wager in one of the local theme parks. Not exactly the kind of jobs that prepare you for an end of the world scenario, but somehow here we are.

Fortunately, Chase remembered some of his ROTC training from when he was younger and loves camping. Sunny has a far more common sense and foresight than the two of us. Her worries and problem solving keeps us alert and in the game. Her teal eyes seem to soak in the world; except when she wields the "Mom Glare". It's that look that your mom can throw your way to make you stop dead in your tracks no matter what you're doing.

Sometimes, I tease her that if she'd just use that look on the Dead, they'd wander off all downtrodden and remorseful. It usually earns me the look, but they say good morale and a sense of humor are important to keeping sane under bad conditions. Between our combined knowledge, skills, and gear we have become the underdogs that endure. Even Vegas wouldn't have bet on us.

Our first day together, we all agreed on a basic survival plan: avoid staying in major cities, guns, and hospitals, as these were the things we felt the masses flocked to.

The theory is large crowds of people are likely to draw large crowds of zombies. Not to mention the high odds that someone in their midst is already infected and their friends are simply unwilling to do the necessary deed. Military installations also draw the multitudes, first the living and then the Dead. Before the news reports stopped, the bases and hospitals were High-def cesspools with crystal clear death rattles echoing through the barricaded homes.

Every so often, another person or group would cross our path. A guy we call Bubba comes and goes frequently. He says he likes to travel through the wreckage of civilization in search of adventure but I always thought adventure was code for a special someone. Some people joined us, a few moved on, and others died. Life went on.

It was a month or two after the dearly departed refused to stay gone, before the Vampires decided to announce themselves. I suppose the human overpopulation problem stopped being an issue a lot quicker than they'd originally expected.

Learning about the existence of a race of people who drink human blood and live for centuries, is much easier to accept once you've already come to terms with things like your deceased babysitter chasing you down the street with her intestines snagging debris on the ground. Either that or it will thrust you over the precipice of sanity and you'll be dead within the week. It happens.

CHAPTER 3 NOVEMBER YEAR 1

Cal's arrival was epic in its simplicity. That fall night, as the three of us huddled around the squat fire planning our guard shifts, he merely: walked between Chase and me, sat next to the pit, dropped a sack, and declared,

"I brought you all some dinner."

Just like that.

Five silent minutes later, I thanked him as we began cooking our surprise meal. Sunny asked our guest his name as Chase started to watch the darkness for others.

Over the crackling meat, we heard the reply "My name is Caelinus Gaius. I am a vampire and would like to propose an opportunity for your group."

I would like to say we acted swiftly and calmly at these words; but we didn't. All at once, three things happened while Cal looked on: Chase fumbled with his axe (cutting his hand in the process), Sunny toppled off the rock asking "seriously?", and I just turned the smoldering raccoon over and stirred the can of corn.

The vampire held out his hand to help Sunny to her feet and spoke.

"Yes, it is true."

Chase was at his feet — his axe in hand with a drizzle of scarlet along the handle — eyes riveted on his wife. She saw the blood and grabbed the bandages, cautiously keeping from turning her back to our guest. The vampire's eyes glimmered with a red tinge as he watched the rivulet of blood. I checked around the darkness for signs of more surprises and set out our bowls.

I was spooning the concoction into dishes when I opted to break the stillness.

"Well this is awkward. Thanks for the dinner. Um, just to clarify is this a last meal to fatten us up?"

Cal laughed at me, his eyes returning to a light hazel color; my heart slowed back to a moderate pace.

"It is meant more as an olive branch to begin our conversation peacefully".

Satisfied with his response, I thought with my mouth.

"Okeydokey. Guess we'd already be drained if you wanted to kill us and you probably wouldn't have wasted time getting us chow, so I'm willing to listen."

I threw the couple a glance, they nodded their consent, and Cal took the floor.

"I would like to offer my skills and strength to you in exchange for your providing me with sustenance. I assure you, my considerable age allows me to need very little blood to survive. I am also vastly experienced in combat and maintaining an encampment. I can protect you from the rising Dead at night if you cause me no harm during the day. We can aid one another's continued existence; all that is needed between us is trust."

I don't think I even asked for any proof he was actually an immortal super-being before I blurted out "sure". It appeared possible given all the other strange occurrences. Sunny and Chase leaned their heads together to discuss their concerns.

By the time the supper had cooled enough to eat, we'd all agreed to a tentative bargain. Our conditions were basic: Cal would follow our rules about guns and crowds, we would still stand watches with him, and he would drink only what he needed. The pact was born and we became four.

***

Cal was already a middle-aged Roman under-commander in the legion when he was brought across. He maintains his blond-gray hair short and posture stern even centuries after the empire's fall. The Roman Undead has nearly two millennia of wisdom and experience in camping, combat, and leadership as well as pristine control of his powers. He used a display of his quickness to catch us some extra dinner and seal the deal.

It didn't take long to realize that teaming up with a guy wanting to drink some of my blood is a much better deal than facing down the monsters that are trying to consume all of my body parts. Plus, I really like to sleep.

Knowing that a vampire will keep me safe has allowed me to wake up feeling refreshed and well-rested. You can really underestimate how much a good night's sleep does for the mind and body until you have gone a few weeks without one. And you definitely need to keep your mind sharp when setting traps or scavenging for supplies. The Dead never sleep or think, they just keep coming like bill collectors.

CHAPTER 4 DECEMBER THROUGH APRIL YEAR 1

As other survivors wandered into our little patch of hell, our community began to grow. At last I realized the world was not going to change anytime soon; we chose to build a more permanent fort, rather than a transient camp. The first month, we erected an outer wall of sharpened steel — Cal insisted on getting us metal panels from town instead of using wooden posts. We celebrated a meager Christmas holiday by sharing a dinner of scraps and working together all evening on the protective barrier. New Year's was spent replacing the chain-link fence section with a sliding steel gate. It was rough work with the dry air sapping the moisture from our hands; I began wearing gloves when Cal started staring at my bleeding knuckles too intently.

Only in late afternoon and nightfall, would we dare to hammer; it allowed the vampire to dispatch any roaming Dead that found our makeshift home as we tapped with our cloth-wrapped mallets. With each strike, I thought of helping my family with building projects at the house; I held the pain and tears inside as I redoubled my determination to survive this lost world.

Over the next month and a half, we gained three more people, a cabin, a large fire pit, a weapons chest, a storage shed, and two outhouses. Our two species began to rebuild a (mostly) living society.

By March, our community had grown to include two more families and Caelinus assured the group children wouldn't be part of the donation schedule. The familiar Orlando humidity rejoined us and I found it odd to be so comforted by the sensation of drowning on dry land on a warm spring day. We started to plow a field outside the North wall. All winter, Cal raided the nearby city for provisions as we hunted, trapped, fished, and trained for our new way of life; now we would provide for ourselves and arrange for the next winter's survival.

We lost a few that first winter to stupid stuff like the flu, but the training Cal provided kept most of the zombie-based deaths to a minimum. I can still see the look of exhaustion and peace in Jorge's eyes when he accepted his fate; he knew what the fleshie's bite meant and gave me a weak smile while placing the Colt .45 to his forehead. The smoke from his pyre stung my eyes even as the stink of his burnt remains brought me to my knees retching.

The next month was a blur of mundane tasks, interspersed with fleeing or combat.

During the days, I'd help with the food or training with my sword and bow. Evenings were spent sitting around the glowing trench of embers and discussing our plans or techniques for survival. Entering this life of a fresh new night, or Nova Nocte (Cal's term, but I especially like it), has given me a new awareness for all the time I wasted drifting through existence — content to be moderately average, if slightly dorkish.

    We only ever talked about our existence since the Nova Nocte began; it's as though we had no lives before that day. No one asks about pasts, just the current day and maybe the day beyond. People that tend to dwell on the past find themselves surrounded only by shadows and misery. David was like that.

    When I looked in David's eyes, I knew he wasn't going to make it; he was dead when he found us, his body just hadn't caught up with the truth yet. It's because of him that I stopped learning names of the new people until I'm sure that they're determined to survive.

    David was only fifteen; ordinary except for the jewels he wore as eyes. The sadness in his face failed to hide the glimmer of optimism for the world to right itself; his hopes encased him as a shroud.

    That morning the sky had pallor in place of its usual hue. The shade covered the open field we cultivate and air was oppressively still. I stood alert when I noticed the silence, where the chirping of wrens and buzzing of dragonflies should have been. The minuscule hairs on my body danced in anticipation of intruding danger.

David appeared to be in the spin cycle of his thoughts and unaware of the heaviness in the air. We trudged down the path to check our fishing lines. I maintained the quiet as we walked; my hand clutched my sword hilt while I surveyed the forest edge.

It was the scream that tore the stillness apart. It leapt above the trees and hung there for what felt like eons, until the blood pounded the nauseating sound from my ears. My partner sprinted towards the screeching without any hesitation. I drew my weapon and followed, arriving moments after him.

Too many; there were way too many Dead for us. Nearly a dozen of the fleshies were ripping and gnashing apart a small boy who'd been trying to poach our line. The child's shriek fell hushed, as we came into view. It was too late to save the kid; David had to know that. Still he charged in, swinging his axe at the lumbering corpses like Paul Bunyan in a junior varsity jacket.

The boy had already been devoured and dissected by the time the young teen reached the assailants. David seemed possessed by fury and grief, belligerently yelling at the zombies who couldn't understand him as he fought. It was as I called out to him to run – drawing the fleshies' attention away – that I saw David fall.

He slipped sideways on what must have been a piece of the kid; I was just close enough to hear the moist whoopee cushion sound before the thud. The freshman scrambled to get to his feet, and I saw the nearest zombie sink its pearly teeth into David's flailing arm. The zombie's mangled braces reflected sunlight between spurts of the teen's blood.

I fled back to camp and left David behind. He'd been dead the minute the world changed and seeing that bite made it official. His enraged shouts tapered off before I reached the gateway.

Chase was at the edge of the wall with some of the others when I barreled up the hill. They made a move to follow the trail, when I waved them off. Everyone understood and the congregation sought out the relative protection of our walls. Slingshots, bows, spears, and machetes materialized in each person's hands.

I hurriedly showed I was not infected. Grabbing a bow and quiver on my way to the lookout platform, I joined several other archers at the top. We spent the day — and nearly a hundred arrows — fending off a mob of fleshies. By late afternoon, the carcasses around our steel barrier were burned and all was calm again.

When Cal arose from wherever he retired during the days, he noticed the smoldering piles and extra guards on the tower. Looking around for a minute, he asked,

"What transpired today? Who hasn't returned?"

"Some Dead attacked a boy down by one of our lines. David and I got there too late. He went after them; I left when he got infected." I answered.

All eyes were downcast. The Roman breathed deeply before he spoke again.

"The lad's equipment?" he asked.

"There...there were over a dozen zombies near the water," I stammered out my explanation. "None of us wanted to venture past the field after they came up to the fort. Dav...he had his axe, knife, and not much else on him." I suddenly felt like I was ten and was busted by my Dad for not doing my chores.

Cal looked past me.

I hate when he looks through me like that; feels like the grim reaper is checking his appointment book.

"I will be back shortly. I'm going to check if there is anything to salvage of his belongings and clear out any other Dead nearby. Go through the boy's other possessions in case there is anything the community can use. Tomorrow is another day; we start anew right now."

~ 20 ~

With these muted words, the vampire flew over the wall and we returned to our normal duties. Sunny and a few of others began boiling water and cutting plants for dinner. A handful of bass fried in a pan as the heads went into the water for stew. The scent wafted over, driving away the stench of burnt zombie remains, as Chase and I changed the subject to methods of accurately aiming our blows with different blades.

The few parents in our bunch were getting their kids ready for bed; deflecting the questions about the day's events. The children were afraid of monsters in the darkness and no one would be able to tell them monsters weren't real. The littlest girl cried for David and asked when he would be back to eat us. I was thankful not to be that parent and went to gather the teen's stuff.

CHAPTER 5 EARLY MAY YEAR 1

Over the next few weeks, the camp fell back into a rhythm. More traps were set — as much for food as for protection — and we checked them daily. Our gardens were yielding carrots, tomatoes, and herbs; Sunny even found a small grove of oranges and guava a bit west of the fort. Most of us had become adept at fishing and hunting, supplementing our groceries with raids into the city. For a short time, we even had vitamins and power bars from a Walgreen's to keep our energy up.

A handful of other wanderers joined our camp. It didn't seem that we had any major stresses; it began to feel as though our lives had always been this way. And then it all came crashing down – literally.

The sounds of treetops cracking and a string of obscenity-laced gibberish interrupted the party for Ellen's seventh birthday. The stars were just coming out as the cloak of night faded to a deep violet. The fire was kept just large enough to light the festivities. Chase was carving up some of the assorted waterfowl for dinner while Sunny pilfered snatches of egret wing.

Our entire assemblage was on alert as the pale figure plummeted into an outhouse screaming "Son of a doxy fish-monkey bastard!"

Instantly, Cal was next to the gaping hole of filth, armed with his fangs and a Terminator glower. Out of the waste, a young man climbed; his leather jacket and jeans thoroughly plastered with rancid muck. The strange vampire grimaced, as he stood upright and looked at himself, arms out in disgust.

Finally, he noticed Caelinus was only an arm's reach away and the rest of the camp was staring at him. We all bore a weapon, except for Ellen who still had a present in her hands and a bejeweled princess tiara askew on her forehead. She blinked her azure eyes several times before dropping the gift and latching on to her mother; that particular Mom Glare could have stopped a bullet better than Superman.

I struggled not to giggle at the look of embarrassment on the poop-covered intruder looking at our birthday royalty as though he expected the girl to yell 'off with his head'.

The outsider put his hands in his pockets, sunk his head down and mumbled,

"Uh, hi everyone. Sorry about the landing, I'm still pretty new to this whole flying biz and an owl kind of startled me. I see you already have a vampire here so, um, cool. I guess he probably already has dibs. Nice crown princess, very sparkly. You guys enjoy your festivities. I'm just going to wander over to that river and tidy up."

Is this really happening or has the summer heat knocked me out and I'm in a weird dream?

I felt my hip for my sword and drew it. I noticed other hands being wiped on jeans to keep the weapons from slipping in the layer of sweat. The intruder was inching backwards now; we continued to stare at him like a sideshow attraction. Chase looked like a lumberjack with his axe held so resolute in front of his chest and Sunny was standing perkily next to him, grinning like a jack-o-lantern at the sudden entertainment; her spear was nonetheless steady in her stony grip.

He rambled more rapidly.

"If it's cool with the group, I'd like to come back later and maybe join you. I'll absolutely fix your crap-house, of course. My name is Daemon by the way. So, um…yeah. Nice to meet everyone and sorry about disrupting the fun time. See you soon." Daemon paused to glance around. "Unless of course I should run, in which case just let me know so I can get a head start and wash the goop off first."

I burst into laughter (along with a few others). Daemon resembles a 1980s rocker Lestat but clearly had the grace of Jack Black; his pale, toned flesh is offset by his long black locks and piercing green eyes. He stopped his advance-to-the-rear motion and smiled; Cal even smirked a bit himself.

Cal spoke first.

"It will be up to the humans here and you would have to follow the rules we live by, but I am agreeable to discussing the options with you. For now, I will lend you fresh clothing and walk with you to the stream and back."

Caelinus led the newcomer away through the large sliding gate, stopping only to sprint into his storage for an outfit. By their stances, they appeared a father and son strolling through a stadium entrance.

While the vamps were away, the celebration was concluded and an impromptu town meeting took place. Ellen and the other two children were sent to bed with their plates and their parents hurried back out to have their say in the matter set before our group.

As soon as the two couples returned, Chase began.

"Alright everyone, we have some things to consider. We'd have a lot to gain by having a second vampire in our community: raids into town, security at night, and even simple chores around camp would be more efficient with Daemon here. That is if we all agree to his presence. Conversely, it would also mean more blood would need to be donated."

Sunny piped in, nearly propelled in the air as though the thought stung her,

"We should consider that he may be less than helpful, too; I mean, if you take his stylish entrance into account. On the reverse, Cal seems unconcerned about the guy being a hazard and he's actually Roman Empire old, so he's probably accurate in gauging his own kind. I'm willing to trust his judgment on this one."

I waited for the next person to speak, only to find all eyes fixed on me. At some point, I must have become a de facto leader; it was both flattering and disconcerting.

I cleared my throat to stall for time.

"Well, I think we should consider that this Daemon guy is a stranger and we've got no idea how he'll react if we say he can't move in; this guy will still need blood to live and if Cal's off on a raid, we could end up dealing with him ourselves in a nasty way."

I popped and rubbed my knuckles to ease the pressure.

"That being said, fang boy appears to be honest enough. He easily could have waited a day or two until Cal left if he just wanted to drink his fill and bail on us."

Brows were furrowed as the rest of the group listened, the gears in their heads whirring. I blathered on, my nerves forcing the words out in an attempt to appear more confident than I felt.

"I think as long as Daemon agrees to do a couple of things, we should admit him to our little society."

I counted off my fingers.

"He'd have to: follow our pact, fix the outhouse he decimated, and - for the sake of our toilets - get Cal to teach him how to fly. Besides, we could all use some luck and this dude was lucky enough to somehow get out of that collision without impaling himself on any of that wood planking."

There were five or six smiles in the mass of bobbing heads. "Granted, he didn't walk away scot-free, but coated in crap is far from dusted."

Chase broke the silence after a few moments. I was so overjoyed to be out of the spotlight, I almost didn't hear him.

"Okay, we all know what repercussions we could be facing for any action we choose. We ought to vote for now to see where the majority stands before the vamps return. First, hands up if you opt to let Daemon become a resident."

It was a clear decision.

"Well, all but two hands. Let's hear your concerns against and any alternatives you might have, but at the moment, if he agrees to our terms, the new guy is in."

The woman stepped closer to the fire pit, letting the glow surround her. I recognized the other person as her husband; his stance as timid as hers was unyielding. He stroked his comb-over while his wife spoke for them.

"There are children here; not just our Lonnie and Amber, but also their Ellen." She gestured over her shoulder at the rest of the community as she talked, "We're not comfortable having another blood-drinking demon around these innocent children. To be truthful, I'm still not keen on having that other one here either."

Please don't let her keep talking. We need to keep the peace with Cal. We need the pact to survive.

"It would be healthier for us to have just our kind living here. We should just kill both of the fiends during the day and be done with it. I'll not raise my children with even more of these monsters; if you let this Daemon stay, my family will leave."

The husband gawked at her, shifting his weight from foot to foot, and surveyed the crowd as though looking for someone to save him from wedded bliss. She didn't notice.

Cal and Daemon strolled between Sunny and me, effectively dissolving the standoff. The younger Undead broke the silence,

"Sorry again about all the trouble I caused. Cal filled me in on how you guys do things and what this pact entails; I'm totally square with the rules you keep at this fort."

He raised his hand in a Boy Scout salute.

"I agree not to feed more than I need and never on anyone under 18. No shooting guns and we avoid staying in areas where the zombies tend to be severe."

Daemon dropped his right hand and fidgeted while his babbling persisted over the murmur of chuckles. The elder vampire silently raised an eyebrow and tracked the youth's gestures with an amused crease to his lips.

"Cal even said he'd help me develop my powers. I'm going to fix the john I broke, so you don't have to make like bears and poop in the woods. Also, I'm Kosher with staying in the woods during the day like he does, if it makes the group more comfy with my presence.

That's assuming I get the go ahead to call this home. If not, I would ask for a few days to get the hunger down and learn a bit from Cal; I only learned a little from my sire due to an extreme dusting by Molotov cocktails."

Cal gave his new protégé an approving look and stepped forward. The quiet laughter broke off. He took his time before speaking, each word felt deliberate, yet unrehearsed.

"I have spoken with Daemon during our brief jaunt to the stream and back. It is my opinion that he will make a fine addition to our populace. I acknowledge personally feeling a certain responsibility to guide the young man in the ways of our species, in light of his sire's untimely demise."

He halted and looked into everyone's eyes directly.

"Ultimately, the decision of his acceptance is endowed upon the majority; nonetheless, I have given Daemon my word to act as his mentor until he is adept with his new abilities. I am honor bound to remain with him, wherever that may be, until that level is realized. We will leave you all to discuss the matter further. Please inform us once a decision is reached; we will be disposing of the shattered latrine and it's... contents."

With a gentle hand upon the shoulder, Cal led the fledgling vampire out of the fire's illumination. The rest of our assembly remained in silent reflection, the glow flickering across our faces, thoughts flashing in our minds. The only sound was the stacking of fragmented wood and a bullfrog in the distance.

Sunny drew a slow, deep breath before taking the floor.

"It's time we tally up where we all stand. We know all of the pros and cons we are facing with either arrangement. We either trust in Cal's judgment and have two vampires in our society or we lose both and are human only. Hand's up if you choose to bring in Daemon."

There was no reason to feign counting; the only hands not raised were crossed in front of her chest. We all knew that our deal with

Caelinus greatly helped our odds of long-term survival. Chase announced quietly
"Only one against."
The defiant wife snatched her husband's arm from the air so swiftly she was a ninja. I glanced at Sunny and Chase; they held hands as they urged me to make the declaration.
"It's resolved then," I proclaimed, hoping it sounded official. "Daemon is the newest member of our community."
I locked eyes with our sole dissenter,
"It's your call whether your family stay and accept his presence or leave to fend for yourselves. I think I speak for everyone here when I say, we'd prefer for you to remain here; we have the numbers and defenses to protect one another. It's your right to do either, but no one would think any less of you if you chose to stick around."
I surveyed the crowd, I checked my watch, and excused myself to sit my turn as sentry.
From my perch on the tower in the center of the fort, I saw the bunch disband after a few minutes of chatter. Sunny and Chase immediately welcomed our new resident as I waved my greeting.
Guy looks pretty good without the layer of crap.
They were accompanied by some of the other denizens for a few moments, before the

community tapered off to rest for the coming day.

I continued to scan the tree line, intermittently checking inside the wall as well. An hour before dawn flooded our hamlet with its radiance they left.

The family wore their rucksacks. I could make out Lonnie's Sponge Bob backpack covered in stickers from my vantage point. The father took a spear from the weapons shed, in addition to the katana on his left hip. The other guard at the gate took off his canteen and gave it to Lonnie. He then knelt down to give something small to Amber.

I suppose it was a nice trinket because she gave him a hug, her stained sock monkey pressed against his shoulder. The kids shuffled sleepily out of this haven, Amber reminding me of Cindy Lou Who as she held her doll close. I always try to remember them that way…

***

The following day the tension in camp was palpable; every person was unsure how the night would pan out. Little things like misbuttoned shirts and burnt meals signaled how restless the sleep had been. It was already too late to change what happened the previous night; we could only hope for the best and mentally prepare for the worst. As I went into the cabin for a short rest, I secretly wished we would see that family again.

It was lunchtime when Sunny popped in to rouse me. Someone made a lunch of roasted fish, squirrels, frogs, and assorted plants. I launched into my supper with a vengeance. As I was chomping on a squirrel, Sunny looked over.

"Cannibal" she teased while Chase grinned wide enough for a Buick to drive through. The laughter made me sputter and my eyes water; the strain lessened, but continued.

Although we went about our regular rituals, the pressure was building as twilight approached. Eventually, the sun bowed out and the full moon took the stage. Time to see what havoc we had unleashed.

CHAPTER 6 MID MAY YEAR 1

Daemon arrived before Cal. He stood outside the gate. I chuckled slightly at seeing the powerful immortal humming and stretching – while clad in a Hawaiian shirt and camo pants — to pass the time. The nervous energy poured off the guy like Niagara Falls. He exercised for nearly twenty minutes before the elder Undead arrived.

Through the open gate, I heard Cal mock his protégé.

"You are aware that calisthenics are quite unnecessary once you have been turned, aren't you?"

The Roman smiled as Daemon laughed and they ambled through the open wall together. You could see relief wash over him. Cal waved me over to them as they entered. I brought two papers out of my pocket.

"Hi fellas, I have new calendars for you both." I stated as I held out the new donation schedules. "I rewrote these this afternoon. Daemon, some of the community is a little wary of how much blood you may need, so the first five names are all volunteers. After that, everybody has agreed to the regular rotation; but if any concerns arise, the five of us will have to be specifically your donors and everyone else will take turns as Cal's entrée. If that happens, they've agreed to cover some extra guard shifts in case we start to get too drained."

I think I forgot something again. Flicking away the love bugs, I pressed on.

"By the way, Sunny is on this list but Chase insists you feed on him instead if the Hunger is particularly strong. Also, I'll be assisting Caelinus while you get situated, so if you need anything or have a question that doesn't need super powers or centuries of wisdom to answer, let me know."

I noticed Daemon was staring at the loose-leaf paper in his hand like it was a puzzle with the pictures face down.

"Um, Daemon, is everything alright?" I looked to the other vampire for insight, but he just shrugged. Daemon opened and closed his mouth twice before communicating a response.

"How do you have a calendar? It's a real calendar with exact dates and days of the week; I get knowing the time, watches are still running with the batteries from before, but a calendar? Why would anyone grab a calendar of all things while fighting or running from flesh-eating dead dudes? Seriously, where the hell did this come from?"

I gawked at him, dumbfounded. The whole thing amused the bejeesus out of Cal; he clapped my inquisitor on the back exclaiming,

"By Jupiter, you will add some entertainment to our drab existence!"

Daemon abruptly appeared sheepish and a high-speed prattle flooded from his mouth.

"I'm sorry. I just tend to fixate on random stuff and it seemed so odd to me. And you came up all professional and I don't have a clue who you are and you hand me a calendar with names of my next week's meals. It was too surreal that with all this serious survival crap that you have, like, office supplies."

Cal continued laughing and I watched a pair of the flying pests narrowly miss being swallowed by the Roman as he guffawed. After being distracted by Cal, I tried to follow Daemon's parading explanation.

"...sort of freaked me out by making drinking a stranger's blood sound like a corporate merger and there was even paperwork and I got all confuzzled in my head and all joking aside how did you keep up with the correct date in all this mess? I can't even get power to charge my phone."

By this point, the Roman was bent over in stitches and I struggled to restrain my own snickering. Cal composed himself long enough to breathe out,

"That is Squirrel."

Daemon excitedly looked around asking "Where?" and it was too much for us; I let out a fit of giggling and the ever-serious Caelinus of the Roman Legion snorted and wiped his eyes. Some of the camp was beginning to gather nearby at the sight; their confusion matched the expression on Daemon's face. After several minutes, I was able to catch my air inside my aching ribs.

"My mistake. I'm Squirrel, that's the name I go by around here." I forced the hilarity from my mind. "I completely forgot to introduce myself. The calendar thing is a long story and it's a bit hard to explain why I kept one; I'll tell you another time, I promise. For now, let's just go about our evening. We need to show you around the fort and get you acquainted with our Nova Nocte."

The newbie interrupted.

"Why do you guys refer to this as Nova Nocte? I mean it sounds kind of cool and all, but why Nova Nocte instead of Awesome Ville or Camp Badass?"

The elder vamp answered first.

"It's my phrase. We spoke one evening about the need to start fresh instead of attempting to regain what is already lost. The words translate roughly to fresh new night; each night we help one another is a new chance to remake our existing civilization."

Cal noted the fledgling's nods and changed the subject. "Perhaps we should all get some supper soon so we can take a tour of the area. Afterward, I can show you how we uphold our end of the pact."

The two vampires looked at their calendars like tourists reading a theme park map; I half expected one of them to ask what time the three o'clock parade was. I grinned at the mental image; Daemon's current attire lent itself far too well to the imaginary scenario.

It would be just starting to get busy at work right now. The tour groups from Brazil, kids from schools that get out early in the year, and business folks from the conventions would be swarming the parks if the zombies hadn't already beaten them to it this season.

Arriving at the cabin we found Cal's donor waiting. They were in and out of the building in only five minutes. The human pressed his hand to his neck to stop the trickle of vital fluid and the Roman's skin had become flush. As they exited, I walked inside, Daemon trailing behind me like a stray following a child home.

Aware that a question was coming, I explained.

"It feels less awkward for everyone if the feeding is done privately. We clear out of the cabin at dusk except for the person donating that night."

He was shifting his weight back and forth, fidgeting with his hands.

"That makes sense. It just feels kind of strange for me; this is really intimate and I almost think people outside are wondering if we are making out or something. It's sort of odd." He blushed and looked around the room, "So, I just bite you?"

"Unless you can suck out blood from there, yes. You drink what you need, I get some dinner myself, and then we get our chores done."

He took a step forward, tripping over his feet a bit before baring his fangs. This guy really was young; he seemed so nervous it was as though he'd never fed before. It was cute seeing this powerful being so flustered. I felt Daemon's breath on my neck as he lingered a second and then the familiar twin pricks.

He was right, despite efforts to make this just another necessary chore; the act of sharing your lifeblood like this is very personal. The fledgling vampire drew several large gulps and I sensed the tug on my veins.

I started to feel lightheaded and considered what he said about the calendar to distance myself from the intimacy of the moment; the room went out of focus as I remembered what it took to track the dates. I felt myself floating back to that day as the room tilted away.

I don't know why the exact passage of time matters so much, so abruptly. I simply need to get a calendar. I slip through the library door and my backpack gets wedged in place. Pulling myself inside I curse. The calendar should go a few years ahead just in case. In case of what, I don't know. It feels like not knowing what day actually would be my birthday, or Christmas, or the anniversary of the recent day of rising death would be as unbearable as laying naked on asphalt in summertime.

I scamper to the computer stations. Power is still on in the building, so maybe the Internet still exists too. It's only been three days. Maybe. Maybe I could search up a printable calendar for the next five years. Hit the power button. Thank goodness for a buzz and glow and glimmer. "Load faster you out of date piece of junk." Searching and found. "Good signal for an apocalypse."

Why this even exists I don't know but I could weep for the comfort of it. It's like knowing time will still exist. Print to station 1. "Enter print credit code? Crap-tasticness on a Communion Wafer." Circulation desk must have an admin override. Search the desk, toss a book, open the drawers. "Under the register maybe?" Manual for operation of register and blank code cards in a file. "Pay dirt." —thud thud crash— "Really? More zombies, ugh." Outer door. Lights are off in the lobby. I must've made too much noise (knew there was a reason to be quiet here). Basic instructions... scan card add $1-5 *to card with admin code 0037. Enter twice, scan again, —Thud Thud— "um okay, not good" agree to terms. Okay done. "$2 max for new card? Whatever, fine, just do it." Again button button yes $2 and on. Bolt to the computer and enter code...printing total is $3.60. "Dammit" sprint back to register —Thud THUD crack scrape— I'm not looking, not looking, just move quickly "hurry hurry" $2 added. Dash to station. "Computer printing...faster faster"— THUD THUD Crack scrape moan— "Time to bail like the bar tab is coming" and... printed. "YES!" Four years of time. If I can get out, I have four years.*

How to leave? "Ouch! Stupid chair". Looking looking... meeting room window! Any fleshies out this side? Nope. Clear and climbing out. Lower the bag as silently as possible. Two books on wilderness survival and medieval weapons fall out. Okay here I go. "Ummph. Big drop, little legs." Made it. Stuffing the tomes back into my pack. Sword out, backpack on, hauling ass towards the woods. No Dead are following and I've got all I need for now. I feel better just knowing today is September 19th.

Something was different; there was a handsome vampire half-holding me and Cal stood over us. My senses were coming back to my body. Daemon, that's his name. I tried to remember, but my mind was foggy.

He must have drunk too much; when had this guy last fed?

It felt like forever before I realized Cal was spooning me stew and feeding me pieces of orange. All I heard was the young vampire apologizing profusely while holding me upright; his grip on me was delicate and warm.

I vaguely understood him say he'd been without nourishment for over a week and hadn't wanted to worry us before.

I would've rather been given a warning.

I took the remaining fruit from Cal's hand and finished it on my own as the silver-haired vampire gave a sigh and leaned back. His worry for me eased for the moment.

"We will work on your control first, I think." Cal announced to his student; it was as close to a reprimand as I heard. Daemon nodded quietly, his expression penitent.

Soon, I had completed my dinner and my focus returned. I joked with the overwrought vampire.

"Okay, that wasn't a bad trip, but it wasn't much fun either. Let's not do that again; if the hunger is that strong, give me a heads up next time, alright?"

He still wouldn't look me in the eye, but remained crestfallen and almost whimpered; he was a scolded puppy.

I tried to lighten the mood.

"I'm fine now. Let's just pop out of the cabin and knock out the rest of this tour. If anyone asks, you just asked a ton of weird questions about your new powers and about taking guard shifts and raids or whatnot. We'll be the only ones who know how much you drained; no need for any alarm, it was only due to the lack of meals. Let's go outside all happy and you two can compare fang-size or whatever."

The sad little puppy beamed so much I checked for a wagging tail.

Not a bad view.

After a cursory tour of the camp, our trio ambled over to the gate to initiate Daemon's vampire practice – he referred to it as bloodsucker boot camp. I placed items Cal instructed me to pick up on the ground just outside of the gate. There was a candle, a steel rod, and some arrows placed in a straight line.

I sat on the ground nearby with my hand on the grip of my sword; I took no chances, even with a sentry watching from the gate and two vampires to protect me.

Watching Cal attempt to instruct Daemon in the finer points of being Undead became a great source of amusement in the coming months. I have to assume that the elder vampire had never brought across anyone who asked so many questions. It reminded me of a t-ball coach dealing with a child who keeps asking why he should hit the ball, instead of just grab the ball and run. His experience as an Under-Commander in the Roman Legion was evident in the way Caelinus initiated the training.

"Primarily you will be learning the following: flying, glamour – also referred to as mind control - and how to control both your feeding and your strength. As you progress, I will also assess any secondary powers you may develop over time. This would be skills such as telepathy, animal control, telekinesis, and in rare cases shape shifting or pyrokinesis – control of fire."

Daemon raised his hand, cutting short his teacher's spiel.

"So can I get X-ray vision and invincibility like Superman?"

The elder answered in a soft tone.

"No, this is not a comic book. While it is difficult to kill one of our kind, we are not invincible; we merely heal at an accelerated rate so long as we have fed enough. We will still be injured and the pain is likewise quite vivid. As I was saying…"

"But are there Werewolves or Leprechauns or Dragons out there too, because I still haven't seen any. Creepy pulse-less guys doing leper impressions, yes, but none of the cool entities."

Cal pinched the bridge of his nose as he spoke, aggravation coloring his voice.

"Again no. This is reality; there are only humans and vampires, no radioactive superheroes or aliens or magical beasts. Just us."

Before I had time to think I blurted,

"And the zombies, don't forget they're real, too."

He glared at me, eyes shimmering a bright green with scarlet flecks.

"Yes, and the Dead. **Thank you for reminding me.**"

The fledgling chortled as I shrank back on my seat; the phrase 'seen-but-not-heard' resounded sharply in my head. When Cal looked for the source of the muffled laugh, he saw a hand again in the air; it fell as soon as eye contact was made.

"How are you so sure that those other beings don't exist? I mean, I never believed vampires were real until I became one, and I'm sure you didn't think the dead could rise until they started chomping on people. Why discount the possibility of other paranormals?"

Cal. Lost. It.

"WE ARE DIFFERENT! We're not magical fairy tale creatures, despite what we may have let the idiot masses conclude for centuries. We are legitimate, flesh and blood people. We think and feel and have a history and a culture; those others are just imaginary figments."

It felt like I was watching a car plow towards a wall at eighty-eight miles per hour; someone was definitely going to have a bad night.

"But we used to be human, so how did we get changed? I remember what was done, I just don't know why it worked if not for some kind of magic. If magic allows our existence, then other magical beings should also be possible."

The guard was backing further into the camp, probably alarmed by the sight of a vampire shouting and gesticulating wildly. Cal rebuffed his protégé, his fists clenched and eyes burning red at the edges.

"It succeeded because that is the nature of our existence; we do not bear children so we must bring across other humans to carry on our lineage. When we turn them, our vampiric DNA overruns and changes their human DNA. Our blood works more like a virus as part of our procreation; hence the reason we can only feed on human blood. Their biological components replenish ours.

Our species evolved to adapt differently and – unlike other offshoots of mankind that failed — we are able to thrive. We develop powers because of our differing genetics; some abilities are simply tapping into more of our brains and others are far more complex adaptations. Essentially, we maintain a certain amount of stem cells in our blood throughout our lives. They allow us to heal and function at a higher level than our human counterparts.

It is not magic but simple science and nature at work. That is why we exist, and those supernatural creatures are pathetic stories told to scare children into behaving so their parents can get some sleep."

He ceased his rant, fury cascading off of him as he scowled at the fledgling. His nose flared and his final statement was more growled than spoken; the seething could be felt from where I sat staring wide-eyed.

"Cool. Thanks Cal. So what do I learn to do first?" Daemon asked with the innocence of a toddler.

My sword hilt jabbed me in the stomach as I rolled over cackling; my eyes watered and sides ached from the laughter. Both immortals looked at me as though seeing me for the first time. I wondered if all sires had to train new vampires like this.

Probably would limit their population growth.

Cal strode off towards the forest shaking his head,

"I'm taking a break. Squirrel, please check the camp's perimeter and traps with Daemon."

In an instant, the young Undead was at my side.

"You always have to screw with the teacher on the first day; it's like a law." He explained with a smile.

I rubbed my ribs as we patrolled, the pain was minor but distracting. Daemon turned to me. "So what kind of ninja genius were you before the outbreak? Everyone seems to follow you; your skills must be killer."

I shook my head.

"Not even close. I'm just a regular twenty-three year old woman who worked a cruddy job in theme park sales. I had to wear cheesy polyester outfits and have my hair in a ponytail just to work a register. When our little Zombie Apocalypse started and everyone fought over guns, I raided gaming shops for swords and axes. That's it. I'm the dorky chick who hit up the library for a calendar and some books. How about you?"

He chuckled and gave me a grin that made my cheeks feel warm.

"Some girl I met at a party after junior prom brought me across. I only recently tracked her down after she bailed on me; before she got killed of course. Sucky part is, I still didn't get laid; she was fine with guzzling my blood and changing my species, but a little nookie was pushing the line. But it's okay; I figured out how to fly."

I raised my eyebrow at him. "Okay, I need some practice, but at least I remember some dirty jokes from high school."

We chatted until we heard Cal returning. He was holding a possum and looking more composed.

"Were there any issues on your patrol?" he asked politely. I told him all was quiet as we looked at the animal in his arms. For a good three minutes, we stood watching Cal hold the struggling marsupial. He took his time before answering the unasked question.

"We shall continue with training. This time, however, there will be no questions until I ask for them." He added under his breath, "Probably sometime next century."

I sat back down and Daemon gave a thumbs-up that he'd received the message.

"Good. I will start with a demonstration of proper control of the various powers. Firstly, I will manipulate this animal's mind, forcing it to perform basic movements. Mastery of this secondary ability requires gaining proficiency of the glamour skill beforehand."

As he spoke, the Roman dropped the critter to the ground. It froze for a moment, and then began to do what looked like a tap dance of sorts. The animal switched to rolling and lastly dragged a foot in the dirt, making a smiley face on the ground. I clapped at the unusual show I was observing. The possum made a bow and scampered off towards the trees.

After a few seconds, I realized that could have been dinner and stood to hunt it; a pale hand stopped me.

"I need the creature for my next presentation."

I returned to my stiff seat in the dust and nodded Cal to press on.

"Moving without making any sound and faster than the human eye can see proves very useful during a hunt or ambush. Once you focus on your senses, finding your target is simple. All that it depends upon is practice and being mindful of your surroundings."

He now stood inches from his student and held the possum an inch from Daemon's face; the boy was so startled, he shot up about ten feet and hovered awkwardly in the air. The Undead mentor smirked.

"And that brings us to our next lesson: flying."

***

After twenty minutes, Daemon was able to land without crashing, but only slowly and directly below where he was floating. Following his crash course in not crashing, Cal lifted the steel bar.

"Now we move on to using vampiric brawn responsibly."

He bent the large rod into a perfect square and then back again as though it was just a pipe cleaner.

"The trick is to know how much to reign your muscle in as you create the exact angle you intend. Take your time and focus on how little strength it now takes to destroy the things you touch," he paused as his face was clouded as though by memory, "especially the living ones."

The mentor handed the bar to his pupil and beckoned him to repeat the task. Daemon's face screwed up as he slowly shaped the metal, the tip of his tongue playing peek-a-boo as he concentrated intently on every atom in the steel.

"This isn't so bad" he mumbled as he finished the first bend and began the second. "Oops. Bloody bags of kitty capers!"

The student grumbled as the rod snapped in two. Cal set a hand on his shoulder.

"Actually, it's quite good that you completed the initial bend. Most vampires your age break the bar within the first ten seconds. Well done; it requires practice." The youth beamed at the praise and set the pieces down, ready for the next display to begin.

"The candle will be used for the next two powers: pyrokinesis and telekinesis." Cal spieled. "The basic movement of an object from a distance - referred to as telekinesis - is the easier of the two. It takes some practice and strong concentration, but its uses are well worth the effort."

The candle now wafted the ten feet to his outstretched palm. "Lighting the candle by mentally generating fire - called pyrokinesis - is extremely difficult, however. This is a rare ability amongst our kind; once nurtured, this power is a game-changer. Only a handful of Undead are able to create and master flames. Those who do are considered the most dangerous and skillful who live and are given status as such."

The wick glowed slightly and a meager trail of smoke drifted up from the candle as he spoke; once he stopped speaking, it grew into a tiny flame that went out after three seconds. I noticed Cal was sweating and out of breath from the effort.

As the other vamp rested, Daemon played with the candle; it reminded me of seeing my little brother trying to figure out how a toy worked on Christmas morning. I thought of him building roller coasters with his video game that day.

I arrived at my parent's house after I first saw a Dead rise; I needed to know everyone was all right. Dad was yelling at the police over the phone, Mom's hand was wrapped in gauze, and my little brother was blissfully playing with his game. She was crying because the stranger's bite mark was throbbing; I turned the TV to cable.

Over Owen's arguing for me to switch his game back on, the news reports informed my family for me. Tears flowed from our breaking hearts as the truth set in. There was only the sound of crying and my Mom praying the rest of us survive.

The memory brought a pang of anguish to my heart before I pushed the past behind me and focused on the pair training nearby.

Cal rose again.

"I believe we have come now to glamour. All vampires learn this skill early in their training; it is needed as part of survival. Using glamour to control a human's mind is an instinctive way to avoid too many questions causing trouble, gain easy feeding, and gain freedom during legal disputes or when traveling war-torn areas.

Although it likely will not work on the wandering Dead, it may be useful in defending our community from human enemies that may arise. Glamour is essentially hypnotism. Squirrel, will you please be my volunteer? I promise no harm will come to you."

I faltered a minute - giving over your free will to someone is not a terribly comforting thought.

"Yeah, I guess."

I shuffled over to Caelinus's side. The next thing I remember is that standing on one foot with my arms in the air and singing Loch Lomond.

"Did I miss the stage show or something?" I asked, feeling my face burning a bright red. Both of my companions grinned, assuring me that was all I'd done. I reclaimed my seat in the dust and shrugged the experience off; all I could do was trust them. The sentry in the gateway clapped.

Cal rubbed his temples as he spoke.

"And for the last demonstration, we will cover telepathy. Afterward, we will set the arrows up as markers for Daemon to practice moving stealthily as well as the other basic abilities we have covered. There will be no show of shape-shifting due to a complete lack of this talent on my part; it is exactly what it sounds like and is also exceptionally rare but advantageous."

It was nearly midnight and I was ready for sleep. Suddenly, I realized Cal was speaking to me and responded drowsily.

"Sorry, where did you say you need me to stand?"

They both looked at me like I'd asked what time the Martians would be landing. Cal chuckled while Daemon answered.

"No one said anything. Cal just looked at you and you responded. It was trippy. Did you really just hear his voice in your head?"

Taken aback, I nodded quietly.

Cal proffered his hand to help me to my feet.

"Squirrel, that will be all the help you need to provide. Have a good night's rest. Thank you for your assistance."

With that I waved and marched back to the gate, allowing the vampires to continue training. I felt honored to have been one of the only mortals to ever witness such an education.

CHAPTER 7 MAY 26TH YEAR 1

Daemon's first test of his abilities came a few weeks after he began training. It was our weekly meeting an hour after darkness fell; the vamps had fed and we humans were sharing a meal around the pit, basking in its incandescence but sweltering in the spring heat.

There were almost twenty people in our camp, as more people trickled into our community by twos and threes; poor little Ellen remained the only child. Bubba left us again right after Daemon arrived. He said something about wanting to track down other survivors or provisions.

The aroma of roasting wrens, pigeon and snail stew, and raccoon wafted around us; it engulfed the throng in wisps of steam and smoke. The smoke lingered in the thick humidity. I listened to the Roman Legionnaire regale the girl with ancient tales of Jupiter and Mercury and their kin. It struck me that it must be odd for Cal to tell this kid these things she would regard as fairy tales, when it had been the state religion when he was her age.

As soon as dinner ended, Chase stood and called the town council to order.

"Okay everybody, let's get this meeting done so we can get some rest before tomorrow."

The conversations stopped and all eyes were focused on the reddened man.

"Squirrel has put the new donation schedule up in the main cabin. The second cabin is almost finished and a copy will be posted there in a day or two. Sunny is still working out the kinks in our guard rotation. Anyone having a problem with the calendars, ask around to trade and let Squirrel know who you are switching with and when. Questions?"

Chase looked around; a sea of blank expressions and half-shrugs stared back. "Easy enough. Cal and Squirrel have an issue to address and we'll go from there."

We both stood at our introduction. Chase reclaimed his spot next to Sunny as the Undead nudged me to go first.

Coward.

"We noticed that we are running low on certain supplies, mostly things we can't get out here." The weary group sat straighter and leaned forward. "It's time we organize another raiding party to go into town."

With few exceptions, everyone shifted their feet or crossed their arms. My heart jumped to my throat as I saw Ellen hug her parents tightly. Sunny and Chase clasps hands and peered into one another's eyes; they were having an entire conversation in that gaze. There was a short duration of murmuring, followed by modest nods from a half-dozen citizens.

Drawing a slow breath, I pressed on.

"We're asking for volunteers; the list of supplies we are searching for will be finished by morning. As always, if you see other items you feel like carrying, grab them quickly."

A fellow who had wandered into one of our pits a few weeks earlier – I think his name was Jake or Jack — stood unevenly on his sprained ankle, a faded Epcot hat tilted on his sandy hair.

"Are both vampires going on this expedition, or is one staying here at the fort? We want to be sure that everyone who stays behind will be protected, too." He scanned the crowd. "I mean, now we have Daemon here."

With a sideways look to his pupil, Cal answered the man's question – leaving me relieved to be off the hook for this one.

"I will remain here to aid in our defense while Daemon will go scavenging with the other volunteers."

Several people made faces of concern; clearly not what they'd hoped to hear. Cal picked up on it immediately and his response was peppered with mild annoyance.

"His powers are developing well and he has been practicing control quite successfully. I have every confidence that Daemon will be fine on the journey, without needing my guidance.

We've already discussed the matter and agreed the young man is up to the task."

The fledgling vampire waved at the conglomeration of doubters and smiled awkwardly, one corner of his lips quivering. Jake – or Jack, maybe — took his seat; I'm still not sure if he was satisfied or just worried about bugging Caelinus too much. I took the minute of silence as an invitation to continue.

"So, on to the fun part, who feels like going on this field trip?"

Again with the blank stares, the place was a mannequin warehouse.

"C'mon people, all the fleshies you can flee from…"

Daemon, Sunny, and I looked to see who would be joining us; five hands were raised. We had decided beforehand that Chase should remain in camp. The couple was displeased with being apart, but his skills were best used preserving our little village and Sunny had proven to be an adept scrounger; she was swift and resourceful on these missions.

"Eight people will be great. We're going to leave tomorrow evening. Dane needs to trade someone for donating tomorrow, so get with him if you're willing; if no one's willing, we'll draw lots out of a bag. Let's finish our shopping list and rest up."

Dane talked to several people, brushing his red tufted black hair to the side, whilst the rest of the group stated the things they thought we should search for in the city. He stood a head above the others, but their postures and eyes betrayed how much the rest of our population disliked him. Within five minutes, Dane returned. He checked out Daemon while he talked to Cal and I.

"Chase is covering my donation tomorrow, and I'm taking his turn at the end of the week. By the way, we need to pick up some more condoms, the only ones here are expired and you never know when a person may need some."

He shifted in his skinny jeans and winked at Daemon before walking away. The vampire spoke through the corner of his strained grin.

"Someone please protect me from that guy." Cal chuckled and patted his protégé's shoulder. "Even if I was into dudes, that Dane guy weirds me out."

Cal sat at the table for the night's errand, ignoring the plea. I took the fledgling's arm and led him to a seat. We spent the next hour planning our foray through the suburban nightmare and further on to the urban unknown. Our shopping list grew from the usual items we always looked for – medicines, bandages, weapons, etcetera – to include a large variety of other things. Our raiding party was now also searching for: dental floss, spices, clothes, a cooler, Ziploc bags, canteens, blankets, pillows, seed packets, ink pens, condoms, nails, a skillet, birth control pills, and a storybook for Ellen.

The sheer number of folks who requested birth control or condoms appalled me; I have no idea how they all found the time, energy, and privacy to use them. I was aware of how many couples and single adults were in our community, but it never occurred to me that they were actually managing to have sex.

Maybe it's become a way to entertain them or to find comfort despite the zombies and communal living.

I joked that it was good everyone was at least being responsible, last thing we needed now was an epidemic of STDs. Daemon seemed unnerved by the whole situation.

Once the list was finished, everybody went to sit watch or crash for the night, except for the two vamps and myself. Cal went out to patrol while Daemon helped me write out copies of the potentially fatal scavenger hunt.

"Aren't you at all concerned about this?"

I looked at the vamp quizzically.

"About what? Did we forget something?"

He furrowed his brows to match his sulking expression.

"Every adult in this town of ours is desperate for birth control. Doesn't that bug you?" I set down my pen and pondered for a minute why this would upset the guy so much.

"I don't see why I should be worried about all the condoms and pills. It's not like we can tell everyone not to screw. Why is it bothering you?"

Daemon brushed his dark hair out of his waxen face.

"I don't care that everyone is having sex, that's fine. Actually, I'm a little jealous. My fear is they all want to avoid pregnancies." He stared at me like it should click in my head and I should be frantic with anxiety.

I was a deer in the headlights.

"So, you're worried because there won't be any babies in camp if everyone's practicing safe sex?"

He beamed and nodded.

"That makes no sense to me. Babies are cute and all but…"

"No, it's not like that. I understand not wanting to raise a kid in this kind of world, and a screaming baby would probably draw fleshies to us in an instant; no arguments there. In the long term, though, some people are going to need to start having kids if the human race is going to survive. Without kids, this whole pact and fortification is just a stall.

I worry because no one's willing to just let things happen so life can go on. How is there a fresh start without new life? Besides, if all humans die out, us vampires go extinct as well."

He fiddled with his pen as he focused on the list he was copying.

All I was able to do was roll mine back and forth next to the papers, taking in the surprisingly profound remarks.

"I can't speak for the others, but I do know that birth control isn't always effective and I will probably be unable to find any tomorrow." I caught my fellow scribe's gaze. I got the impression Daemon wouldn't be finding any Trojans either.

As we finished the list, Daemon hummed a song I recognized as Rockabye by Shawn Mullins, and in short time we were having a horribly off-key sing-a-long. Tomorrow would be an interesting adventure.

CHAPTER 8 MAY 26TH-27TH YEAR 1

The next morning, I woke early to gather some extra provisions for the camp to use while we'd be gone. It seemed half the community was driven by the same impulse; we sat together, sharing a quiet breakfast around the dying fire. It would be put out soon. The wood supply was safe again until lunch was being prepared.

With the temperature already moving the mercury up into the mid 70's, I doubt anyone looks forward to starting the fire.

The sun warmed our skin as it crested over the gleaming barricade. One by one, we finished eating and dove into work. My mind raced through checklists of what was left to do tonight and who was going; the pressure of keeping them safe turned the muscles in my neck into pretzels. I walked through the camp rubbing it and found Sunny near the gateway. She must have been waiting for a partner to exit the barrier.

"You feel like a little fishing, Squirrel?" She held a spear with a long thin point in her right hand – I assumed she wasn't looking for bass this time.

"Sure, I'm game."

We began to stride down the familiar path to the water's edge. Sunny looked around at everything, only it wasn't with a look of concern for danger, it seemed she was taking in all the details of the dawn. Her smile shone calm and natural; it was almost creepy. As we reached the water, she took the lead, turning towards the marshes downstream – yep, she intended to catch a gator this morning.

"Felt like starting out rough and tumble today, did we?" I taunted as I saw the downed bait line.

"Is there any other way?"

Cautiously, I went around to the wood planking we set down for a foothold and grabbed the line. When I glanced up, Sunny had the spear lowered to just above the bubbles; her face was all business.

I began to draw the line out hand-over-hand until the gator on the end jerked and the fight was on. I braced my legs, leaning my weight back as I strove to get the reptile's head above water.

It wasn't that big – three maybe four feet – and in a matter of minutes, our battle was done; Sunny had jabbed the spearhead through the top of the skull. She must have been training with

Chase and Cal recently; the kill spot is only the size of a quarter.

"Nice poke there, Ahab." I groaned as we pulled our catch from the water.

"Thanks, but I don't hunt whales; I hear they're endangered or something. Wouldn't want to get a fine."

We laughed as we began hauling the alligator back up the trail, eyes ever watchful for fleshies who may hear us or smell the fresh kill.

We made small talk as we labored up the hill with our prize; the air was already humid, making breathing more of an effort.

"I miss take out. There's something wonderful about just calling a number and having food appear. I would settle for drive thru, though."

"Don't forget the hot & fresh donuts. What I would give for a real donut, or a warm shower. But mostly, its donuts and ice cream."

We could see the others gathering vegetables from the gardens up ahead.

"Maybe one day. Who knows what will happen when the Dead finally die off?"

Sunny's response bothered me; it festered below my ribs and kept me awake on long nights when I sat guard.

"How do you know we'll still be here then? Maybe if we still exist, what about the vampires? They may not all be as nice as Cal and Daemon. We could just be putting off the inevitable." She started glancing around again; her smile looked a little forced this time. "I'd love some food I didn't have to kill first, though."

By lunchtime, we'd already: turned over our catch for preparation, gotten cleaned up in the small wash bins, changed clothes, added our overnight gear to the pile near the tower, and helped put away supplies. Everyone was bustling about, readying for the next couple of days.

Baskets and plastic ware containers of cleaned berries, roots, oranges, and assorted veggies were being loaded into the storehouse. Two people marched towards the cooler, each toting long strands of shimmering bass. This morning was turning out to be a good haul all around.

Ellen was busy helping her parents load a Jansport backpack for her father's use on the trip. As we searched for Chase, I overheard her advice.

"No Daddy, you can't pack the lucky rabbit's foot! You have to keep it in your pocket or it's not any good."

She had her hands on her hips.

He chuckled while asking the blue-eyed Blondie.

"And who told you that?"

"Gammy did back when I was littler. And she's your Mommy so you know she's right."

Ellen stamped her foot, emphasizing her point. He put the trinket in his pocket and hugged her before continuing his task.

I couldn't hear the rest as we found Chase with several of our more skilled chefs. Sunny and I surveyed their progress with lunch like critics for the Zagat's guide before pitching in. Chase beamed at Sunny as he gave her a kiss. They were vigorously carving up the alligator into strips for jerky and tossing random chunks into a few pots of boiling broth nearby.

I looked at the concoction; carrots, herbs, pale gator meat, and what looked like orange rinds were bobbing to the surface intermittently, only to disappear as the bubbles popped. I became somewhat leery of the meal.

"Looks, uh interesting guys. What is it?"

Chase gave me a dumbstruck look as he quipped,

"Supper."

Without further detail, he went back to his butchering. I stared at him and then at Sunny, who merely shrugged, before I sat and started drying the strips on the frame. Riotous laughter broke out behind me, erupting from Chase and the other cooks.

The frantic shouting of the sentry on the tower cut off the happy sound.

"Looks like three strangers coming towards the gate; everyone inside the walls! Hurry, get the gate, one has a rifle!"

Ellen was scooped up and rushed into the main cabin; her mother grabbed a long knife before barricading herself and Ellen inside. Several others took up positions outside the door. Our people bolted into the fort and the gate was slammed.

Arrows were notched on the platform and swords unsheathed below. Shaking hands carried extra weapons. Dane loaded a small stone into a slingshot, accidentally shooting his own foot in the process, before being sent to watch lunch.

I was at the top of the tower in an instant, pressed to quicker speed by the clanking sounds ringing out within the walls. This was not the time for unknown persons to arrive.

I saw the outsiders through the spare binoculars Chase carried up with him. There only appeared to be three of them, but we couldn't be sure. The trio had stopped when the guard had yelled out and they now stood around 100 yards from the wall of our fort.

They were between two of the spike pits. The tallest was holding a rifle out to the side; he placed it on the ground in front of him and hid the other two strangers behind him as they backed up a few paces.

I realized the small ones were children – although not likely his – both had snowy skin where the tall man was a Tyler Perry doppelganger. The group stood still. It occurred to me it could be a trap, but this man was clearly doing his best to protect the kids in case we responded with violence.

"What should we do?" someone yelled from below. I peered at everybody's faces, looking for some inkling of what they all thought.

Chase spoke to the crowd.

"There only seem to be three people, one man and two kids. The guy has already laid down his gun and stepped back. I say we check them for infection and go from there. We just keep weapons at the ready in case it's a setup. Anyone disagree?"

Shaking heads answered the pink-tinted man wielding an axe.

"I'm coming down to the gate, open it slowly and I'll go out to meet them." I stated, climbing down.

"Once we know they aren't infected, we should bring them in. I say we keep the outsiders in camp and under watch until we can get to know them and decide the best option to take. If they're infected, well…we can take the necessary measures."

There was no doubt in anyone's mind what that entailed.

"Correction, we will go out to meet them. No one goes outside without a buddy." Chase added. "Especially, in this kind of situation."

We both turned after descending the tower and were stopped.

Sunny glared at us with her spear at her side.

"Ahem. And I'll be beside you two 'brave hero types' with a spear and machete ready to keep you from getting yourselves killed while rushing headlong into danger."

We both agreed, scolded children that we were, and followed her down the ladder. We passed through the exit, keenly aware that the entire throng within was armed and ready. I was also aware that if it was a trap, the three of us were royally boned; I suddenly wanted to borrow Ellen's rabbit foot.

Sunny took the lead, crossing between the traps to approach our visitors. The man looked concerned as he spotted our weaponry; he retreated back two steps and pressed the children further from us, shielding them with his own body in case of attack.

She slowed to a halt a few yards from the intruders. After quick look askance, and we all set our arms on the ground. My eyes never left the man. The kids looked terrified and kept searching the woods from behind their guardian; fearful of Dead or living, I couldn't tell.

Sunny spoke first, her eyes easing from the man's to each of the children's in turn.

"Hi. Sorry about being so defensive and off-putting, but we can't be too careful these days. My name is Sunny. This is my husband Chase and our friend Squirrel. We came out to meet you. What are your names?" She knelt down to soothe the children's fears, her smile gentle and inviting.

The man visibly relaxed.

"My name's Randolph. This young man is Michael and this is his little sister Barbara, she prefers to be called Bobbi. I found them on the road and we've been traveling together. We didn't mean to scare everyone; we just want somewhere safe to rest."

Chase grinned and waved to the kids. Taking in the scene, I made the call.

"You caught us at an awkward moment; usually, when we're going to town, we don't let anyone in or out of the fort. We were getting ready when you arrived. We're not sure how this is going to pan out but for the time being, we've agreed to let you into our group. Assuming none of you has been infected, of course."

The kids came to Randolph's side, holding his hands tightly.

"Sounds fair to us. None of us have been bitten. Should we just follow you three or do you need to signal someone?"

He bent to retrieve his firearm; Chase stopped him, shaking his head.

"Sorry, but we have to check for bite marks first; not that we don't trust you, but…"

I interjected,

"It's just that we can't trust you. We have others to consider and none of us actually know each other. I'm sure you've got concerns about us, too."

The outsider nodded his agreement before Chase started again.

"Also, we don't use guns. They tend to cause more trouble than good. I promise, you'll be brought into the camp safely, but the gun will be locked away with the others that have come our way."

Randolph stiffened for an instant. Michael and Bobbi took notice and clung to their protector.

"Okay, your place, your rules. We haven't got any other options." Randolph consented, leaving the rifle in the dirt and slowly pulling off his shirt. "Okay kids, these people are just going to look to see if you have any boo-boos real quick. They won't touch you, they just want to see if you're sick like at the doctor."

Michael followed suit, showing that he hadn't been bitten, before helping his little sister. As soon as everyone had disrobed to their undergarments and turned around, we gestured for them to get dressed.

This part was awkward but necessary.

"Alright, just follow us exactly so you don't fall into the traps." Sunny proclaimed, turning and striding back. Bobbi held her brother's hand

and he held onto Randolph's as they played follow the leader past the ensnarement.

Chase picked up the gun and whispered to me as we followed the troupe,

"A signal probably would've been a good idea; we should run that by the others next time."

"Yeah, but let's not do it in front of the new folks, we'd look stupid for not thinking of it sooner." I agreed.

"Okay. Sunny may have had a point about our running out all unprepared. Don't tell her I said so, she'd never let me live it down."

We filed towards the enclosure. I hoped none of the nervous people inside sneezed while aiming arrows our way. It would be too humiliating to die by friendly fire after all the stuff I'd already survived.

Once we got settled in, the gate was locked tight and preparations finished. I felt bad for the newcomers; they walked in with weapons aimed at them and were now being more or less stared at like fish in the aquarium. It had to be a disconcerting sensation.

The entire camp – minus our two nocturnal members and the sentries – ate lunch together; the meal became our unofficial town meeting. While we ate Chase's special 'gator surprise', we spoke with Randolph and the two kids. It was a pleasant conversation laced with job interview and a touch of police interrogation.

Ellen seemed thrilled just having other kids to play with.

By the end of our anxious lunch, I was confident the trio wasn't a threat. Setting down my bowl, I decided we should get down to business and rest up for our trek.

"We all need to catch some Z's before night falls, so let's see where we stand. Who votes we let Randolph, Michael, and Bobbi join us provisionally?"

I grinned widely at the results. "Unanimous. Good deal, welcome to our little Nova Nocte. You can set up your belongings in the cabin to the right, so long as you all agree to live by the rules we told you about."

Randolph showed an easy smile.

"That'd be great. I can deal with the donating thing as long as the three of us are safe. The vampire thing is pretty out there, but I'll go with it. It can't be weirder than the rest of the stuff I've been seeing, I guess."

I stood to stretch before ending the pow wow.

"Obviously, you'll be meeting Cal and Daemon after sunset, so we haven't heard their vote yet. But I'm sure they'll give you the thumbs-up. It will take time before we can trust you enough to let you wander unwatched or give you unchecked access to the weapons."

Sunny must have seen some discomfort at my words.

"Trust with our lives is earned, not given by consensus. Sorry, but it's something we all go through at first. In a week or two, we will know you all better and you'll be part of the community."

Several people rose and began cleaning up the meal or heading towards the cabins. We had more important business to focus on now.

Sunny and Chase helped our new additions find a spot to relax. Ellen skipped along with Bobbi, the pair chattering away happily. Michael blew his shaggy amber hair off his face as he strolled next to his sister, ever the protective big brother. It was time for a pre-raid nap.

***

Five o'clock popped up swiftly. Watch alarms hummed and buzzed, the cacophony reverberating in the still cabin. I stretched away my slumber and crawled off my bunk. The other foragers meandered from the cabin to the fire pit; we were on schedule.

Our brief dinner was followed by see-you-laters and the hushed tones usually reserved for cemeteries. Randolph sat to the side, speaking jokingly with his charges about the fun they'd have when he got back. Bobbi fretted a little, her dainty feet becoming pigeon-toed; Michael stood stiff and tall, as though assuring Randolph that all would be well with his stance.

It reminded me of seeing a soldier take command. As difficult as it was to separate the trio at such a tenuous moment, the children couldn't go scavenging and we couldn't trust a new adult in camp yet.

Fed, packed, and properly sent off, the eight of us gathered our arms and departed. It was forty-five minutes until dusk would draw out our ninth pillager.

We marched in quiet, each person alert for danger, white knuckles clenching sword hilts and ax handles. Randolph appeared relaxed as he carried a spare machete; the blade suited him better than the firearm he previously bore. He and Sunny hacked at the overgrown pathway.

Concern rose in me that the trucks may not start. Cal regularly came out here to check on our vehicles and run the engines so they didn't lock up, but none of us were mechanics.

The fingernail moon spied on us as we entered the small clearing where three trucks and a moped sat. The grass had climbed up to the bottom of the truck doors; the moped was entirely engulfed in what looked like kudzu vine.

We only used two of the trucks; the Dodge was only good for storing extra fuel and our portable gas retrieval kit. The air hung heavy with apprehension as we marched in quiet.

"Water break?" Sunny asked no one in particular.

She had already pulled out her canteen and taken a large swig. Several of us drank deeply after the hike.

Rested, we loaded our gear into the truck beds and gave our transportation a look over: two low tires, one headlight was out, bloody smears and scratches marred the paint from earlier endeavors, and neither tank had much more than a quarter tank of gas. Dane crawled into the cab of the F-150 and turned the key; a puff of exhaust and the engine roared to life. His skull pressed against the ceiling he shut the vehicle off and slid back out, a look of disgust etched on his face.

"One down, one to go." I exclaimed, opting to be captain obvious for a minute. "Who wants to test the Ranger?"

Sunny climbed into the scraped and gore-laden pickup.

"Dibs. This one plays CDs." She beamed as her ride turned over on the third try. Journey was playing low on the speaker system. "Needs gas but it can carry a tune."

I checked my watch.

"Alright, let's get the tires pumped and spare gas flowing so we're ready when Daemon arrives."

"Too late, Squirrel. But you guys can do the grease monkey stuff anyway." The fledgling vampire hovered several feet over the sedentary Dodge, grinning; he was the Cheshire Cat reincarnated.

He tumbled (relatively) gently onto the roof of the cab as the rest of us chuckled. The youth jumped down off the rusted automobile and offered his hand to the stunned new guy.

"Hi, I'm Daemon and I will be your bloodsucking undead ally for the evening."

Randolph stared at the hand, then the smirking face, and finally shook the outstretched limb while muttering - what I think was - a greeting. I watched the pair make difficult small talk for a few minutes, before settling on sports as a safe topic to discuss. All the prep work was done by eight and our road trip was underway. I sat in the bed of the Ranger next to Daemon. He tells me he knows a joke.

"Eight humans and one vampire drive towards Walt Disney World for condoms; stop me if you've heard this one..."

***

We rode our gas guzzling chariots up the stony road, being jostled and juggled with our baggage. Soon we came to the paved street and our party tensed at the view. The asphalt bore patches of grass, immobile vehicles, wild flowers, and dozens of Dead. The zombie population would only get worse as we traveled further into the city.

"Let's get the fuel taken care of before we attract to many corpses." Sunny said through the cubby-sized window as she pulled up between the cars.

"I hate this part." I exclaimed as we jumped out of the trucks.

Sunny and the other driver stood watch in their doors, prepared to start our getaway, their weapons firm in hand. Daemon flew straight up and circled like a vulture as he surveyed the area.

Randolph and Dane crawled under the two nearest autos and cut the fuel lines as everybody took position. Four others collected the flowing liquid in steel mixing bowls; they passed them to the last woman and myself. The two of us used our beer bongs to pour the fumy substance into the gas tanks.

Everyone continuously scanned to check the distance of the decaying wanderers. As I clicked shut the gas cap, Daemon swooped down. In a blur of motion the vampire tore off the head of one Dead, causing a sound of snapped celery before returning to the sky.

"Ewww." I heard as he ascended again.

The head lay on the pavement twenty feet from me; it was still blinking and gurgling as a thick black substance oozed from its ragged stump. I hadn't realized it was so near. The process was repeated on three more cars and several more carcasses. A couple of fleshies got unnervingly close to our party. Gassing up left us so exposed; I felt I was on a stage naked in the spotlight.

Sunny was almost bitten by what had once been a young girl. The creature dragged its half-missing leg, leaving a wake of pus, tissue, and stink. It had crawled beneath the truck and was only discovered when the tiny hand clasped her ankle.

Sunny leapt sideways as the thing pulled itself out in the open and drew upright. It chomped its mouth open and closed; crooked baby teeth reflected the scant light. A pink plastic bracelet and several brightly colored bangles decorated the discolored child's remains. Someone's dried blood coated the creature, a stark contrast to the glittered fingernails that reached out for Chase's wife.

Someone added vomit into the aroma encircling us when she jabbed her spear through the zombie's bleached eye. Immediate peril being neutralized, our group completed the task and mounted our metal steed to begin our search.

Our drivers pulled into a subdivision; it was a pastel nightmare with a community pool. There weren't many fleshies in view, but sometimes that was worse. I silently prayed that the Dead hadn't learned to hide.

We stopped at the first house that was unmarked from previous ventures. It was bright pink with teal shutters and the front yard had bone shards strewn about; they gleamed under our headlights.

Daemon and I took the lead for the sweep of the house, all but the drivers trailing us closely. I drew my broadsword as he pulled the door off the hinges and tossed it onto the misshapen hedges. The azaleas seemed to be thriving.

"You couldn't try the door knob before going for the horror movie effect?" I asked.

He shrugged and answered sheepishly,

"Sorry, I've been wanting to do that ever since I got turned."

With a half-smile, the vampire disappeared into the suburban deathtrap. I crossed the threshold and checked the kitchen, pantry, and garage for hungry cadavers. Upon hearing the all clear, I stepped into the doorway to give a wave to the drivers. They acknowledged call and guarded the trucks and extra gas.

"Alright, we all have the list so let's load up whatever we can use. We need to move quickly, there are a lot of items we need and it's a big neighborhood to search." I instructed.

Our team became a tornado, drawing everything into the center of the room. I carried a green reusable grocery bag stuffed with Ziploc bags, spices, pots, pans, Ramen noodles, and some cans of corn out to the trucks. Between the first six houses the party also found: toiletries, bedding, pillows, a new shovel, some tools, and a lot of tacky decorations (which we left behind). So far, every house on the block had been stocked with IKEA furniture, cheesy knick-knacks, and not much else. Sunny looked over our haul.

"These must be vacation rentals. They're way too empty and ugly to have been lived in."

Her observation echoed in my thoughts; there had to be a better way to do this. I approached the doorway. Carving a large X on the door with my belt knife, I put the choice to the group.

"This place is done; how does switching neighborhoods sound?"

Everyone leapt into the trucks and the decision was made. I sheathed the blade and walked to the Ford. Daemon plopped down next to me wiping his gore-drenched hands on someone's sailboat towel.

"This is messier than I thought. Anyone find hand sanitizer?"

I responded with a goofy grin before settling in for the next potential hazard. We turned down the street away from the site of the accident from September 16th.

I was driving home from work; the theme parks had been closed and evacuated without explanation. All of the cheery background audio shut off and an announcement sent us home to the nearest exits. Every radio channel spoke of the outbreak of Z-bug; I thought it was just a silly hoax.

The Pontiac in front of me ran over a man on the side of the road and streaked away. I threw my car in park and ran to help. I dialed 911 as I ran to the motionless form. The victim was mangled, unconscious, and had several ribs exposed. As a small crowd gathered I checked for a pulse. Finding none, I ran to read the street sign for the 911 operator and the deceased man reached out to an onlooker.

I dropped the cell phone and jumped back in my car while the Dead victim began devouring his rescuers. Seeing other fleshies approaching, I gunned it for my parents' home.

  I was shaken from my reverie when Sunny plowed down two stumbling Dead. I felt an elbow in my ribs as Daemon pointed at an approaching zombie; it kept falling over its sagging Rocawear jeans and still bore several pieces of bling around its bony neck. We laughed at the sight as it penguin-walked towards us and tripped before pulling itself upright. The corpse repeated the cycle every four steps.

  "Someone gonna kill it or what?"

  I could feel the Mom Glare from the front cab without looking.

  "Yep. I got it."

I notched an arrow and fired. The tip went through the creature's neck as the hip-hop wannabe stumbled again. "Dammit." I took aim again, crouching in the truck bed and loosed the arrow. It found its target in a spray of gray matter and coagulated blood. The penguin was now extinct. I considered taking the gold necklaces as I sat back, but they had no value.

"Nice one, but now what will I do for fun?"

Daemon pinched my side playfully, his smile relaxed and reassuring. Our eyes locked and held for a minute, his smile changing from playful to intimate.

Sunny cut short the moment.

"This one looks good. Everyone out!"

The scavenger hunt was back on. We cascaded out of the pickup and poured into the cream house in the cul-de-sac. After the sweep yielded one already destroyed body, we split up to search. I grabbed several pens and pads of paper off the desk and started opening drawers.

"JACKPOT!" somebody yelled from the master bedroom.

I ran to see the cause of the outburst and was instantly overjoyed. The walk-in closet was full of desired supplies. As we unpacked the wardrobe we found it contained: cases of water, MRE's, two wind-up flashlights, a new beer bong, playing cards, a first aid kit, fishing equipment, two sleeping bags, a large cooler full of Jack Daniels and Bud Light, a box of condoms, puzzle books, canteens, and board games.

Not only had we found a place someone actually lived in regularly, but also that person had kept hurricane supplies in stock. The motherload was carried into the backs of the trucks; we all had smiles super-glued on our faces.

Sunny's jaw dropped while she evaluated the procession of goodies.

"Holy crap."

After forty minutes, the house was emptied of everything we needed and then some. We'd even pulled the battery out of a golf cart from the backyard in hopes of powering a couple of rigged lights at camp. I strode up to the door to mark it and froze as a familiar clicking sound echoed through the night. I turned slowly.

A muscular man was standing behind Dane with a sawed-off shotgun pressed against the back of his head. The stranger was dressed in a black shirt and camo pants, a Yankees cap pulled down over his eyes. They stood ten feet from me and I hadn't even seen the gunman.

"Step away from the trucks right now!"

We stepped back a little but I knew we couldn't let him take the supplies and vehicles; we might not make it back to camp in one piece. The look on Dane's pale face revealed panic.

He started pleading with his captor.

"Please, just let me go. You can take my bag, just let me go. They might not give you the trucks, but you can take the stuff. Don't shoot me, just take what I have, please."

Dane broke down sobbing as the interloper gripped him tighter, the veins visible both there and in the assailant's thick neck. A gush of urine darkened Dane's khakis and pooled around his feet. Every time he moved his feet, they squished.

The brawny man growled his threat at us, spittle flying into Dane's black hair.

"I'll blow his head off if you don't toss those bags into this truck and back up. I'm taking this truck and that pretty girl with me or this scrawny bitch in front of me gets some real sloppy brain surgery."

I tried to negotiate with the cretin; Dane was aggravating, but he didn't need to die.

"Look, we can't do that. We can give you a portion of what we gathered, but we need the trucks. Others are counting on us and we need to be able to get back to them."

The goon adjusted his brace on the weeping man and flared his nostrils; I took slow steps towards him.

"You aren't taking her with you, I'm not going to let that happen. Sunny won't either, I'm sure. And there's no way I'm telling her husband we let you kidnap her at gunpoint. We can work something else out. Just lower the gun and we can come to an understanding."

Tears rolled down Dane's face as he wept, sucking snot back up his nose while he whimpered. Sunny's face oozed fury and her spear tip was pointed at the Herculean intruder; she was a Valkyrie ready for war. The man sneered at me and blew a kiss at Sunny as the shot sounded.

Everything slowed down for an instant, while Dane's face was rent asunder by the shotgun round exiting through his tear-streaked face. His left eye landed on my shoe as the taste of pennies filled the air. The eye stared up at me and the body collapsed in a pile.

"Now I get my way, or you'll be..."

Daemon materialized behind the murderer and cut his sentence short. The vampire grabbed the gun and tossed it aside, engulfing the outsider in a fatal bear hug. His eyes shone green and he sank his sharp teeth into the attacker's throat, shaking and ripping the holes wider like a wild predator.

No one moved; we were too stunned by the events we were witnessing. The slurping sound betrayed how deeply the fledging drank as he took the stranger's life. Vibrant eyes looked through me as the vampire unceremoniously dropped the body. His face was covered in crimson and his dripping fangs remained bared. Scraping sounds were coming from behind us;

the blast had drawn the fleshies right to our location.

Daemon ran the back of his hand languorously across his stained mouth and chin, gathering the remaining blood, and licked it from his knuckles. A low growl of contentment escaped him. His eyes flickered red as his smile widened.

In my peripheral vision, weapons were being drawn while I instinctively took a stutter-step back. Realizing the potential outcomes, I took a gamble and drew the tiny bottle I'd located from my pocket. As the hand sanitizer somersaulted through the darkness towards the vampire, I saw the first of the blundering Dead traipsing between the driveways.

A blood-streaked hand caught the little plastic container; he looked down at the contents. The gentle breeze circulating did nothing to relieve the stillness trapped in the apex of truck lights. The departed edged closer, their movements slow and jerky, but steady nonetheless. Daemon closed his eyes and took a deep breath, his fangs receding into his gums.

"Thanks, Squirrel."

His usual upbeat tone and innocent smile returned as he cleaned the sanguine fluid from his hands and rubbed his chin clean on the inside of his shirt collar.

Eyes went wide in confusion and blades were lowered insignificantly; only Sunny squinted with distrust. The young Undead looked around and blushed – although he may have simply been flush from the blood he'd consumed.

"Sorry guys, just lost myself for a second there." He stared at the weapons still aimed in his direction. "I'm going to work on this with Cal when we get back and I'll keep it together for the rest of the raid."

Silent looks passed from person to person.

"Um, shouldn't we relocate someplace a little less unfriendly?"

Daemon gestured at the growing swarm of cadavers in varying stages of decay. He was right, Dane's killer may not have been alone and these zombies were already too many to make a stand. I wiped the splatter from Dane's cranium goop off my cheek and barked out orders.

"Someone grab the gear off those two bodies and let's get to an elsewhere while we can. This place is too dangerous."

Randolph and Ellen's Father lightened the corpses of all things useful and our troop receded into the truck beds. We set out in search of a haven for the coming day. Dawn would arrive in a few hours and we were already down one person on the first night. Ellen's Father sat across from me, clenching the rabbit's foot as Sunny drove over fleshies while making our retreat.

At least there was no one back home to grieve Dane's demise.

We drove five miles in search of an adequate place to barricade ourselves for the daylight hours. Randolph spotted it first; it was a tan house with the blue windows boarded up and the garage door half open. Both trucks would easily fit inside.

Our drivers stopped in front. Daemon and I leapt to the ground, preparing to check the potential sanctuary. I looked back and found everyone else hanging back; they stared at the young vamp with unease. Fear crossed his face as he gazed at our companions. Watching this wordless conversation, I decided to act like the leader they seemed to think I was.

"Daemon and I will clear the house for enemies: living or otherwise. When we're finished, I'll come out and we will all secure the building for the day. From here out we're also going to buddy-up so everyone has someone to cover their backs."

The pack started pairing off with whomever they trusted.

"I call dibs on the guy who's been watching all of our asses; you know, the one who killed the douchebag with a shotgun who murdered a member of our community. That asshole that tried to rob us and carry off Sunny for God-knows-what. You guys consider all that while Daemon and I are inside."

I turned on my heel, drew my sword, and stormed up to the door. The vampire followed. The home was empty of anything but furnishings. We turned back to the door outside and I took a deep breath. I steeled myself to face the probable backlash of my earlier rant. With my hand on the doorknob, I felt fingertips softly run up my forearm and grasp my hand.

"Thanks for what you did back there. You're the only person they would've listened to. I owe you major and I'll make it up to you."

Tendrils of warmth and red climbed my face. I returned Daemon's smile and proceeded outside. We rejoined the others and lifted the garage door the rest of the way open, guiding the trucks into their daytime storage. The sole Undead carried a few bags into the living room before excusing himself to patrol the area. We worked without sound, making pallets of bedding and unpacking some of the food. All minds were churning over the night's events.

An hour before dawn, Daemon knocked on the front door; after checking the peephole, Randolph let him in. The fledgling shoved his hands in his pockets and cleared his throat.

"There aren't any fleshies roaming about nearby and I found a place to crash that's close, so if it's alright I'm going to bail now. It's pretty obvious that I'm making most of you uncomfortable. I'll come back after sunset.

Sorry again for not being able to keep my cool earlier; and for not preventing that dickhead from shooting Dane. I was dealing with some zombies and wasn't aware of the danger over there. I'll be more vigilant and composed from now on. Night all."

He stepped back out the doorway and disappeared into the predawn fog.

We all knew his reason for sleeping elsewhere; the guy was afraid of what we might do to him. Daemon was immortal, fast, strong, and petrified of us. I understood his concern; while the sun was up, he'd be helpless and there was no trust between him and the group. I drifted off in a Despicable Me sleeping bag wondering what it would take for us to all feel safe again. Somewhere outside I heard what sounded like a bobcat defending its territory.

It was almost noon when I was roused for my turn as guard. I looked around the dim room. Ellen's Father was adding toys and children's books into his backpack; his face was drawn and he seemed despondent. It occurred to me I should learn his name soon, as I walked into the kitchen to join Sunny for some gator jerky and oranges. She and the other driver had just finished their turn on duty.

After we quietly fortified the residence in case of multitudes of dead or gun-wielding maniacs, we'd agreed to return to camp the next evening. Our scavenging had already yielded everything on the list – including condoms — as well as a shotgun and shells, various books, booze, and toys.

The firearm was in the cab of the F-150 until we got back to the camp. Once we got home, it would be locked in the case with the others we'd acquired throughout the chaos (we only kept them as a final response for when all else fails). I thought about the return trip, my thoughts only disturbed by the snoring from the next room and the occasional moans from the exterior of the structure. The day was long and uneventful, but far from peaceful. I wondered how Daemon was resting.

The Sun had set twenty minutes prior when three little knocks tapped on the door; the team had already gathered in the truck beds, ready to leave. I saw it was our late arrival and proceeded out the door. Daemon had changed into a pair of Levis and a blood donation tee the Red Cross was handing out last Halloween. As we strolled around the house to open the garage door and rejoin our party, he noticed me checking out his new attire.

"Yeah, met some icky people on the way over and had to do a little clothing shopping. My other outfit got kind of gore-splattered, but we won't have many Dead in our way for at least a block. Besides, I couldn't resist this shirt."

He smirked as he pointed out the logo of fangs and the phrase: donate blood. It fit him well.

I shook my head and lifted open the metal door. I was a little jealous he was the only one whose shirt hadn't stuck to his back awkwardly in the Spring air. Both vehicles roared to life and everybody found a spot for the ride home. I pulled out the bow and quiver of arrows and got comfy between Randolph and Daemon; I hoped the weapon would be unnecessary as we backed onto the glistening street.

The drive back to camp went by quickly and Daemon had been correct, we encountered only a handful of zombies for the first several blocks. I noticed some were hardly decayed; they must have been successful at hiding until very recently. I felt a miniscule pang of remorse for these people. They'd managed to survive the first tsunami of infection, only to be absorbed into the zombie masses weeks later.

A moment of terror and depression compressed my chest as I saw the bleak future ahead for our community. How long could our fresh start last? These people seemed to believe I was able to lead them into a new life, and I prayed to a God I no longer trusted, that they were right.

Failure wasn't an option, not when so much was at stake. I breathed deeply and slowly. My eyes focused on Ellen's tiny rabbit foot, as her father rolled it in his palm, to keep my world from tilting me over the edge. Feeling a slight nudge at my side, I realized Daemon was trying to get my attention.

He whispered into my ear.

"Are you okay? Your heart is pounding like a freight train; it's deafening."

I caught the hint, and just gave him a little smile and nod. He'd been discrete so that no one would be alarmed. I pressed the fears down into the deepest compartments of my psyche, and concentrated on scanning for approaching enemies. I kept the shotgun along my right leg, in case the hostility came from another human.

Pavement receded as the brush became trees separated by gravel and soil. We'd be at the clearing soon; then work would keep my inner thoughts locked tightly away as bags and equipment were schlepped back to our people.

I noted that the vampire to my left hadn't needed a donation this evening, even though he vibrated with energy. I wondered how long that one man's blood would keep the hunger at bay. If the strength held, he could probably fly two or three loads of this treasure to the camp before us humans reached the gate. Tonight wouldn't be too rough a hike if Daemon brought Cal back with him to lend a hand. Of course, the younger vamp would need to land without damaging his cargo, or himself.

CHAPTER 9 MAY 28TH–31st YEAR 1

To say our return was triumphant would be a bit much, especially considering I'd lost a guy, and there was palpable tension of distrust between one of our vamps and a half dozen of the humans. Nonetheless, as soon as we unpacked our prizes the community shook off those things and rejoiced in our safe reunion. The issues with Daemon were lessened, both by having his mentor near and the previous dangers far.

As far as Dane's messy end, none of us really liked him; he was an annoying dipshit and no one was terribly sad or shocked to hear of his passing. Our mourning for the deceased was brief and general. I felt guilty at having lost a person, but I never actually grieved over him; it was like the feeling one gets when accidentally running over a stray dog.

As the added bonus of beer and whiskey was displayed, past downers fell away like leaves on an ignored houseplant and were replaced with the anticipation of Christmas morning. Our settlement had worked hard to last this long. Now we'd play hard before crawling hungover to our chores at dawn. Not being much of a drinker, I volunteered to lock up the shotgun and store the last of the supplies. My hands grasped a sack of canned goods and Ramen noodles and I felt a cold palm on my shoulder. Turning expectantly, I was surprised to find the Roman next to me.

"Oh, hey Cal. How can I help you?"

"I merely wanted to offer you some assistance. You seem shocked to see me; were you expecting someone else or did I happen to startle you?"

He peered at me as though trying to read my hand at the poker table. I felt my cheeks redden as I realized his words were closer to home than they should be. I opened my mouth, but the vampire waved his hand and grinned.

"Never mind, I see the answer already. It's probably due to being in such close confines these last forty-eight hours. May I?"

The box of cookware at my feet floated up to his arms. I trailed behind Cal as he marched to the storage shed, mentally reminding myself not to play cards with him in the future. Once the packages were put away, the elder Undead blocked the doorway. He ran a hand through his blond-gray hair before speaking.

"Squirrel, I know there is a growing affinity between Daemon and yourself. To become romantically involved with a vampire, particularly with a young one, is perilous. I encourage both of you not to pursue this as it can only end badly."

I opened my mouth to pretend I didn't know what he meant, but couldn't find any words.

"You don't know the obstacles to such relationships; the most basic being that he could kill you if he relaxes his restraint. Remember the steel rod during our training sessions?"

I was blindsided by this birds and bees speech. I think I nodded or something because Caelinus continued his warning, each word making me acutely more embarrassed.

"It takes years and even decades for an immortal to maintain control with emotions. As soon as we become enthused by a person or idea, the hunger grows with each pump of our blood. Whether it's due to anger, or passion, or actual starvation, the hunger is a dam waiting to burst.

At this point, Daemon's dam is made of twigs and mud; it will be a long time before he can build it into concrete and steel. Do you understand what I am attempting to say to you?"

He stood straight and his anxiousness was visible in the pained expression he wore. It appeared he spoke from experience and not from an arbitrary code of vampiric living. Shadows of his own life fluttered in his eyes and sorrow walked in the lines of his frown.

"Yes. You've made your worries clear. I wasn't even aware how attached we were becoming until you called me on it. I won't do anything stupid; you know I'm a survivor. Daemon and I are good friends and that's all. You're probably right, it's mostly just our having been so close these last couple of nights."

He moved to exit the room and I followed. Walking back to the pile alongside him, I asked,

"Do me a favor and when you talk to Daemon, leave this part out of it. I want to be able to keep the friendship and I can't do that if he's uncomfortable around me."

We lifted two more bags while the children were being shown into their cabin for bed.

"Of course. It would be my pleasure."

After three more trips, the supplies were all in place and the party was raging. Although the sentries were only allowed one beer max, everyone else was sharing the bottles of Jack Daniels. I witnessed a riotous game of charades around the fire pit as Cal took his protégé to check the perimeter and discuss the prior night's activities.

I got a sinking sensation in my navel, knowing that it was going to be an awkward conversation. When my turn came around, Chase had to prompt me to stand for my improvised mime session.

The rest of the night went by quickly. I traded guard shifts and sat on the tower with my binoculars after failing miserably at charades.

Seriously, how do you pantomime Forrest Gump?

They gathered around the illumination, telling stories and jokes below while our fangy friends soared overhead. For an instant, the world seemed simple.

Then all the thoughts that had been compressed into a tiny box in my mind rushed out and overwhelmed me. I tried to keep busy by scanning the edge of the woods, but got distracted when it occurred to me that that pointing at the forest would've been a useful way to win that round of charades.

Even though I was sober, a kind of mental drunkenness overtook me as I perched on the platform. Things were getting so complicated, despite our lives getting more secure; vibes of foreboding rippled within me.

As suddenly as the impulse began, it turned to mist. The woods were dark but not overtly dangerous, the camp was in high spirits, a couple was finding use for those condoms behind the latrine, and the children slept soundly gripping their new toys. Life was normal and pleasant.

I shook off the panic and began humming with the sing-a-long that was starting around the embers; it was a medley of Disney songs. Sunny was surprisingly good at Hakuna Matata.

My watch alarm went off at 9:00 AM to create an impromptu serenade of groans from my dehydrated bunkmates. Slipping out of the cabin as unobtrusively as possible, I checked my armaments and cleaned up before breakfast.

Within an hour, the rest of my companions trickled out to attempt downing a meal. I noticed Chase was moving slower than usual. In stark contrast, Sunny seemed her usual perky self, despite having been my relief for guard rotation only a few hours prior. As the couple grabbed plates of my admittedly poor cooking, she teased her disheveled spouse.

"What, no appetite today, Mister-I-will-feel-fine-tomorrow? Did the big bad whiskey make you feel sickies?"

As he stared at the lumpy mass on his plate, Chase briefly shared the complexion of the Incredible Hulk. I laughed along with his wife before joining the game.

"Nah, he's hungry. He simply doesn't like how greasy the raccoon meat looks, sliding around his dish. Or maybe it's the texture of the stewed tomatoes."

The sunburned man held up both palms. His lips were clenched as he steeled himself against his tumultuous stomach. Finally, he suspended our fit of giggles.

"Okay. I surrender. I was wrong, you were right. I give up; just please stop. I need to keep something down so I can get the new fishing gear out and check the old lines."

He resembled a child pleading for a toy or to stay up late. Chase had managed to perfect wounded puppy dog eyes. Sunny beamed as she handed him some water and set a bottle of aspirin on the table. All eyes were fixated on the tiny white container with the childproof cap.

"This will help everyone have a better day; it was in the medicine cabinet in our safehouse yesterday. Everyone take two, eat, drink water, and get moving." She turned to Chase, "Feel better soon Honey."

She finished her last bite and kissed his forehead.

"See you later. Squirrel and I are going to get some firewood and maybe get a little hunting done. Love you."

Chase smiled as he shoved another forkful of stew into his mouth and waved. The bottle had already rattled its way around the table, giving hope to the masses. We grabbed an axe, my bow, and a gunny bag from the shed on the way to our chores.

We exited the safety of the glimmering steel wall, and wove our way between the pits and Chevaux-de-Frise (a structure I learned about in a book about civil war defenses; it looks like a series of sharpened X's with a tree trunk connecting them in a row). I mentally noted that our patchwork of wooden prongs needed to be repositioned and sharpened.

As I examined the condition of our protective measures, Sunny pointed at one of them; there was a fleshie partially impaled twenty feet to our left. It was still ambling after us from our raid – the Dead often followed the sound of the trucks until they found someone to eat.

It was bringing the framework closer to camp glacially as it threw all its strength into the spike with every step. When we moved closer to destroy the carcass, it became aware of us and started tugging sideways and reaching its tattered arms.

The thing had clearly been infected for some time; the skin had receded from its fingertips, leaving talons of bone and nail. The face was sunken and ashen, an eye swung with each movement; it was a bulbous pendulum. A twinge of recognition wavered in my gut, but no name came to mind.

Probably someone who I'd seen at the parks before the world died. Don't try to remember, just deal with it.

My sword was drawn and Sunny adjusted her grip on the axe as we drew beside our detained quarry. The police uniform it wore was stained and torn; I noticed the collar still held a little crease. Suddenly, my partner gasped and recoiled; the color drained from her face. I gazed at her, startled by her loss of composure.

"Are you alright? What happened?"

She was unresponsive as the zombie made a guttural noise. My concern grew as I took a hand from my sword and touched her shoulder. Her eyes welled up with tears as she stammered out a reply.

"It-it's my brother-in-law, Kyle. I thought…I thought he and his family had…I know it's foolish, but I thought they…left. Found somewhere safe. Chase and I hoped…maybe." She trailed off as the truth sank in and grief overtook her.

That was the recognition; he looked like Chase. Sunny's fortitude had crumbled. This was family. My heart ached for her as the departed, formerly known as Kyle, dragged the edged rails in our direction. I thought carefully before disturbing that quiet.

"Turn around. I'll put his body to rest. Remember, that isn't Kyle anymore; it's the infection that took him away. Just turn around and watch the horizon."

She barely had the axe handle in her hands as she fixated on his remains. I wasn't even sure Sunny had understood me.

"Sunny?"

She finally shifted her gaze to me.

"The rest of the family isn't here. They could still be fine. One day they may even wander here, safe and sound. I'm sorry, but Kyle is long gone; that isn't Kyle anymore. Please just turn away and keep watch. I promise I'll be quick. His remains will be at rest and his spirit will be able to find peace."

I heard a sniffle as she rotated away and dropped the weapon on the ground. Moving swiftly, I closed the distance to the zombie and drove my blade through its skull. Weeping instantly drowned the squelching sound of the blow; it was over.

I waited a moment to be sure it wouldn't rise again before pulling the corpse free and dragging it to a dip in the ground. There was nothing of use to remove; I pulled the lighter from my pocket and cremated the body in the small trench. There was no vegetation to catch fire, so I walked away.

Gathering Sunny from where she'd collapsed, I half-carried her back up to the entrance of our village.

As we made our way past the field being tended, all work stopped. The sentry shouted for Chase. Entering the camp, the weapon dropped from Sunny's trembling palms. Randolph picked it up and took my sack as well; he tapped another man and they left to do our task. Chase flitted through the meager crowd and grabbed his wife. With panic etched on his face, he belted questions at no one and everyone in a flurry.

"What happened? Are you all right? Is she hurt? Was there an attack? Were you injured or bitten or something? Sweetie, are you okay? What do I need to do?"

She hugged him and sobbed. Chase seemed to lose his voice in her sorrow. I could see faces checking for wounds around them.

"I'm sorry, Chase. There was a Dead in one of the C-frame defenses; it was your brother. I, um, dealt with the situation. Sunny isn't hurt, but she's devastated. I'm sorry for you both. You two should take some time. The remains are being cremated to the left side of camp if you want to say goodbye to Kyle."

It was disheartening to see our strongest people in consummate agony. Chase held her to his chest and cried with her. They rocked slightly as the rest of us peeled away, afraid to bother the despondent couple. When I left, I saw the kids near the second cabin.

Their play had halted while they watched everyone's worst fear striking low the toughest amongst our number. Michael led the girls inside, hiding the sight from his sister with his cupped palm. Ellen's Mom scurried to hug her child. The rest of the day, no one complained about hangovers or aches or their work.

Chase eventually walked with Sunny to bid farewell to his brother's ashes. After that, they both remained within the fort, cooking and cleaning until the Sun slept. Words were sparse in the community as everybody threw themselves into their errands. Where their thoughts were can only be guessed.

I forced visions of my loved ones in similar state into that tiny compartment in my head. Two of my closest friends were hurting, and nothing I could do or say would change that. Instead, I went out to fix the traps with one of the Jamaican men I could hardly understand – I called him Marley Guy. Thankfully, he liked the nickname. We filed the spikes and lined the rail walls up correctly. It was like preparing for the next bad thing somehow made this one less painful.

Checking the pits, we found two more fleshies to destroy. A third had landed with the spike through its brain, rendering it permanently deceased. The two of us gathered what was left of the infected fiends in the burning patch and added some more kindling.

When we returned, no one mentioned our findings: the two children had resembled Chase and the other had been a woman. Even though we couldn't be sure of their identities, we didn't want to risk snatching away the last scraps of hope from the grieving pair.

There was no scheming or plotting, just an unspoken understanding that they'd be spared from that despair. I saw the sparkle of the guard's binoculars as we carried out our dismal errand. If he saw our doings, he kept the knowledge to himself.

Night fell and I realized Cal and Daemon would be arriving soon. I strode to the portal in the wall to meet them first and recount the day's events; it seemed wrong not to warn them of the change in our friends' demeanors.

That night was as somber and cheerless as the prior night had been enthused and jovial. Over the coming weeks, the camp eased back into its routine and the couple transformed gingerly into their old selves. Occasionally, a wisp of clouds envelops their gaze, but they always returned to the present.

CHAPTER 10 EARLY/MID JUNE YEAR 1

The spring was flying by and hurricane season charged forward. There was a lot of work to be done if we would get through the storms without a warning system. Our storage was full of provisions to weather the potentially deadly season.

We stockpiled fresh water, salted meats, tools, and medical supplies as well as extra arrows and stones for the bows and slingshots. The weapons building brimmed with knives, swords, spears, axes, and equipment for traps. We reinforced the wall and rehearsed our emergency plans. (To die from a storm during a zombie apocalypse would just be too pathetic for words.)

As preparation for natural disasters was in full swing, the unnatural disasters continued to disrupt our community. For some reason – Daemon guessed lack of food – the Cadaver Fest began wandering out of the urban areas and into the more deserted marshes, parks, fields, and forests. Every day a handful of Dead had to be burnt in the clearing to the left of camp; thankfully, it is far enough downhill that the stench doesn't drift into our home. The hard part was burning them as soon as the sun was up so they'd be done before the afternoon downpour.

Undead training turned into a more practical, on-the-job kind of thing for Daemon, since he and Cal had more targets to practice their skills on. The pair never travelled out of sight of our tower for long. Watching his progress from the gateway or platform became one of my favorite things about sentry detail.

Every so often, the elder vampire would give me a look and speak to me with his mind; it was always the same reminder to keep my feelings in check. Sometimes I'd see him give Daemon the same expression and his protégé would nod. Despite the warnings and restrictions on what our relationship could be, I felt most connected with the young vampire.

One evening, as I finished reinforcing the new awning to cover our meal tables, Randolph sprinted over.

"Chase needs you. There are a bunch of strangers in the woods. Came back to tell you; he and Jamaican guy went to keep tabs on them." He wheezed and leaned on the table. "The strangers have bats and pipes. Not sure if they plan to attack or are just wandering around.."

The panting messenger jogged towards the gate, urging me to follow. I yelled instructions to the guard on the tower.

"Outsiders approaching from the woods. Get everybody armed and ready. We're going to meet up with Chase and Marley-guy to see what these people are up to. If the vamps get back here first, send one to check on us."

The camp transformed into a swarm of movement as we rushed away. As the sun dipped below the horizon, we found the pair of allies. They lurched behind a copse of moss-laden oaks, surveying the half dozen people several yards off. I waved to Chase, informing him of our <u>Mission Impossible</u> presence. Randolph and I scurried to their hiding place, crouching as we ran. The theme to played in my head; making me smile despite the gravity of the matter.

"What do you think; do they seem hostile?" I whispered. Heads shook in unison as Chase answered in hushed tones.

"Looks like a bunch of lost tourists. They've got pipes and bats, and that short one is carrying a shovel, but these days everyone is armed with something. No signs of guns or that they're aware of our village. These people don't even seem to have much gear."

He tilted his head and softened his eyebrows, it was clear to me Chase thought we should help; he'd turned off battle-mode once he assessed them as harmless. I thought for a moment and agreed with his judgment.

"Should we all pop out and say hello now, or head back to camp and make introductions in the morning with an extra couple of people?"

Someone spoke gently into my ear,

"Let's make friends now."

Startled by the proximity, I twirled on my heel as my fist made contact with flesh and I heard the bone crackle beneath my clenched hand. I'd yelped with surprise at the intrusion of my space. My knuckles throbbed as I instinctively reached for my sword.

An icy hand grabbed my arm, preventing me from drawing the weapon. Looking up, I realized Cal was the one grasping my wrist to end my attack. He gazed down, scolding the pale figure that knelt cradling his jaw.

"What exactly was accomplished by dashing silent as a mouse if you then proceed to cause a ruckus with foolish pranks? Serves you right, having your face fractured."

The Roman assisted Daemon to his feet.

"Shake it off, the bone will mend in a few minutes. Come now, you are making our species look embarrassingly feeble."

Relaxing my stance, I laughed loudly and shook my head.

"Dude, you just got beat up by a human girl; your macho vampire card is revoked." I teased as I stepped towards the encampment of outsiders. "Well, judging by the noise over there, the tourists know we're here now; may as well go make nice."

I led our little exploratory detail to formally greet the intruders.

Once I stepped into the flickering illumination of their small fire, the girl with the shovel stepped forward; she held it as a lance with the metal edge aimed at my chest. I paused and held my hands up with the palms openly facing her. The other residents followed suit and gestured their peaceful intent as they came alongside me into the light. After what seemed like eons, their leader lowered her improvised spear to my great relief.

"Sorry to scare you. We have no interest in hurting any of you; we just want to make sure your group isn't a danger to us. You appear to be leading this bunch; they call me Squirrel, what's your name?"

I held my hand out to the petite young woman, intending to make full introductions after inviting them up to our encampment for a parley.

A lightning fast parade of foreign gibberish ambushed my hearing.

Fuck my life, they don't speak English and have no idea what I'm saying.

Taking a closer look at the rag-tag journeyers, I noticed they all wore green, yellow, and blue shirts, as well as each being in their teens. The picture came together immediately.

"Brazilian tour group? You all speak Portuguese?" I asked as the faces of my fellows cringed and jaws dropped with the revelation.

"Si, falamos Portuguese!"

The leader bombarded me with an avalanche of words I couldn't comprehend. I gestured to her to stop.

"I don't speak Portuguese. Do any of you speak English? Or maybe Spanish, someone in your bunch has to know some Spanish, right?" I pleaded with the now frustrated head of the turistas.

The lone male in the bunch stepped closer, raising his hand.

"Hablo un poco Espanol."

I turned to my compatriots.

"Okay anyone speak Spanish, or do we need to get some backup?" I asked.

I wondered where the other Brazilians from their original group were; these people always hit the theme parks in droves of 60 to 80 with one or two translators/chaperones for each pack. My thoughts were broken as Cal chimed in.

"I speak some Portuguese and fluent Spanish; I acquired many tongues during my travels."

Daemon chuckled and elbowed Chase.

"I'll bet he got some tongue skills while abroad."

Cal glowered at the fledgling.

"I can translate if needed, however, I doubt going through two translators for everything during the daytime will be worthwhile. Perhaps we should simply offer them some basic necessities and send them on their way. Being unable to communicate effectively with these people will only increase the risk to our group."

He stood erect and gestured smoothly with his hands as he elaborated on his advice; I stared in disbelief at his suggestion.

"We're risking the security and safety of everyone – not to mention the increased demands on your food supplies — if we admit them into the populace. Granted, it would increase the source of sustenance for Daemon and myself, but I feel it would be unwise on the whole."

All eyes were on me as the elder Undead finished speaking. He looked at me for a decision, while the South Americans shifted their gaze between us; I think they were aware that the course of their existence was being debated and chosen for them.

Everything Cal said made perfect logical sense, but it felt as though I was being asked to abandon a box of puppies on the side of the road just because they weren't housebroken. I thought for several moments.

"Cal please translate for me; I need to ask some questions before this goes any further."

The vampire nodded, his expression blank.

"First, what's her name? Where are the others they came with, specifically their guides? I thought they stayed with them to handle the language barrier."

He faced the shovel-bearer as he spoke. I had no way of being sure of what he was actually saying; I simply had to trust the man. She answered him but never took her eyes off me.

"Her name is Maria. She says they all were eaten by the Dead or fell sick during the trip. A zombie bit her guide while they were at the hotel. She and her friends ran away when the men with guns started shooting everybody with bites.

She says Fernando knows some Spanish and a few words of English, so he can translate. She wants to know if we will leave them alone now. She doesn't want to fight; she just wants to find a place to sleep before they try to find a way to get back home to Sao Paulo."

I've never had a real decision to make until that moment. Even deciding who to trust has been simple: go off body language – signs of deception, don't trust; no deception, trust until given a reason not to. If someone breaks my trust, that bond can't be rebuilt.

Choices have actually become easier since the outbreak of rising Dead. Anyone infected or hostile gets killed, and everyone else is considered an ally until shown to be otherwise. Leaving these kids unprotected and without aid is tantamount to death sentence.

"Cal, gimme a second over here please."

The two of us stepped aside into the darkness to converse. An owl hooted its warning in the distance, drawing Daemon's attention from our mini-conference; he was the only person not intently zoomed in on the meeting. The Roman vampire motioned for me to speak.

"We can't just deny them a chance to join us in the fort because they don't speak English; it feels, well, wrong. If they keep wandering out here alone, they'll be killed. I don't think I can handle being responsible for their deaths."

"Squirrel, I will talk plainly with you. Everyone in Nova Nocte sees you as our leader, myself included. You are the final say, not myself or Chase or Sunny, you are. Although my experience and advice are freely given to you, this judgment must be your own."

"Look, the communication thing is important; we have to be able to understand each other to make our society work. It adds a lot of risk to bring the Brazilians in, but keeping them out feels inhumane."

I was begging Cal to give me a better reason to abandon these adolescents; or for him to make the ruling without me. His demeanor softened and I saw the sadness trapped in his gaze. He answered my plea the only way he could.

"Making painful choices, even with others' lives, is the reason the mantle of leadership weighs so heavily upon the bearer. I've carried that burden as well and do sympathize with you right now; but you must do what will be in the best interest for our people. Are these six lives worth risking all the others?"

He gently patted my upper arm as he skulked back into the amber glow.

I stood in a swirl of lonely shadows, the murmur of my thoughts buzzing through my head. I felt the bright eyes fixated on me from the recesses of night. With a deep breath, I announced my decision.

"I agree with Caelinus; these half a dozen turistas pose a greater risk as our neighbors than as passing strangers. They're trying to get home so let's help them on their way.

They won't be entering camp; we'll bring the supplies to them and give them tips on survival while guiding them away from our community. The potential hazard to our group outweighs the desire to provide more assistance."

I threw my head back slightly, signaling the Roman to translate the message. Stepping closer, I watched the petite girl who'd been forced into leading her friends; Maria exhaled lightly and put on a false smile as my words came to her through the vampire. She maintained eye contact with me until he finished each word. She seemed to grasp why I made this ruling, but I doubted she was aware of what an opposite judgment could have meant.

I pushed away the sound of my parent's voices in the back of my mind; they would've wanted me to help these kids.

But they aren't here anymore.

The popping upwards of Daemon's hand fractured the seriousness; he nearly quivered himself off the ground in excitement. I heard snickering from several spots at once. I was almost embarrassed to be friends with someone dorkier than myself. I jokingly played teacher.

"Yes, the hyperactive child in the first row."

His usual ramble of thoughts poured out as smoothly as uncorked wine.

"I can fly up now, get the bag and canteens ready, and tell everyone else to relax. Then I'll be back in a few minutes and Cal can tell them camping tips and stuff while I'm gone. And then I can show them how to leave through the orange grove; I've always wanted to be a tour guide, I just didn't really know until now. So can I? Please?"

He was so energetic at the prospect of having a new task to do I thought the guy might wet his jeans.

He grinned widely as laughter erupted from one of the tour kids; at their urging, Cal had translated.

"Sure, go ahead. Have fun."

I barely restrained my amusement. It actually hurt my abs trying not to laugh during such somber conditions.

Daemon shot up and flew towards the guarded hamlet. He really was gaining control over his flying. The warbling of frenzied Portuguese erupted from the other teens as Daemon crossed the dim heavens. I could make out his silhouette as he stopped mid-flight and pulled a shaky U-turn. Cal tried to calm the agitated tourists, his efforts thwarted as his protégé landed.

"What happened? Is everyone all right?" Daemon asked, his face awash in puzzlement.

Maria shouted and thrust her shovel edge at the bridge of his nose in response. In the same instant, the fledgling moved to his right and Cal was at his side; it seemed like he'd materialized from the air itself.

The Roman snatched the weapon from the girl and bared his fangs with a hiss reminiscent of a cat being bathed. The shovel was embedded deeply into the ground as Daemon recovered from his astonishment and took a fighting posture. Their eyes burned a furious green as they snarled at the assault.

Everyone around the dying fire was poised with arms drawn. Maria stepped back and flicked out a small pocketknife as she muttered viscous foreign words at our detail.

"Cal, what the hell just happened and what is that bitch saying?" I asked through clenched teeth.

Although my vision was tinged with crimson and my heart thundered in my ears, I tried to restrain myself from gutting the girl who I'd argued to protect a moment prior.

"Apparently, these brats were unaware of our kind. They are now under the distinct impression," he paused as he threw their leader a disgusted look, "that the entire society we have here is composed of demons. She also claims this meeting was a trap to devour her and her companions. They reacted by denouncing our survival and attempting to remedy the situation."

The posse of teenagers began chattering amongst themselves. The lone male baby-stepped to his left and leaned down, hefting a bag onto his shoulders. The other Brazilians followed suit and gradually loaded their belongings before edging backwards from our crew. No weapons wavered.

The diminutive Maria spoke at Cal; disdain and hatred dripped clearly from each word thrown at him. The elder vampire retracted his fangs as he sneered his response. He translated as the wandering pack of teens retreated haltingly into the trees, disappearing into the inky obscurity.

"The head urchin said they don't want help from abominations like us. They're leaving and refuse to consort with damned beasts or worthless traitors to the human race. Maria added her intent to cleanse the entire community from existence at the first opportunity. She also tossed around some other threats and insults I will not deem to impart."

Chase and Randolph moved towards the tourists at the threat on our loved ones.

"Personally, I would like very much to rip her self-righteous tongue out of its cacophonous hole, and rend her apart until her blood ceases to gush and there is nothing left for the mindless Dead to ingest. However, it is your decision."

The fury seethed off of Caelinus in droves, each wave tactile as it rolled through the vicinity. The miniscule hairs on my neck stood at attention, an army prepared for war. I still struggled to maintain composure and think clearly after the initial assault.

She nearly killed Daemon.

I felt myself moving towards the tour group's exit route but halted the advance after only three steps. We needed a plan. I wanted to hunt them down and destroy them, but that wasn't the best course to take.

"No. We're going back to the fort. We'll put out this fire, go tell the others what just happened, and add some precautions to our routine. Daemon and Cal, you'll both need to sleep either within the wall or just outside where we can protect you during the day. We haven't been holding up our part of the pact and I'm sorry.

You've been left unguarded when you are most exposed. We can add a cabin if it makes things more comfortable, but I won't let anyone slaughter you while you sleep."

The team withdrew a bit and the Roman eased his stance.

"If these punks are foolish enough to cross our paths again, do whatever the fuck you want to them. They're getting one chance to leave in one piece, if not peacefully. If they're too stupid to take this opportunity, we'll call it natural selection. Let's go."

I kicked some dirt into the coals and plodded angrily back through the bushes to the entrance of our fort. My mind raced with thoughts of beating the girl into unconsciousness for her attempt on Daemon's life. He was my friend and that dumb brat nearly ended his existence. For her sake, Maria should have stayed away.

Upon entering the fort, I realized both vamps had positioned themselves at either end of our line; Cal watched our tail and Daemon walked directly behind me. I was stunned neither of the vampires had argued about changing their daytime address. If I hadn't been fuming over how the evening had gone, I probably would've laughed at the silliness of two such powerful beings following the commands of my five foot two, meek self.

Immediately calling the town to a meeting, the six of us relayed the events. Looking around, I noted several flinches and wide eyes as I announced the new precautions. Thankfully, a handful of smiles and agreeable nods were interspersed among the nervous residents. The mosquitos politely stayed out of it and went on with their buffet.

If Cal noticed, he didn't show any response; he wore a soldierly posture of indifference and a noble's bearing. Daemon was busy playing rock, paper, scissors with the three children. He only acknowledged the announcement by shooting me a thumbs-up. Turning back he adopted a befuddled frown and furrowed his brow; the kids were winning every round.

CHAPTER 11 END OF JUNE/JULY YEAR 1

It only took six days to complete a small cabin for Daemon and Cal to live in. Until the construction was done, they stayed in the main cabin with most of the early members of our group. It was agreed that the second cabin with the kids added too much potential for issues.

Chase and Sunny switched their beds to the entrance of the room so that the Undead tenants could slumber in back. Even without windows, opening the door at the wrong time could pour too much sunlight into the bunkhouse – another reason not to stay with the children, as they constantly ran inside and outside.

This sleeping arrangement revealed something I hadn't thought of; vampires don't just pass out when the sun rises, they merely have no resistance to sunlight. The first day the vamps stayed inside the camp's barriers, I came in from my guard shift to find Daemon lying on his back and tossing a baseball in the air next to his snoring mentor. The fledgling signaled me over, sat up, and brushed his dark hair from his pale face. As soon as I sat on the cot next to him, he giggled.

"You look really funny when you make that face." Daemon whispered.

Taken aback, I looked at my watch and then Cal before responding.

"How come you're awake? I thought vampires slept during the day?"

He sprouted an ear-to-ear grin.

"During the day and all day are two very different things. We can't go outside, but we don't fall under some magic sleep spell at dawn; you heard Cal, we're natural creatures, not mystical demonic fiends. No matter what the turistas think.

Cal likes to crash early and be up by three or four, but I like staying up and sleeping in. Neither of us really needs much sleep, but it kills time."

I nodded along letting the logic of Daemon's words roll over me.

"That makes sense."

I plopped onto my bunk.

Reclined on my left side, the two of us talked about nothing and everything until my watch alarm buzzed loudly. I pressed the snooze and yawned, "Oops, no nap for me today. Got to get back to work. You should probably catch some Z's while you've got a chance."

We exchanged smiles as I rose and tossed my unused pillow at the vampire.

"Yes, Daemon, you should sleep; you two hens have been clucking all day whilst some of us have been attempting slumber." interjected Cal from his mattress.

We apologized and I rushed outside. Once the door shut behind me, the Roman's hearty laughter rippled through the heavy air.

***

The weeks that followed provided an inside view of vampiric life; I found it surreal. Apparently, I wasn't the only one who'd presumed our fangy friends hit the dirt at dawn. Chase actually walked into the cabin, saw Caelinus pacing one afternoon, and walked back outside blinking rapidly and saying,

"Ok there's a lot of weird stuff I've already accepted, but sleepwalking vampires is too much and I'm too tired."

Sunny's husband wandered over to the second cabin while she and I laughed; dishwater splashed as a pot cannon-balled from my hand into the washtub.

That evening our community discovered why the Roman had been pacing. Cal stood near the radiating fire pit and cleared his throat for attention. His protégé at his side beaming with his chest puffed like a peacock.

"I have an announcement for the camp patrons."

The usual murmur died as focus was drawn to the elder vampire. I nodded my enthusiasm and sat back to observe his speech's impact.

"Today Squirrel, Daemon, and I agreed that he has become proficient enough in use of his abilities to patrol untended from here on. Therefore, we believe that it would be in our collective best interest for the two of us to alternate nights on duty. We can patrol individually six days per week and use the seventh for both defense and training together.

This would allow each of you more assistance from our specific skills as well as give us a better chance to interact on a personal level. Thus far our two species have cooperated in this village but we have remained – with little exception – detached socially.

There is currently minimal human/vampire involvement other than donations. Obviously, we don't have to be best friends, but I would enjoy the opportunity to form more intellectual and emotional bonds. There is more to life than just surviving."

Daemon scanned the crowd like a nervous groom at his wedding when they ask for objections. Cal stood straight; his body language projected calm, except for his eyes, which flicked from place to place wildly. Michael raised his hand and rose. My head tilted in amusement at the situation as much as at Cal's face. I couldn't tell if the elder Undead was amused or just bewildered.

"So, from now on, either you or Daemon will be here with us at night?"

"Yes, that's correct."

The boy was prodded to continue by his little sister.

"So, um, would you be able to tell us more stories those nights you don't hafta work? If you can't it's okay, but you know all the cool war stories and all about other countries and stuff." He shuffled his feet uncomfortably, all eyes plastered on him.

"It would be my pleasure to tell you and Bobbi and Ellen stories. Does anyone else have any concerns about this new arrangement; I promise, the adults are welcome at story time as well."

Laughter rang out and the boy resumed his seat, satisfied that the tales would occur regularly. With no further issues, Daemon swaggered out to begin his first solo shift and Cal sat by the children. They listened intently as he regaled them with the story of Romulus and Remus, dinner gradually disappearing from their plates.

Randolph teased that the kids were getting dinner and a show before stacking his dirty dishes and taking his post at the gateway.

Most evenings began with both vamps for the first hour, during which they increasingly participated in camp talk and revelry. (Daemon's jokes were banned until the kids went to bed.) An evening almost a month after the Coffin Cabin was done, as Daemon called it, I joined the gathering with my grilled otter and roasted peppers, overhearing the debate as I sat down.

"There's no way the Mummy is a better monster flick; it's just a wrapped up magical zombie, it's not even gory or anything. If we go zombie flicks, it's either the Dawn of the Dead remake or the original Night of the Living Dead. Personally though, I prefer werewolf films; I'm sort of over the zombie thing now."

Sunny was arguing with one of the newer guys. Her arms were wielded in conjunction with each word, swift and precise as in combat.

The coed kid with a Gators tee shook his head and sneered half his mouth in retort.

"Most werewolf movies aren't that good. And the Mummy is a classic. Besides, it's creepy. A retro creepfest can be way more entertaining than a stupid effects gimmick like with werewolf flicks."

I took the opportunity to stir the verbal embers.

"Vampires make for cooler films. You get not just classics like Dracula, but also great stories and effects. I mean, look at Interview with the Vampire, The Lost Boys, and Queen of the Damned; those movies rocked! Besides, vampires make for better television. Maybe not something like Dracula: the series, but True Blood or Forever Knight are definitely better than those other monster shows."

Several heads bobbed their assent or shook off my debate emphatically. Chase stood and held his palms out to the group.

"Okay, granted I liked the Twilight movies, but…" he was cut off abruptly as the elder Undead was suddenly on his feet.

Chase paused, startled by Cal's appearance; the Roman clenched his fists and snarled. His nostrils flared and eyes glowed in the dancing shadows of the fire pit as he growled out his rant.

"That Twilight crap is the most offensive, insulting pile of horse shit I've ever experienced in two millennia on this dusty rock. Real vampires don't sparkle like a disco ball and whine like babies to over-dramatic expressionless bitches. We don't go to high school over and over for eternity; that's an absurd waste of time and sanity. From what I can tell, no one wants to go through matriculation the one time."

Chase held up a hand in an attempt to slow the tirade; Sunny pulled it to his side.

"And who the Hell would randomly decide to become responsible for a dying brat without a decent reason? I've never met anyone of my kind who was that big of a fool. That horrible series tarnished the image of vampires. How can you claim to actually like something as abysmal and insolent as Twilight? I had thought you had some taste."

Cal's hands shook with rage as he stopped pacing and yelling. He locked eyes on Sunny's husband and he panted from his avalanche of annoyance. Chase's pink face turned a burgundy. The air was thick as Chase opened and closed his mouth several times before shrugging in surrender.

Sunny held her palm over her face and mumbled to her husband.

"I told you not to tell people about that."

He just glanced at her and then back to the infuriated vampire, his eyebrows lifted his eyes wider as he muttered.

"Sorry?"

I've never been sure which person he was apologizing to, but both exhaled deeply and accepted the concession simultaneously. Chase looked at his feet while silence engulfed the diners. Sunny resumed eating her fish, prompting the rest to follow suit.

The Roman looked about and it seemed to dawn on him how harsh his speech had been. His stance deflated and he hung his head; his eyes dimmed as he turned away. The kids finished their dinner and were rushing to clean their dishes when Cal sat back down.

"I must ask forgiveness for my outburst. Although the subject is very agitating for me on a personal level, it was unacceptable for me to be so coarse, particularly in front of the children. I hope that you can all excuse me this incivility."

The penitent vampire was almost knocked down as Ellen abruptly hugged him. The energetic little princess both forgave and scolded the Roman as she clung to his side.

"Of course we forgive you; that's what you're supposed to do when a friend says sorry and really means it. But you're still in trouble for interrupting and using the bad words."

She released Cal and stepped back, her hands at her hips and elbows sternly out at right angles.

"Now look Mr. Chase in the eye and say sorry for talking during his turn and then you two shake hands. Then you go to your room and think about why you were mean 'til someone lets you out."

I never knew a seven-year-old could throw out a Mom Glare until that instant. Caelinus awkwardly did as the diva ordered and sulked away to his bed. As I sat stunned by the dinner show, she signaled her two playmates and they merrily bounded away to start a new activity. As the trio of youths left the silent mass of grown-ups, Ellen shouted to us.

"In ten minutes, someone tell Cal he can come out and tell us our stories, m'kay!"

I bobbed my head and laughed. We allowed the powerful vampire to end his time out in accordance with the child's instructions. He still looked confused and ashamed when I paroled him from his windowless cell.

"Cal, time out's over." I called from the doorway. "The kids are ready for story time, but I think after that your rehabilitation will be complete; just check in with your parole officer first." I couldn't resist giving my pal a hard time.

"Thank you. I think I have been adequately humbled now, so you can stop vexing me. I think I'll check on Daemon once the little ones are in bed."

Caelinus ambled off, a tiny smile playing briefly across his pallid cheeks. Macho as he tried to be, it was clear to me that the old fellow loved entertaining those children.

Always having one vamp inside the fort eased the trepidation that had been building. Everyone began seeing Cal and Daemon as just two more people in our band of survivors. Each night, we learned more about our immortal companions and the imbedded fears dissipated. By the time the suffocating heat of summer peaked, our hamlet in the ocean of decay felt like a family.

CHAPTER 12 AUGUST 3RD-10TH YEAR 1

    During our late afternoon storm, Cal flew into the camp with another person in tow. Carefully putting the drenched person on the ground, the vampire shouted to the handful of us under the food canopy.
    "All is well, he is a familiar friend."
    The man shook the drizzle from his raincoat and removed his wide-brimmed hat; enthusiastic smiles welcomed him.
    "Hi y'all, how's it been here in old Nova Nocte? Looks bigger since I was last here. Bit wetter than my last visit, but least its washed 'way all them love bugs. Fang boy here already done give me a look over and took my new guns. I mooned him good, just in case, heheh. Don't suppose any of y'all missed me?"
    Forrest Jackson, AKA Bubba, helped himself to a late supper of rice-thickened possum stew as he drawled out his greeting.
    Cal clapped Bubba on the back as Sunny and I put away our weapons.
    "Nice to see you back with us safely. I'll catch up with you tomorrow evening; I must get

back to my vigil, particularly given the information you have provided."

The elder vampire set Bubba's rifle and pistol on the table along with a box of rounds, and took to the air like a streak of lightning in reverse. Forrest waved his freshly emptied spoon in reply. Sunny and I exchanged nervous glances; I blurted out my worries first.

"Uh, Bubba, I'm glad you returned from your adventuring safe and sound, but what info did you give Cal that sent him shooting off to guard duty so enthusiastically?"

"Oh, yeah that; about fifteen miles from here there was 'nother camp set up outta a big condo complex and, one morning last week, a big herd of murdering folks raided that camp and ever'thin nearby they could take. Handful them bandits was wearing Brazilian tourist shirts and was ramblin on while the boy with them translated to Spanglish. The rest was all camo-dressed macho types with guns-a-blazing.

They burnt the place down and staked a vamp that was protectin the complex folks, then shot up or beat down the humans. Drew a helluva lot of fleshies to the camp, so I scooted out quick as deer and come back this way to check on y'all. Dunno which way they gonna go next or even if they survived all them roaming corpses, but figured we was all good friends so I ought to put out the alert to be cautious."

Sunny glanced at me as she responded.

"Thanks for the warning, Forrest. We'll get ready for attack just in case. I think we may have met some of that group before."

I choked down my fear around the lump in my throat. I reluctantly considered the possibility that numerous other survivors were now dead thanks to my earlier choice regarding the Brazilian teens. I'd been unable to think of a better solution after the misunderstanding that night. I probably should have killed Maria and her friends then, I just didn't want innocent blood on my hands.

They're not innocent anymore.

"Squirrel, you alright there? Yer face been overcast since I told y'all the about them pillaging bastards in town." Bubba asked, shaking me from my reverie.

I blinked rapidly before the words sank in. I became aware I was now the sleepy lion at the zoo; everyone watched for me to do something interesting. I shoved the frog down my narrowed gullet to force verbiage to my tongue.

"Yeah. Sorry, I just zoned out a minute. I'm thinking up a temporary plan until we can have a town council in the morning and iron out a solid arrangement."

Several people nodded and leaned back. I took it as encouragement to elaborate.

"We should start having two people as sentries at the gate instead of one. Daemon and Cal could patrol closer to the fort, as well. The vamps would also be the only ones to deal with the Dead for now; anything with a pulse, they'd return for backup."

Sunny smiled and jumped in.

"Thankfully, we've already reinforced all the structures here and stockpiled provisions, so we won't have to scramble for that stuff. We will need to upgrade the traps and prep for defense from rampaging assholes instead of just run-of-the-mill zombies though. And maybe Bubba can check out the arsenal of guns for us in case it comes down to a shootout."

I stood to put the plan in action.

"I'll tell Cal our game plan on my way to help out at the entrance and Sunny can fill Daemon in. If one of you could relieve me at the end of watch as well, that would be awesome."

Forrest guffawed and stomped his denim-clad leg.

"Hell, I'll do that watch. Sure did miss this place, may as well help keep it from gettin burnt to cinders. Besides, there's nuthin like a tough gal planning fer a fight. Reckon I'll even stay a few weeks this time so I don't miss out on scrappin with them hooligans."

He stood and stretched towards the waxing moon as he finished speaking. His graying hair poked out under the worn hat, betraying his age more than his lifestyle. Hefting his bag onto his shoulder without a sound, the country thrill-seeker strutted towards the cabins to rest before sentry detail. At dawn, some of his bunk-mates would be startled to wake up next to his grizzled face again.

As I rose to my slumbering feet to join the guard up front, Sunny joked,

"It's nice to have Forrest back. He's fun, he works hard, he's a true southern gentleman, and he always shows up with Hell licking at the soles of his feet." The quiet laughter followed as the remainder of residents dispersed for the night.

I've had about enough of Hell for a lifetime. Maybe this new pile of crap will land on someone else's door.

For a week we waited and prepared for ransacking lunatics and tourists. Both Undead volunteered to scout the ruins of the condo encampment; Forrest was gung-ho to lead them to the location until Chase pointed out how weak everyone would be if we separated.

Daemon and Bubba both continued to press the matter until Sunny stepped in and admonished them about unnecessary risks and tossed a few grimaces their way. Cal thought it was hilarious; he stood behind her pantomiming her scolding for almost a minute before she realized. The elder vampire may heal quickly, but that slap must have been painful; the mark was visible from five yards away.

All three signed up for extra sentry details immediately once their quest was canceled. I noticed that not only had they begun to battle train daily, but the whole community had also taken to practicing more thoroughly for combat. Forrest even cleaned and checked the working condition of all the firearms accumulated in the locked chest. The growing hamlet of Nova Nocte was ready and equipped to defend; we simply lacked an assailant.

The daily grind made the meager relaxation periods more satisfying. Most evenings without work, I just joined in the talks around the fire, played board games, or listened to Cal's story hour with the tykes.

Six days after our hillbilly wanderer's arrival, I passed the time playing cards with Daemon until we were supposed to sit guard. Even with preternatural speed, he was horrible at sleight of hand.

"Stop cheating! I can see you bottom-dealing, Daemon."

He grinned as he shrugged like a toddler covered in paint.

"What, I'm not cheating, I'm just lucky tonight." He denied as I reached for the deck. The young vamp pulled the deck up over his head and teased.

"Oh you want the cards? You want to see what's coming up next for your hand, huh. Who's cheating now, Squirrel?"

I grasped after the blue bicycle deck causing the already played cards to swirl around the blanket of the small cot. He smiled sweetly as he continued to hold the stack beyond my reach. I matched his laugh and tried to climb over him to grab the cards.

"Come on Daemon, you just don't want to admit I caught you again."

I lost my balance and nearly fell off the bed; firm hands gripped me as a shower of spades and hearts cascaded around us. Daemon looked into my eyes as he caught me, his smile changed as his cool lips grazed mine gently.

Without a thought, my hands wrapped around his shoulders and my mouth found his. His kiss was gentle but passionate. His left hand wrapped in my hair and his fingers massaged the back of my neck; his skin warmed against mine. The right hand slid from my back to my waist, rubbing softly as our lips parted.

Slowly, Daemon brought me over the cot, our embrace continuous. The tips of his hair tickled my cheek as he trailed butterfly kisses along my neck and ear. The vampire's fangs scraped teasingly along my taut flesh with each touch of his lips.

We shouldn't be doing this. I need to stop us.

My brain tried to force my thoughts outward, but all I could comprehend was how much I wanted Daemon.

Almost as though he heard my concerns ricocheting through my mind, the vampire abruptly stopped. I felt him inhale deeply and his body tense. I turned my head to face him. Our eyes met even as our faces pulled away.

The longing to be together like this was visible, but I could see him struggling with his control already.

Cal was right. We couldn't be together, at least not now. I didn't want to die — even in his arms — and he didn't want to kill me.

"We…we can't. I'm sorry, I want to. Desperately, in fact. But, I can't risk…" His words tapered off as his eyes went to every corner of the room. He eased his hands away from me. Daemon stood and went to the doorway. "I think I'll go help Cal until my shift; I need more training anyways. From now on, I don't think we should spend time alone together. It's just too tempting." In a blink, I was alone.

CHAPTER 13 AUGUST 11th-31st YEAR 1

The shouting woke me.
"Strangers and Dead, everyone inside!"
Pulling on sneakers and buckling my sword to my side, my legs carried me into the bright day before the sleep dust fell from my eyes. Running towards the gateway, camp members clamored inside the glimmering wall. They huddled near the tower and checked who was still missing.

A frantic bellow pierced the air as I reached the entrance. The two guards and myself quickly scanned our fellows for infection as they approached. Looking towards the sound, I found its source. There were eight or nine people running from several dozen zombies.

Half of the zombies appeared to be infected very recently and kept a close pace; rigor mortis hadn't even set in to make their movements slow and jerky yet. One had a rucksack on its back and a rifle dragged the ground behind another, the shoulder strap knotted around the creature's wrist.

I noted a familiar pattern of blue, green, and yellow on the shredded shirt of a young female corpse. My mind whirred as I tried to process the clusterfuck of bad news stampeding towards us.

I heard orders being given before I realized they were pouring out of my mouth.

"Slide the gate shut until only one person can fit through. Get three or four people on the tower with bows and slingshots. No guns, it will just make things worse. Big stones only. If your aim sucks, start grabbing the stockpile of arrows and stones, you are going to cover ammo for the shooters on the platform; use the pulley system, it's faster. Anyone who comes in had better be clear of infection."

"The four of us," I pointed at the guards, Sunny, and myself, "are going to funnel the living inside and cut down the ones who are infected if they make it past the gate. Someone let the vamps know what's happening and get the kids in their cabin with the parents."

Every muscle in my body tensed as the adrenaline coursed through my veins. My vision focused on the humans closest to the fort.

"Strip! Show no bite marks!" The first sentry began to shout at the fearful runners.

Clothes peeled off without question as the first three reached us and were admitted. Randolph stood a few feet behind our entrance gauntlet tossing spare clothes at the survivors. Small rocks began to fly and arrows were loosed. Cadavers dropped like anchors at port, giving the next few people a chance to draw near. A frazzled man carrying a small boy ignored the instructions and I pushed him back.

"Please, you have to let us in! Don't do this!" He yelled over the repeated directions to show us they were not infected with the Z-bug. I realized the child wasn't moving.

"Is he dead? Is he going to reanimate?" I shouted at the crazed guy as I pushed him away for the third time. "Either show us you're both clear of infection or keep running from the fleshies."

"No, you have to let us inside. My son is sleeping, he isn't dead, he's my son. Please help us, help my boy." He ranted as he continued attempting to shove his way past me; I pushed him back with a kick. The boy stirred, opening his eyes and tilted his face up towards his father.

I stepped back, unsure of what to do next. The child dug its crooked teeth into his distressed father's neck and tore a chunk out while his small hands clawed at the man's eyes and cheeks like a rabid animal.

My blade cut right through the small cranium and into the dying guy's collarbone. Kicking the remains off the sword, I swung it around to ensure they wouldn't rise again, before punting the corpses clear of the pathway. The archers and shooters were blotting the sun intermittently as they rained down a more permanent death on the progressing cadavers.

Only one of the recently deceased still pursued the newcomers. Its more decrepit counterparts flowed towards the encampment like a tidal wave of stench and low groans. The noise was so guttural, I wondered if it was merely the continuation of the infected's death rattle escaping the cracked lips.

In the minutes that felt like years, two others made it to the gate, the man with a German Shepard at his heels. Another stranger with visible bites tried to force her way in, only to be met by Sunny's spear.

In a single thrust, she shoved the spearhead through the woman's temple and out the other side. A gush of blood flew through the air and a squelching sound marked its abrupt removal. Sunny's face was set in kill mode as she hastily harpooned the body in the chest and dragged it out of the gateway.

The last of the recently turned gained on a woman and boy. The kid was around ten or eleven years old and practically carrying the woman against her will. I assumed it was his mother; she kept trying to push him to leave her and run. I felt a shove from behind as Chase dashed out towards the pair.

Sunny and I shouted after him, while I held her back from pursuing her husband. He was yelling to the strangers as he approached and they hurriedly tore off their shirts while fleeing. Chase reached the pair and hacked at the zombie with his ax. After a few strokes on the mangled remains, he looked over the family.

They grabbed their belongings and dressed in mid-run. A mass of other fleshies was stumbling after the trio from the edge of the forest. Chase realized the danger; they could be cut off from the camp and engulfed completely in a mass of ripped limbs and gnashing teeth.

Sunny was frenzied as she dropped her spear and reached for her husband, screaming at us to let her go. The sunburned warrior lifted the woman, nudged the boy to run, and sprinted for the gate. The boy galloped just ahead of them, looking over his shoulder to see that his mom was still close.

He turned to his side as Chase came up next to him and was suddenly gone. Chase had passed the child and was yards from the gate when he noticed. The boy had tripped on one of our snare traps, taking out his ankle.

Chase thrust the mother to me and bustled away before Sunny could grab him. The groans of the Dead grew as the towed their rotting bodies closer, the reek of decay and filth invading our nostrils. Having untied the rope from his foot, the kid was crying and limping as best he could, only to fall and drag himself forward on his elbows.

In one swift movement, Chase slid in the dirt, scooped up the injured boy, and flitted back towards the gate. His ax fell from his hip while he leapt to his feet. The archers were trying to aim for the zombies in his path. An arrow grazed Chase's right shoulder as the shot came to close.

The thin red streak dripped as Chase set the boy on his good leg and helped him reach the wall. Two fleshies clamored after them. Chase handed the boy to me to be shuffled in to safety. Hearing the corpses at his back, he drew his Bowie knife and turned.

A broken jaw missing several teeth wobbled and bit down on his left hand as the skeletal zombie stumbled from the side of the wall and latched onto the limb.

Chase brought the blade down, leaving his hand to the moaning fleshie and retreating within the gate.

I heard Sunny screaming behind me as her spouse bolted past. She picked up her spear and rushed after him to the fire pit; hastily, a burning log was lifted and the bleeding stump was cauterized to the soundtrack of Chase's agonized yells. I slammed the gate closed and the guards barricaded the steel frame, while I ran to assess the situation with my friends. The dog circled around them, sniffing Chase every few moments; his owner watched intently with furrowed brows.

Five yards from the couple, Sunny reared on me with her spear aimed at my throat. I dug my heels in the dirt and threw my arms in front of my chest to halt my stride. The canine growled low, his handler flinching. Randolph and Bubba raised their weapons slowly. Sunny looked around with her head and hands unwavering; her nose flared as she addressed us.

"You are not going to hurt my husband. He cut off the arm immediately; there wasn't time for the blood to pump the infection through. Chase is okay and I'm not letting any of you kill him."

The amputee whimpered as he cradled the charred stub of his forearm to his chest. He rocked gently as he sat by the inflamed trench. The smell of his burnt flesh reminded me of overcooked pork chops; the sight of the jagged ash-covered sear at the end of his arm transformed my stomach into a trapeze artist.

I could see the others taking small steps forward in my peripheral vision as I choked down the rising bile. I had to intervene or this would get vicious.

"Okay, maybe you're right." Everyone paused and her eyes studied me for signs of trickery. "If he isn't infected, of course Chase will be fine. All we have to do is get the vamps to check him first."

I was suddenly surrounded by blank stares. The twang of arrows and pfft of stones flying over the chorus of moans receded into the backdrop. I could hear every tiny sniffle from the distraught amputee and the sharply held breath from Randolph; my heartbeat grew steady and calm, no longer attempting to erupt from my chest.

"What are you saying, Squirrel?" Sunny lowered the tip of her weapon a fraction of an inch, just enough for her muscles to relax.

"Simple test for all our sakes. If he's clear, we patch up that arm and do our best to prevent regular infections from killing him. If not...Chase will die either way; our way is less painful, quicker, and allows the man some dignity. We get Cal or Daemon to take a few little sips and see if they taste Z-bug. Those two can taste death in the blood, remember?"

I held out one hand with the palm up and used the other to wave Bubba and Randolph away.

"Will you lower the spear and the two of us can get him over to the coffin cabin?"

It seemed eternity that my arm hung there, trapped in apprehension, waiting for a reply. Chase drew himself up gingerly, ambled to us, and set his remaining hand on his wife's shoulder.

"We have to try it. Squirrel's right, Cal and Daemon will be able to tell if I'm...they'll know if my blood is tainted. I don't want to die that way. I can't risk hurting you or the others and I don't want to end up like Kyle. If I'm going to die, I want it swift and painless."

With that, Chase walked past her and headed towards the second cabin. Randolph let out his breath before sprinting to help elsewhere – I don't think he wanted to witness the results if Chase wasn't cleared. The stranger and his dog followed the three of us to the vampires' quarters. I stopped the new guy at the door to the building.

"Why are you following us? Go help with the arrows or get water or something; this isn't your business."

"I'm a nurse, if that man isn't infected, I can take care of his wounds before checking on Jordy's ankle. Besides, Sindbad here can smell infection overtaking the body. This is where we're most useful." He answered confidently as he made a gesture and the canine sat at attention.

"Fine, it'll be nice to have a medic on hand and a trained pup could be handy. However, if Chase isn't given the A-Okay, you leave. Take care of that kid and leave this to us if it goes that way; Chase is a close friend and we'll handle it ourselves."

I entered the sparse room without waiting for a reply. Both vampires' eyes shone bright red at the amount of blood covering our patient. I assume the scent of it set them off. Daemon stood with his back against the far wall; I could see the risen hunger was pushing him to the edge of his restraint.

Cal leaned over Chase and nipped his neck. The Roman held the sanguine fluid in his mouth a moment as though critiquing a fine wine, while his protégé shifted uncomfortably with his back against the wall. Daemon's sharp fangs were pressing into his bottom lip. Sunny's chest heaved as she awaited her spouse's fate. I could hear her panicked wheezing from across the room. The nurse behind me strode over with his dog, watched the animal's motions, and smiled.

"Not infected." Cal declared with a smile as he calmly eyed they state of the young vampire across the room. Daemon had tears rolling down his cheeks as he kept his back pressed to the wall, wringing his hands, and his gaze fixed on the floor. The couple hugged tightly and wept. The nurse agreed while drawing himself erect and giving out directions.

"I think it's time I took care of Mister Chase. I'll need some medical supplies or at a minimum: clean rags, painkillers, and sewing items. I may need to redo that cauterization and the pain of stitching and cleaning of that wound will be excruciating."

He gazed at Daemon before continuing. "First, we should move the patient to another building; it would be unwise to add more blood to this environment given that those two are already struggling to keep their fangs to themselves."

Our new medic took hold of the injured limb and began a precursory examination of the extent of damage while aiding Chase to his feet. All gazes converged on me as the stranger repeated his directions.

"The guy's a nurse, do what he says. Get Chase and that boy into the main cabin and help him patch them up." I turned to the hungry Undead before continuing. "As soon as night falls, we need you two outside. Daemon, I'm your donor tonight, so just find me; Cal, yours was scheduled to be Chase so tell Sunny to do it instead. Any problems?"

Even the dog's head shook. I gave a firm nod and hurried out to defend the perimeter; it pained me to see Daemon so distressed. The only sounds were the intermittent muffled screams from Chase, the noise of projectiles cutting the air, and that horrible moaning from the zombies assembling around our steel walls.

The children stayed in the secondary cabin with Ellen's Mom; soon the boy with the sprained ankle and his mother joined them, a torn shirt wrapped the limb. Randolph kept everyone fed, filled the canteens, and loaded stones and arrows into the pulley-buckets for the rest of the day. Every hour or two, he would jog over to the cabin to check on Michael and Bobbi.

The Dead kept coming. They didn't climb, but they could easily walk over the mottled remains and reach up the side of the wall. It was like being in the middle of an ant mound. Most of the fleshies were long since infected and easily destroyed, but the few who weren't threw themselves at the gate with the force of a meth addict looking for a fix.

I placed a ladder against the wall near the entry point and climbed to the top of the barrier, dragging my defense with me. It was a sack made of gator skin that I'd filled with around ten pounds of smooth river stones. It was lashed closed with a six-foot strand of rope that had several knots and loops at one end.

I put a loop over my wrist, gripped just under a knot, and lowered the sack over the side of the partition. Swinging it back and forth as a pendulum, I crushed in the skulls of those zombies who reached the wall.

The moist cracking sound of their heads caving in kept my adrenaline flowing. Every half hour or so, I would heave the gore encrusted bag up and move to a different wall, taking short rests in between. The sight of the bag swinging usually drew the creatures right up to the weapon.

All day we slayed the corpses in near silence, waiting for dusk to bring our reinforcements. Everyone knew that we couldn't depend on the living to save us; the vampires were our only hope to escape today's atrocities and see tomorrow's fresh horrors.

The last rays of light dimmed out of existence as the last of our arrows struck the neck of its target; it shambled closer, unaware of the protruding missile. My forearms burned like acid and shook as I withdrew the sack and dropped it to the dirt along the bottom rung and climbed down. My back popped with every stretch and twist. Several of our shooters came off the tower and went for the weapons shack. I placed myself in front of the door.

"Don't touch those guns! We have almost all of them eradicated, if one shot's fired, this mess will start over."

At that moment, twin streaks lit out of the coffin cabin and over the shimmering steel partition. Hacking and slashing, the vamps annihilated the lingering Dead as they circled the wall.

Cal jabbed his short wasp-bladed sword into half-devoured faces as Daemon swung an ax like Paul Bunyan, felling fleshies as the blade separated the top of the cranium from the jaw with each swipe. The pair moved like lightning, shredding the attackers furiously and edging their way further and further from our encampment.

After nearly an hour, they returned and tossed their weapons aside. Their clothes were matted with shards of bone, coagulated blood, and the occasional patch of scalp. Both looked ravenous, having still not fed. The dog gave a low growl as Daemon stepped towards me. The fledgling regarded the canine with a stare; the dog whimpered and sat by his master while the young Undead spoke.

"We need to clean and feed. Squirrel, I'll meet you in my cabin in a minute. Cal will be there, too. Bring his donor with you, please."

He flew off in the direction of the stream as the last word left his pursed lips. His mentor glanced at me with his blazing eyes. His voice echoed in my mind. "I will make sure he keeps control and you are unharmed. Please get Sunny." Cal followed Daemon to wash away the battle.

Sunny and I stood in the small cabin for ten minutes. The room was quiet as a tomb and as uncomfortable as borrowed dress shoes. I stared at the door, unwilling to look at her after our earlier standoff. The door launched open. Caelinus strolled inside.

"Sunny, if you wouldn't mind, I would prefer to wait until Daemon has fed. It would be best if I ensured the Hunger did not cause any further issues this evening."

She said nothing, but nodded and sat awkwardly on the end of the nearest bed. I noticed she was looking in every nook and cranny that was not a view of the feeding. Cal joined her as Daemon stepped towards me; he was clean, but the flames in his eyes still raged;

the desire for blood wreaked havoc within his every cell.

The feeling of embarrassment at having my donation observed promptly shifted to fear. His face showed no sign that my friend was even aware this feeding was being monitored. I wasn't even sure he still knew it was me standing in front of him.

Daemon's fangs scraped his bottom lip as he reached out to push my hair aside. I felt an iron hand gripping my waist as he pulled me closer. I closed my eyes, and leaned my head to the left for him.

The familiar gentle pricks were replaced with a fierce bite; I startled at the savagery as much as the pain. He took two or three deep pulls from my vein before I felt my knees waver. Warm hands caught me as I felt Daemon's grip disappear.

I forced open my eyes. My head struggled to steady itself from the buzz I was feeling. Sunny held me upright and kept giving my cheek light slaps. She was asking me something; it sounded like she was speaking underwater.

I giggled at the concern on her face. Earlier that day she shoved a spear in my face, ready to kill me without a thought, and here she sat genuinely worried for my health.

Looking over, I saw the vampires scuffling. Cal smacked the young vampire in the face. A bicuspid somersaulted through the dim room and landed against a small tower of dog-eared books. The Roman walked over and rubbed his palm a moment before picking up the tooth with the tips of his forefinger and thumb.

Daemon was on his knees holding his mouth; his eyes were back to their usual brilliance. Examining the prize, Cal turned around and presented it to his protégé.

"Put this back in the hole in your gums. It will be agony for a minute until it heals, but only a minute."

With a whimper, Daemon did as instructed. Cal sighed and held out his hand to Sunny.

"Are you ready to donate? I assure you, they're both fine now and I only need my regular quantity of blood."

Sunny looked around the room at the three of us before helping me back to the bed and offering her vein to the elder vampire; her eyes flitted about as he took a few tiny sips. She gripped the dagger on her belt with an unsteady hand. I gazed at Daemon across the cabin; he sat hunched with his back against the opposite wall. His cheek had returned to its normal pallor, but the thin streaks carved by his tears remained visible.

The fledgling rose to his feet as soon as his mentor was done. Daemon's eyes were glued to the floor as he spoke in a muted tone.

"I'm going to start clearing up the mess outside. I'll leave the useful stuff in a pile by the gate and drop the corpses in the burn zone for you humans to torch during the day. It'll probably take all night. Both of you should get some rest. Especially Squirrel. I'm…I'm sorry I lost control again. It won't happen anymore."

He hurried out of the cabin to his task with the door slamming shut on the final word. Cal merely looked deep in thought and said goodnight before following. Sunny and I sat in the coffin cabin, immersed in silence, until my legs cramped up and brought the exhaustion I'd been ignoring crashing down on me. I stretched my legs, stood, and ambled to the exit.

"How is Chase doing?" I asked.

Sunny flinched.

"He's okay. That nurse guy patched him up before wrapping that boy Jordy's ankle. Kid only sprained it, so that's good. Chase is enjoying a little rest thanks to a couple of painkillers someone scrounged up on the last raid."

"Good to hear. By the way, it's okay what happened. I get it; he's your husband. There aren't any hard feelings about earlier."

Sunny let out the breath she'd been holding and a weak smile appeared.

"Just know that if you ever aim a weapon at me again, one of us will be getting cremated. No ill will, just a fact. Otherwise, we're fine."

I strolled out to the main cabin for some rest, leaving her silhouetted in the doorway with her eyes wide and mouth open. "Have a good night."

CHAPTER 14 SEPTEMBER 1ST YEAR 1

Half a dozen wristwatches blared their alarms at 6:30AM to rouse the cabin from our restless dreaming. I pulled on my jacket against the dry, cool air. I had to step over one of the new arrivals to exit the cabin; all of them lay wrapped in blankets in the walkways except for the boy with the sprained ankle.

Sunny sat beside her husband all night in a collapsible chair to allow Jordy her cot. His foot sat elevated on the foot rail of the old bed, while Sindbad the dog slumbered underneath.

I considered waking the entire cabin so we could get our town council out of the way, only to realize that if these people had been dangerous we'd already be dead. I'd failed to set a watch over the strangers or keep them separate until we knew they weren't a danger.

Some leader I am.

I looked at the others who were waking to the chorus of buzzes and beeps. They showed no signs of concern about the lack of precaution.

Maybe they're still too drowsy to notice.

I shook the second-guessing from my head and left the peace of the cabin to plan for another day's survival.

The sentries on duty were haggard from the marathon of defense and the dullness of the night. We all stood clad in the musty clothes from the prior day. At seven in the morning, half the camp wore a five o'clock shadow under their frowns. When the outsiders rose to join us for breakfast, I noted the puffy eyes and tear-stained cheeks.

Our camp hadn't lost loved ones – yes, an arm was gone, but our people remained alive. Our counterparts had witnessed the deaths of friends and family a matter of hours before. It was surreal to sit next to these wanderers and try to decide their fate.

The nurse and his German Shepard were the last to arrive at the table. Sindbad circled the assembly, sniffing each person, before settling by his owner. I noticed many residents tracked the canine's progress; the kids petted the dog as it passed.

None of our visitors approached the food. They sat to one end of the table and stared at their surroundings, each eventually stopping their visual tour on me. The sensation was disturbing; I felt like I'd been put on display.

Forrest saw my discomfort and chuckled loudly.

"Hell, y'all can have some breakfast. We ain't 'bout ter kill you for havin a bite to eat. We gotta have a meeting to see where we all stand, but until then, y'all are guests. So eat up and stop starin at Squirrel like she's gonna turn into a big purple clown and eat your hearts."

The funereal atmosphere evaporated as the nervous strangers laughed and helped themselves to some deer bacon, berries, and oranges. I grinned in spite of my exhaustion. I raised my strip of venison in thanks and Bubba nodded in return.

In a matter of minutes, everyone in the fort was breaking figurative bread and chatting lightly. The tension easing, I waited for everyone to be seated at the tables.

"I think this is a good time to start."

The small talk tapered off and I stood to be better heard. "We have seven new people here…" Sindbad's barking cut me off, "…and a dog." I finished over a soundtrack of giggles.

"We need to decide a few things: do you want to stay, will you abide by our rules, and do we trust you enough to let you stay." I paused to study the reactions of the conglomeration. The newcomers' eyes shone with fear at the thought of leaving. Of our residents, only Sunny seemed disinterested in the options. The nurse quickly looked at his cohorts and stood.

Found their leader.

"I think I speak for all of us when I say, we'd like to join your village." He received several emphatic nods. "Our shelter was destroyed by those murdering bastards; we don't have anyone or anywhere else. All of us agree to your rules and will pull our weight if you all allow us to stay."

I watched his Adam's Apple wobbling as he swallowed.

"We have a lot of valuable skills to offer: I'm a Registered Nurse, Jonah worked as a carpenter, and Levi is a mechanic. If you all choose to let us move in, we bring all of our abilities and hard work with us."

The dog barked as his master sat down again and pet his head. "Also, Sindbad can alert us to the presence of zombies and infection."

I watched Chase and Sunny as she helped him with his meal, stalling to gather my thoughts.

"You must really want to stay; you didn't even ask about our rules before agreeing to them for not just yourself, but your whole bunch. Seems kind of hasty."

The outsiders looked to their spokesman as he leaned back a little. His eyebrows rose in the center creating an arch of doubt.

"Then again, I was so stupid last night, I didn't even have the sense to keep a watch on the group of strangers who led a mob of corpses to our gates before letting them sleep beside us. Not all mistakes turn out badly."

Nurse looked at me with wide eyes as my own neighbors now glared at me for the potentially dangerous oversight. I ignored the steely eyes boring into me as best I could.

"Our rules are simple but non-negotiable. We have a pact with two vampires and every adult takes turns donating blood to keep them alive and well. We maintain firearms only as a final resort and focus on silent weapon usage. Also, everyone contributes to the community, every adult stands watch according to the rotation, and any infected…" I turned to Sunny "…no matter who they are or how much we love them – dies."

Sunny lowered her eyes and grimaced slightly at my statement. Chase reached his remaining hand down to stroke the canine as though affirming his status as healthy.

"Let's take a quick vote of where we stand and go from there." Chase declared without looking up from the animal's face.

I smiled and followed his cue.

"All in favor of taking in these eight raise your hands."

I scanned the assorted limbs; Chase nodded his assent as he continued scratching behind the dog's ears. "So far none opposed," the new arrivals let out a collective sigh of relief "anyone want to volunteer to get a vote from the guards and vamps?"

Michael shot up off the bench like a rocket and I heard him say, "I will!" The boy ran to the tower, gate, and cabin in a blur of energy. Laughter cascaded through the moist dawn air as we all watched the child sprinting around with that fervor only kids possess. Returning out of breath and triumphant, Michael announced between gasps, "They all said the people and puppy can stay."

After several pats on the back, he sat next to his sister to listen to the rest of the meeting.

"It's official then; welcome to Nova Nocte."

For several minutes, hugs and handshakes were exchanged with introductions and small talk. I remained standing and listened to bits and pieces of the interchanges before pressing on. Holding up and waving my right palm slowly, I caught the attention of those assembled.

"We still have a lot to do today. We need to revise the donation and guard schedules, gather all of the arrows, stones, and other usable items from last night's attack, burn the bodies, and try to settle everyone into a cabin. We also need to gather the crops, clear the fishing lines, check on our traps, and do our regular errands."

The celebration ended and the business got underway. "For now, I think we should buddy up each newcomer with a previous resident to show them the ropes out here and answer questions."

I stopped while the pairings were hastily made. Jordy raised his hand and asked, "Can I stay with my Mom?"

I hadn't considered the kid.

Brain not firing on all cylinders today is it?

I blinked away my self-rebuke and reflected on the options.

"Yes, you can stay together for a few days, but one of us will still be playing tour guide for the two of you. You'll be working within the camp until your ankle mends. At that point, you'll each have to learn to do the other tasks needed to keep this community running."

"At dinner tonight, I'll post updated rotations; in the meantime, everyone show your buddy how to do errands and explain day-to-day life here. By the way, if anyone has a food allergy or medical condition, tell the Nurse. As of this time, he's our only health care professional. I'm going to borrow the carpenter and get plans together for smaller defense platforms for each wall before picking up and cleaning all the weaponry."

I carried my plate to the washtub and strode over to the brawny woodworker. We began discussing the projects needed to prepare our society against the lurking hazards this new world could provide. A loud gunshot sounded in the distance while the group dissembled to their assignments.

Everyone moved expeditiously, arming himself or herself and pulling their partners along. I scaled the tower and grabbed the binoculars from the sentry's outstretched hand.

"I, I don't see who did it. It came from somewhere in that direction I think." The anxious woman stated with a stammer as I scanned the horizon, acutely aware that we hadn't even retrieved the arrows or stones to shoot yet. The guard kept fidgeting and mumbling prayers next to me. I snapped at the poor woman in frustration.

"Just get down and do something useful instead of bugging the Hell out of me with your constant muttering."

Her eyes watered at the edges as she scrambled down the ladder, only to be replaced by Marley Guy. He watched me while I desperately tried to locate the source of the blast. I scoured the area in the direction of our vehicles. A second round was fired.

The source was in my view in an instant, the clamor below lessening as I heard Sunny, Chase, and the Nurse directing everybody to be quiet.

Some idiot was running with a shotgun across his chest. I searched in his wake to see if he was fleeing from Dead or from marauders. It was a black bear chasing him.

It took me a moment to realize I was giggling uncontrollably, and throttle that splintered ball of stress back down inside. I tossed the viewers to the carpenter shadowing me.

"You two stay up here and keep an eye out for anyone or anything those shots drew this way; I'm going out to take that moron's twelve gauge and save him from Smokey the Bear."

Descending the ladder, I picked up a bow and hustled towards the exit. The news was passed to the others and I found Sunny and Bubba at my side when I reached the gate. Bubba just smirked while his counterpart grumbled and held her spear. We jogged across the red-spotted grass and I picked up a few bloodied arrows.

The dew and gore made our feet slip whenever we tried to go any faster. I heard a thud behind us and wheeled about, my arrow notched and ready.

"Sorry, we thought we could help." The young man lay on his side, slick with humidity and blackened blood. I turned back to the task at hand and withdrew the arrow.

"Freaking new guys." Sunny exclaimed as Randolph helped his new shadow to his feet and we hurried towards the failed hunter.

He looked to be in his late 30s, maybe early 40s if the hairline was any indication. The man's face was maroon and drenched in sweat from the sudden bout of exercise. Stopping when he reached us, the fool panted and tried to reload his weapon.

I snatched it from his trembling hands.

"Are you really this dumb?"

He collapsed to his knees as a look of terror washed over him. I dropped the hefty noisemaker behind me and set my arrow in place; other arrows and spears were aimed at the charging bear as we spread out into a semicircle. The creature slowed its assault as we got it half surrounded. Roaring at us, it stood tall on its hind legs.

Two arrows were loosed simultaneously; both finding marks in its chest as Sunny's spear thrust into the bear's heart. A gush of red poured from the wound as the animal repelled its fate. It was over in an instant.

I pulled both arrows out of the carcass and wiped the blood on the grass before turning to the wobbly man.

"I don't have time for this today; have any of the fleshies infected you?"

I held an arrow loosely strung in the bow as our party began to pick up the bear.

"No, no, I was just running from the grizzly. Haven't seen any zombies."

Bubba snipped at the man as he hefted the ursine meat at the shoulders.

"Black bear. Not a grizzly, they don't live this far south and they're a helluva lot bigger.

Just strip down so we kin see you ain't gonna turn into one of them fleshies and help us carry this critter back to camp."

The balding hunter stood slowly and awkwardly removed his clothing. Despite a multitude of scars, the stranger was free of bite marks. While not an adept marksman, he was definitely a survivor of something.

"Okay, you don't die right now. Grab some bear butt and follow us."

I handed Sunny the commandeered shotgun and took up guard the rear of the troop with my bow at the ready. I didn't have to tell him twice.

Upon reaching the camp, Sindbad circled and sniffed the entire party; the frail hunter shook with trepidation. Seeing the dog, I absentmindedly commented to the scared newcomer, "Forgot we have a dog now, sorry we made you strip for no reason." I briefly considered that it was a sorry excuse for an apology and walked inside the wall.

The guy didn't answer but his eyes darted between the canine and the people near the entrance; most of the community had already started their day's chores, giving the awkward man hardly a second thought.

We were cleared of infection and several residents relieved us of our ursine burden. Within minutes, the bear was being drained and skinned. That meat would provide an abundance of food for the now expanded neighborhood.

Putting down the bow, I turned to the hunter; he'd remained in my shadow since we put down the bear. I had too much to handle after the previous twenty-four hours and was still woozy from Daemon's feeding. I was snarky as I thought what to do with the added hardship.

"You aren't tainted with Z-bug, but you've already shown yourself to be a potential hazard to us. For the moment, Yogi, you can help split firewood and cook meals. At dinnertime, we'll decide where to go from there. I'd start thinking about any special skills you have to offer the group."

I turned on my heel and strode to gather and clean remaindered weapons and ammo. My mind whirred away with worries and plans for getting through to the next day.

CHAPTER 15 SEMPTEMBER 8th-9th YEAR 1

Over the next week, Yogi (the nickname stuck) proved to be one of those lucky guys who's survival is a fluke. Having no common sense and limited abilities, we began teaching and training the new arrival by rotating his buddy daily.

So far the frail man with the tiny paunch had only been useful in helping us build the small platforms against each wall and in burning the corpses; although his proficiency in disposing of the outhouse contents had some merit.

It quickly became apparent that something was off about Yogi. Although he'd been cleared of infection, Sindbad perpetually trailed the guy around the camp. During meals, his absence and discomfort with the group made each of us focus on the stranger all the more intently.

It was discussed one evening that his mural of scars may have been part of the reason Yogi was so standoffish; he never made eye contact and visibly cringed whenever any of the adults in the fort drew near.

As theories about the eccentric outsider were tossed around the table, Daemon took a seat and grinned as he observed the banter.

"I could just ask him why he's so strange."

I shook my head, the motion mirrored by a few others in the flickering light.

"No, that would be prying into Yogi's past. The past is moot; if he wants to talk about it, eventually he'll open up to someone. As it stands, the guy is so uncomfortable around us, he won't even eat near us."

Sunny set down her fork and nodded her agreement. The table was quiet except for the occasional sounds of construction on the last defense platform along the opposite wall. Daemon looked thoughtful, his brow furrowed slightly before he spoke.

"Maybe I could just glamour him into relaxing around the rest of the community, or I could ask him why he's freaked out and then wipe his memory of the conversation."

The young vampire cocked his head to the side and smiled widely as he made the suggestion. "That dog isn't stalking Yogi for shits and giggles. Something has to be up; dogs can tell when something is wrong. It's like they just know stuff."

The frogs in the distance and the crackle of the fire were the only noises in the night. A gentle breeze wafted by, stirring a tuft of

Daemon's hair and standing up the tiny hairs on my forearm.

Please not another bitchfest from these two.

"It would be wrong to invade a person's mind like that; it's a violation of his private thoughts." Sunny glared at him from the dimly lit bench. "You can't do that to one of our people."

The fledgling vamp held her gaze as he countered calmly, his words coming out in the metered tempo of forethought.

He must've been considering this for a while before he brought it up; Daemon's arguments are always more of a string of rambles.

"Who said he's one of our people; I thought he's probationary? What if he's a risk to the community? We need to do what's best for the greater good, even when it sucks as an option. Even Chase agrees with that."

The dig at her husband made Sunny's nose flare and I could swear her eyes were about to ooze molten lava; she said nothing as the young Undead pressed on.

"The guy's a grown man who shakes near every adult in the camp, but lingers around the kids whenever possible. It's not normal and we should know more about him. Either he's afraid of us because other grown-ups put those scars on him – possibly with good reason – or he enjoys being close to children more than is healthy."

Faces softened around the illuminated table.

Someone interjected, "Maybe we should think about this."

One of the women added her two cents. "I know he creeps me out and dogs are good judges of character."

Sunny shook her head.

"It isn't right. We all have this unspoken agreement not to pry into each other's past and now you want to not just ignore that, but also screw with his memory. We let him stay here, he's one of us now."

"Look, Sindbad knows something is up, the parents watch the dude like a hawk, I know Squirrel's keeping tabs on him, and he sets off my Spidey Sense. We need to know why. It's not about getting into his past, it's about protecting the kids in camp."

The vampire was snarling at Sunny as she rose to her feet; she maintained the stare-down with a scowl. Across the fort, someone began hammering the final touches on the east wall's platform.

"Despite your feelings, you won't be messing with any of our minds like that. We all voted to allow Yogi to remain here and weird or not, you don't have evidence that he's done anything wrong to warrant such actions."

Daemon crossed his arms and sneered as she ranted.

"Maybe Yogi is shy or scared of all the heavily armed people and vampires, or maybe he is simple-minded and likes to be around kids on the same level; we don't know. Hell he could think he's being protective of the children or they may remind him of a more innocent life. Leave the new guy alone and drop the subject unless you get some real proof that we have a reason to reconsider the topic."

Sunny twisted towards me, her index finger leading the way.

"And Squirrel, you'd better do the same. Keep Fangboy here away from Yogi and stop keeping tabs on everything the creeper does. I don't care if you're in love with Daemon, you are the leader here and it's your responsibility to keep the vamps from overstepping the boundaries of the Pact."

I felt the blush cover me from my head to the soles of my feet as I sat dumbfounded and tried to remember how to breathe. I could even feel it inside my belly button. Sunny whipped away her finger and marched off into the darkness, griping at the shadows. I glanced around the lit trench at the myriad of faces; Daemon's expression had morphed from fury to pained embarrassment.

As I met his gaze, he took to the sky mumbling something about patrol duty.

I can't believe the coward bailed on me; he's really going to regret this when dawn comes and he can't get away from me.

I took note of the sea of confusion, discord, and amusement engulfing the small group. The everlasting moment of discomfort was rent apart and time shifted into fast forward as yelling and the sound of broken wood echoed. I gave a silent prayer of thanks before the worry propelled me in the direction of the commotion.

By the time I arrived at the doorway to the secondary cabin, the skirmish was over. Yogi was hunched against Jordy's cot; a bump protruded from his forehead and leaked crimson. The boy was both hugging and holding back his petite mom. She was an angry bull wielding a cloth-wrapped mallet over her head. Marley Guy and the Nurse helped restrain the enraged woman while Sunny stood next to me with her husband's axe. I took in the scene while trying to halt the crying, screaming, and whimpering.

"Shut up, all of you. You're going to bring a stampede of fleshies this way. Just settle down and we will sort this out."

I turned to the 11-year-old.

"Jordy, what happened?"

His mother clung to the shaking child as he spoke. Her hate targeted at the cowering man on the floor like tendrils of flames from her glare. Jordy sniffled as he spoke.

"That guy came in and sat next to me. He… he said he was noticing I was growing into a man and that all boys needed someone to show them how to become a man." He stared at the floor and wiped away a dangle of snot.

Dammit, don't let this be what I think.

"Then, he was touching the hair near my face and said he was really good with boys and kissed my neck. When I pushed him away he started trying to take of my pants and talking about how I just didn't understand and he was going to make me feel nice and other stuff.

When I screamed at him to get off me, Mom came in and hit him in the head and pulled me over here. She went to hit him again but then everyone came running in."

Knuckles were turning white as weapons were gripped tighter. His mother just held Jordy tightly and rubbed his back while he cried. All eyes in the room bounced from Yogi to me.

Fuck. How could I have let this creep near my people?

"Do you have anything to say?" I faced the puny pain in my ass as calmly as I could manage.

Yogi answered while trying to gain his feet, the blood was running down the length of his face and dripping onto his shirt.

"You don't understand. He came on to me, he flirted with me. I didn't do anything wrong. Jordy wanted to do it; he just needed someone to show him how. You people just don't understand; it's just like the last place. The world changed and we could all use some more love. I was just trying to love the boy…"

I silenced the pedophile with a backhand across the mouth.

"You're done talking now. Jordy, I'm sorry I let this guy in the camp. I promise, I won't make that mistake again; we will deal with him."

I faced his mother, "You two should go eat something or relax or something. Yogi won't be an issue anymore. Ever."

As she guided her son to his feet and they exited the cabin, our prisoner started for the door. Marley Guy pushed him back and Sunny knocked him out with the back of her axe. The sicko dropped to the floor with a thud.

"Nurse, I want you to sew his mouth shut. I don't want his screams later to endanger the group."

I tied his hands behind his back as I gave orders.

"And Sunny, I need that hammer she hit him with before. Marley Guy, please go get Daemon and Cal."

No one moved.

"What, not enough proof for you, Sunny? Why are you all just standing there?"

Sunny blanched and went to her task, mumbling as she did, "I'll get the vamps, too."

The wood door clicked shut as I stared at Marley Guy and the Nurse.

"Well?"

The Jamaican spoke first.

"I cannot be a doings this to another of God's creatures. Is not for I to be harming this man, evil demon that he be likings to be. I go to do the chores and release the Dead from their wanderings, but this is not for me to be involved."

Not understanding him – as much from the accent as the content – I waved him out of the room. The Nurse helped me lift Yogi onto the small bed.

"I'm supposed to help people; I'm a healer, not an executioner."

I thought a moment.

"Fair enough. You aren't going to have to kill this guy; I just need him unable to yell. If you don't stitch him shut, I will. And I won't do it as well or as quickly as you might. Either way, just grab a needle and some fishing line; these stitches are getting done."

He stepped back and his eyes went wide. I waited in silence for him to bring me supplies. I wasn't sure I could trust him to watch the perv.

Sunny burst through the door, ending the standoff.

"The fang boys are on their way, Cal is finding Daemon now. Here's the hammer and the sewing kit. I still say it would've been wrong to mess with his mind but I was wrong about asking. I'm sorry."

The Nurse slipped outside as Sunny and I started darning the pedophile's mouth closed like it was a torn gym sock. He woke after the fourth stitch, his meek body flailing against the rope cutting into his wrists and the needle gliding through his parched lips. The lines were crooked, bunched, and bloody; but they trapped his screams in his gullet.

With Yogi's eyes bulging in time with each muffled yell, we hoisted the captive onto his feet. Looking up, I saw the Roman and his protégé in the doorway.

"We heard what happened," Daemon remarked "what's the plan here?"

He stared at the red splotches on Yogi's shirt. The young vampire didn't make eye contact with me; he just stood fixated on the sanguine fluid, his fangs descended and eyes glimmering.

"Simple plan: this sick fuck is going to be taking on donation duties for both of you tonight. Drink enough to keep you strong, but leave him enough blood to stay conscious for at least a few hours."

Cal tipped his head to the side and raised one brow.

"Might I ask why you two went through the effort of preventing him shouting out if you just want us to drain him dry over the span of a few nights?"

The pedophile stomped on my foot and struggled to get free of Sunny's grip. I cursed as I hopped to the right before turning and smashing his knee with the mallet. Our prisoner collapsed as the bone shattered with a noise reminiscent of pounded celery and glass.

"Because…" I hooked my arm under his shoulder to help carry him through the doorway, "that isn't his punishment. We're taking him out to the spike pits. You guys get a big dinner, he gets both of his kneecaps crushed along with his wrists continuing to be gouged by his bonds, and then we toss him down and leave him to die slowly."

I heard Sunny gasp as the night's humidity engulfed us. The stars twinkled above and were reflected in the eyes of half the camp; my words trailed off as we halted. All around me there were blank faces intermixed with the occasional wide-eyed expression of astonishment.

What did they think I would do about this kind of thing? It's not like we can send him off to mess with another innocent child…

…sometimes you need to be able to destroy the monsters in the world.

Streams of tears were mingling with Yogi's smatterings of blood. No one spoke for what felt like hours; my heart pounded over the hooting of an owl and the sniffling of a pedophile. Slowly, Randolph took two steps towards me.

"I'll give you a hand; someone get the gate, we don't want to waste all night on this prick."

A path cleared as we hefted the limp form and strode to our task. The kids were all in the main cabin, safely tucked away from the wicked creatures out to cause them harm.

The Boogie Man won't be coming back tonight.

We neared one of the pits and both vampires fed on the captive. They took their nourishment harshly. I smashed the condemned man's other knee, feeling it turn to mush under the weight of the simple tool.

With a small kick to the ribs, he tumbled into the trap, a wooden spike impaling his elbow on landing. The muted groans of his anguish floated up to us as our community left him in the darkness.

We ambled back within our walls, back to our loved ones waiting for us in the light of the fire. Yogi huddled in his open grave to await death in whatever form it may take.

Tomorrow was another day. There'd been dangers unforeseen and unacknowledged before. We learned our lesson with Yogi: just because someone is uninfected with Z-bug, doesn't mean they aren't sick.

***

 It didn't take him long to die. When Chase and I checked the pit in the morning, we found a fleshie eating through his torso. As it paused to lunge up at us, I saw one of Yogi's lungs rapidly expanding in the exposed cavity. The half-digested remnants of the man's supper decorated the floor of the pit while the decaying zombie chewed a piece of stomach.

 Both dinner and diner looked at me with protruding eyes. Chase looked away and I choked down the rising bile as the scent of it all hit us like a baseball bat. Reaching into my pocket, I decided to show both fiends mercy. Gathering some brush, Chase and I set the pair on fire within the confines of the deep trench.

 There were no screams. There was only the licking of flames, the sizzle and crackling of wet skin, and for a few moments the ripping of flesh. With a silent look, we continued with our patrol of the traps. When we finished, the fire had burned itself low. We tossed a few shovels of dirt on the embers, smothering the reek along with the fire. There was no point to removing the remains; there was food to be gathered and clothes to be washed. Life goes on.

CHAPTER 16 SEPTEMBER 14th YEAR 1

It was a few days before any other strangers arrived at our walls. Trudging slowly up the low hill in the darkness and dragging what looked like a body, our sentry at first mistook them for a herd of zombies. It was my night to stand duty at the gate. Wiping my sweaty palms on my pants, I drew my sword and lifted my crank-up flashlight; the footsteps stopped instantly and startled faces shone back at me. The thing they were dragging was a drained feral pig in a stick.

"They're not Dead, just not ours." I shouted behind me.

Brandishing the tip of my blade at the small group, I kept them halted about ten yards away. Reinforcements arrived in less than a minute. Chase and Sunny were first with the Nurse and Sindbad close behind.

With a hand signal, the canine was sent to sniff the drifters for contamination. He came back to his master and, with a motion, granted the five strangers a temporary reprieve. Little was said for the next couple of moments; tense expressions and gestures stood in for a meeting.

All eyes rested on me, as I knew they must, so I made the call.

"None of you are infected, but we still don't know you. We aren't letting you in this camp tonight. I'm not sending you away in the middle of the night, but we can't take you in either."

The pack stirred as Caelinus landed beside me. Crude weapons were raised. I stifled a chuckle as I noticed a butcher knife duct-taped to a broom handle.

"Friends of yours, Squirrel?" the vampire commented as he assessed the situation. I noticed that Daemon had landed silently behind the fearful people.

His training really is coming along well.

"Knock off the battle poses." They held their arms steady. "This is Caelinus, he's part of our village. If you folks put away the weaponry, we can have a little chat and figure something out."

Crowbars and improvised spears lowered. The man in front maintained his crossbow; it was aimed at my chest. Daemon's fangs glistened in the moonlight as they descended in response to the threat. I breathed gently, trying to mellow myself out, and sheathed my sword.

"There's no need for this to turn bloody." I maintained eye contact with the bowman. "You'll be unharmed and given water outside the wall until we can have a town meeting. We'll even bring a couple of burning embers out so you can cook your pig. That is assuming that you don't attempt to injure your protectors or myself. "

I motioned at each of the Undead guardians while the young bowman with swirling tattoos withdrew his artillery. There was an audible gasp of surprise as the fledgling vamp retracted his fangs and said "Hello." My point made, the Nurse and Sunny went to bring some water to our guests.

"If anyone's injured, let me know; we have a nurse here and he can patch you up. He and Sunny will be back with something for you to drink in just a second."

The guy hung the crossbow on his shoulder and faced his group.

"Alright we rest here tonight. Start putting out the bedrolls against the wall. I'll take first watch. Quince, show their medic your shoulder once we get set up." The leader smiled. "And someone cook that pig and give our hosts a good-sized haunch."

As his people carried out his instructions, the man approached me and held out his hand.

"Hi Squirrel, I'm Troy. We get the message with fang boy there: you hold the cards. I'll make sure there isn't a problem with my crew and you just keep those guys from making us a midnight snack. Everything else can be worked out tomorrow. Deal?"

I shook Troy's hand with a strained laugh. The tension in my chest eased.

I have to find a less stressful way to make acquaintances.

"Deal. By the way, Cal and Daemon are going to be the ones keeping the zombies from you all night; I'm just keeping you guys from causing us any trouble."

I turned my back to him, signaling for the provisions to be brought out to the small group of interlopers. Forrest and the Nurse strode out to administer aid to the newcomers.

"By the way, any attempt to breach the wall, will result in your swift executions. No offense, just covering our asses."

Chase and I helped tend our guests for the next half hour. No one spoke except for minor pleasantries. Finally, the four of us withdrew into the fort, barricading the gate behind us.

From my post on the small tower next to the entrance, I watched over Troy's group until 1 o'clock. The shepherd sat on the far side of the flock, facing the wilderness, with his bolts at the ready. The stiffness in my shoulders crept up my neck and into the base of my skull. Tendrils of pressure resonated through my head. When Marley Guy took over the watch, Troy checked out the other guard and myself before scanning the clouds for the vampires. The confident, youthful dignitary nodded to me and took his rest.

CHAPTER 17 SEPTEMBER 15th YEAR 1

That night, I stayed awake contemplating how to handle this new group of strangers. While Troy and his four companions appeared to be minimally armed and harmless, they still posed a potential threat.

Could they be acting as a decoy or scout detail for that murderous horde? Are any of them sexual predators? How can I do the right thing to protect my community?

Logically, having the fang boys glamour them into revealing their intentions seemed wisest. I worried about the fallout it could bring in camp, but the role I was thrust into was guardian of their safety.

This sucks, but it is the only way to be certain we can trust outsiders. It's what has to be done, no matter how unpopular. Pasts will have to come out.

I watched the little crew drowsily rotate their guards; the new sentry dozed off within ten minutes.

Ughhh, and I have to train them as well as keep them safe. Fuck.

Intent on mulling my concerns over with Cal, I headed over towards his cabin.

One of the vamps landed a little while ago, hopefully, he's still up to a chat.

Stretching my achy neck to the side, I was greeted with cool palms rubbing the anxiety from the muscles. I could sense his grin behind me.

"Thanks Daemon."

"How'd you know it was me," he laughed, "it could've been Cal. You know he cares about you."

I turned to face the young vampire.

"He thinks of me as a fellow soldier or maybe a daughter; not a neck-rub type person." I forced a playful frown. "Of course, I was hoping it was Cal. But I guess you'll do."

We broke into childish giggling and he motioned for me to take a seat. I shrugged off the remaining muscle constriction and plopped onto the edge of the bed. Experienced leader or not, I felt compelled to talk these worries out before taking action.

Sometimes Daemon can surprise me with some pretty sage advice and he's always been a good listener.

"Can we discuss those guys out front?"

He nodded while he leaned back on his elbows next to me. We spoke until after 2:30AM. We ended exactly where I started; it was the option with the most palatable consequences. Although the burden was eased, it was only a minuscule relief. Stretching out to a chorus of pops and cracks, I braced myself for the full weight of added responsibilities.

By tomorrow evening, either I'll be killing these five and preparing for an attack or working to ensure their survival and usefulness.

"Guess it's time I start the alternate schedule for if they join us."

I began pulling my copy of the calendar from my pocket. The fledgling rose to his feet.

"Okay, I'll grab your notepad and a pen. Back in a sec."

Carefully unfolding the wrinkled paper, I glanced at the date while Daemon bounded out the door.

For an instant, I felt the world drop and my vision form a blurred tunnel. September 15th.

It's my little brother's twelfth birthday.

I heard the door open but couldn't look away from the torn sheet of paper.

Last year I bought him a copy of Thrillville so he could build theme park rides with his PlayStation 2.

Someone was talking to me; something wet ran down my face.

He always loved to see how things were built.

I heard a deep sobbing, a voice going hoarse from misery. The calendar dropped from my trembling hands. The sounds were coming from me, the wetness on my cheeks poured from my closed eyes.

Strong hands wrapped around me. I collapsed in grief against Daemon's shoulder as he caressed my head. He kept whispering gentle words of comfort.

"It'll be all right, Squirrel. Everything's okay. You're safe here, just calm down. Leave this stuff until tomorrow and sleep. I'll take care of you, just get some rest and we can handle everything in the morning."

His words echoed in my ear over and over, punctuated by my crying and the slow rhythm of his strokes.

I couldn't even keep my family safe. Owen's birthday is today and I have to run a village and I can't do it. I'll make another bad choice and everyone will die. I give up; I just want to go home. I want to see them again.

He held me tighter, asking, "What's wrong? What can I do to help?". The fear and affection made his voice cut out.

Mom and Dad would've liked Daemon. If the world hadn't died, I could've brought him home for dinner one night. I could've gone out with him and kept being insignificant, but loved. Can't have either now. No family. No Daemon. Just death, worry, and killing. I have to live to protect others, but I've already failed when it mattered.

My tears lessened as I pulled away from his arms and looked into his eyes. He wiped my tears with his thumbs and gave me a caring smile. I leaned forward and kissed him. Daemon started to kiss back, then abruptly withdrew.

He doesn't understand that I'm ready to take the risk. I don't care anymore; I'm either going to live or die, not just keep surviving.

My lips followed his while my arms draped around him. We embraced as our passion grew. I could sense him holding back his desire even as he pulled me closer. Daemon's hands danced down my spine and along my hips, his silky caress lingering at my thigh. My heart pounded. I dug my fingertips into his muscular back. His long locks tickled my eyelashes as he slowly eased away. His eyes shone green with a different hunger; our shirts seemed to evaporate from the heat between our bodies.

I ran my hand up the back of his neck and into his unruly mane, grabbing it and gently pulling him back to me. As we pressed together on the bed, Daemon sucked my earlobe, his fangs grazing my skin. I felt his warm breath in my ear. He ran his mouth along the nape of my neck while I reveled in the sensations he caused with such little effort. His sharp teeth slid into the vein and there was the familiar tug of his feeding.

After only a couple of sips, Daemon released his lips and ran the tip of his tongue down my neck. He trailed his mouth slowly down to my breasts. I moaned and writhed against him as he began to roll and flick my protruding nipples with his supple tongue. Colors flashed against my closed eyelids as he languorously suckled me, again taking a tiny drink of my blood in the process.

This is definitely a better way to donate.

I pulled his face to meet mine and kissed him fully as we pressed close, my hardened areolas rubbing against his chest. Daemon unbuttoned my jeans and slid his hand inside as his pants dropped to the floor. His nimble fingers made waves in the warm waters within, brought me to the brink of ecstasy, and gradually tapered me back down to sustained anticipation. As my lover grinned and licked his moist finger, I slid out of my dampened Levis.

He teased me with a flurry of butterfly kisses and nibbles along my belly button and inner thigh; periodically using the very tip of his long tongue to lap up the results of his titilation. I grabbed handfuls of his hair, desperate for him to continue. I arched my back while Daemon simultaneously thrust his fangs into my thigh and repeated his show of digital dexterity. The combination of blood loss and near orgasmic tantalization made me lightheaded. His mouth shifted over and my entire body shook with rapture.

I found myself staring into the vampire's shining green eyes; he held me tightly to him as he slid inside me. I wrapped my legs around his waist. With each slow thrust, my climax was extended and heightened.

Daemon moaned into my ear, "Oh God, this is so worth the wait..." while my eyes rolled back. I found myself biting his earlobe as he neared his peak. I tilted my hips with each stroke. Daemon's eyelids fluttered and his eyes took on a red tint.

"Nnffhh...yesss."

He sighed and he drove his teeth back into my neck, this time with a yearning I hadn't felt since that first feeding. I was floating now, my every pore vibrated and bones tingled. He drank deeply as our passion crested together. The cabin went black as I drifted into the fireworks my senses cascaded over me. His loving arms suddenly felt worlds away.

What's happening? Why does Daemon sound alarmed?

***

Someone was snoring on my chest; and drooling, if the feel of the blanket was any indication. As I hoisted my heavy lids and squinted into the dim cabin, images and sounds tumbled through my memory banks like an inebriated dream. The pieces pulled themselves together as I brushed the hair from Daemon's face.

I must have blacked out from the blood loss.

I sat for a time just watching his eyelids flutter and nose crinkle while he slept.

"You gave us quite a fright, Squirrel."

I turned to find the elder vampire sitting rigidly against the wall staring at me. He seemed livid. For a moment I flinched, noticing he wore the expression my Dad used whenever I let him down.

"It's clear you didn't listen to my advice, perhaps you will be less selfish in the future. If you are weary of living, be done with it in a manner that will not destroy that boy or tear apart this small society we have built."

Small spots still floated in my vision and I felt faint, but his snarled words made the sensation worse.

"You're right," I whispered through my dry throat "it was a dick move. I wanted to be with him, so that's what I did. I stopped worrying about how everything could get screwed up and I didn't consider how he'd feel if he killed me in the process. But I'm not sorry."

His eyebrow arched as he reclined on his left side, his right palm gesturing me to proceed. Daemon mumbled something about kilts and Wookies before his snoring resumed. My fingers stroked his head while I drew my argument together.

"We love each other." I sighed softly. "It's not a good argument for potentially ruining or ending lives, but it's what I've got. I've no intentions of having him turn me or…"

"I wouldn't allow that."

Cal stood as he spoke. My startled recoil stirred my sleeping lover.

"Whaa, what happened? Are you okay?" He sat up and rubbed the sleep sand from his eyes. I nodded and he kissed me gently before I could speak. "Good. Sorry about all the biting, I got kind of caught up in the moment."

He looked over at his mentor. Then down at the covers he'd just shaken off. Promptly, we both turned bright red as we reached the same conclusion: we were still nude and Cal was very much dressed and not blind.

Thank goodness I'm still under the blanket.

In a blink, Daemon had clothed himself and my garments were delivered to me with a sheepish grin.

"Um, forgot the naked thing. Sorry again. Cal, can you give us a second please?"

I knew his answer before he said it.

"No. I saw her nude earlier when I helped you put her into bed and elevate her legs so her heart wouldn't stop. Or have you forgotten?"

"No, I didn't. I just, well, I forgot I about the nakedness at the time."

"Nearly killing a lover does that."

The room seemed unbearably warm in the following silence. I dressed under the blanket and dropped my numb legs over the side of the bed. Pins, needles, and steak skewers jabbed through every cell as the blood flowed more freely to my limbs. I became weak and woozy, finding myself held upright by the Roman. He handed me a glass of juice and a plate.

"The juice is warm and the liver cold, but eat it anyway. It's too soon for you to stand, you haven't built up your blood yet." Daemon rubbed my legs while Cal forced me to take the meal. "For the next day or two, you'll need to rest here and consume large amounts of fluids and meat. If Daemon hadn't already fed, we would be burying you right now."

I focused on the food. The rubbing had stopped and I couldn't bring my eyes to meet either of theirs. I slowly drank the juice only to have Daemon replace the empty glass with one full of water.

"Thanks." I murmured awkwardly between bites. The liver was chilly and rare. I choked it down past the guilt that was welling up in my chest. It was like swallowing blood-drizzled silly putty.

Daemon spoke first. His green eyes softened as he cleared my dishes.

"Was it at least good?"

I laughed at his smirk as he attempted to lighten the mood. Cal smacked him in the back of his head and stormed out of the cabin.

"Yes, actually. It was amazing." I responded, giving him a playful kiss on the cheek. "It's just that too much of a good thing can kill you."

The seriousness returned to his face.

"I know. At least we got to make love once. Besides, I finally got laid, so that's nice."

I pinched his arm before cupping his hand. As our fingers interlaced, I forced everything I yearned for into a tiny shoebox in the basement of my heart and hefted my responsibilities back onto my fragile shoulders. I thought of Cal's face, etched with concern and sadness; then of Daemon's, full of love and the knowledge that this was the closest we could be.

"We have to get back to the real world now. Time to clean up my mess."

The elder vampire barged back into the room; Sunny trailing behind him, his blighted hope mirrored in her distressed glare.

What new hell is this?

"Are you seriously this stupid? You almost died." Sunny stormed past Cal and stood so close I could taste the stewed tomatoes on her breath. "And you," she pointed at Daemon "you keep your fangs and anything else that grows to yourself. We have a deal for survival, not screwing around."

"Uhhh, okay. I kinda think this is our business though. Squirrel and I already agreed that this was a one-time thing; I don't want to hurt the woman I love."

He squeezed my hand and lowered his eyes.

"I get it; you two are pissed. Daemon and I can handle this on our own. We appreciate the concern…"

"You could've been killed. If you die at the hands of one of these two, none of the others will agree to keep donating and things will get real messy real fast. This fling was idiotic and selfish."

Caelinus stood like a statue, his eyes following the verbal volleys.

I straightened up and pushed aside the guilt I felt.

"We aren't arguing that fact. I accept that it's true. We're going to keep our emotions in check and maintain the status quo here. So forget last night and let's focus on today's new pile of crap to deal with."

Three silent stares.

"Has anyone been told anything or asked about me staying here last night?"

Cal spoke haltingly, "Actually, no. We told the visitors that the camp was weighing our options and separated them to aid with the gardens and burning any Dead we found in the pits."

He looked past me, his diminished rebuke shrinking his stance. Sunny just shook her head and crossed her arms.

"So the chewing out was for nothing? I'm fine, lesson learned. There isn't an issue here."

Daemon beamed that our nocturnal activities had been without consequence. (Or possibly he was just excited to have lost his virginity.)

"Just tell the others, I took ill and am in quarantine in the coffin cabin for a couple of days; it's already our standard procedure. Then we set up the Q&A of the strangers for tonight before dinner. Cal puts the guys under one at a time, asks the questions we write up today, and we go from there. Problem solved."

Sunny tilted her head and raised an eyebrow.

What the fuck now?

I waited for the question to wind its way out of her.

"Why should Cal ask one by one instead of just ask all five at once and have them nod or raise hands to signal a yes answer? It would be faster and let us handle any of the ones who fail without a struggle."

"Trust. We need them to trust us and we need everyone to trust that they will never be set up like that if Cal or Daemon ever need to Glamour them."

"But…" She started.

"No." I forced my aching body to hold my weight and stood. Daemon held my arm to steady me. "If any of these newcomers get to stay, our lives will depend on them; for that, we need trust. I want these dudes to know the answers their compatriots give and why we take any actions. They have to be willing to accept this camp as their community, otherwise they may opt to kill us while we sleep instead of sitting a guard shift."

Caelinus smiled and gave a small nod of approval. Wordlessly, he picked up a pen and paper and sat by the mussed bed. Daemon rose while his mentor scribbled some questions on the notepad

"Coolies. No harm, no foul works for me. I'll go deliver the messages before everyone starts cooking dinner." He gave me a kiss on the cheek before disappearing.

As I sat back on the bunk, Sunny remained stern-faced. After a minute, she threw her hands up and joined us to pen the big questions for Nova Nocte's new entrance exam.

***

Twenty minutes later, the residents of Nova Nocte — minus the younger kids — were assembled around the cooking fire. I sat on a bench with the Nurse and Sindbad, watching our five newcomers and trying to look vaguely sick as opposed to merely anemic and over-sexed. My light jacket hid the only visible bite marks without being as obvious as a turtleneck.

Cal stood to my side; he held the crumpled list of questions as though it was a scroll announcing a new emperor. The small village was silent except for the occasional laughter of the children playing and the shuffling of chairs. I checked the clouds for any sign of Daemon before confirming that each sentry was in place and watching beyond the wall instead of the inquiry taking place within.

"Okay, let's get these interviews started so we can get on to dinner and sleep. Cal will be using his vamp abilities to put each new guy under individually. Then he will ask them the questions we agreed would be pertinent. Please do not interrupt the process, because it will make this whole thing take longer."

The elder vampire gave me a small nod and began. The first two dudes answered all of the questions so that no red flags were raised. The third guy, the one wielding a butcher knife taped to a broom handle, explained that he left his previous group during the first winter when they turned to eating their sick and recently deceased. He found Troy when he was half-starved and near delirious with hunger; it explained his dedication and obedience to the bowman. It was the fourth man who made the crowd antsy.

"Have you ever forced anyone to engage in sexual acts or been arrested for doing so?" Cal asked nonchalantly.

"Yes, I've been arrested for rape once, but I've taken women at least a dozen times."

The man smiled as though drifting in a fond memory while disgust oozed off everyone in the community like bad cologne. I caught Cal's eye and gestured for him to draw out more information.

"Elaborate on that."

The man's eyes burned as his words poured out with a fervor.

"I like it when the girls struggle. Mostly, I'd take them home and wrestle them down until they'd surrender; it doesn't matter if they say 'no' because I know they really like it. On occasion, I would just find a lady so pretty and the setting was so perfect, I'd just grab them and toss them against a wall or behind a bush and … gururgghh…"

His gushing of filth was halted by the knife jammed through the base of his skull and up through his open mouth. The predator slumped into a heap with the tip of the hunting knife still glistening in the firelight. Troy reached his crimson hand down and withdrew the weapon; it made a squelching noise as the serrated edge was pulled free. Bone flecks and gray matter clung to the blade. With a sneer, Troy wiped the gore and blood on his victim's shirt, placed the knife in its sheath, and stood tall.

"I'm ready to answer my questions."

CHAPTER 18 SEPTEMBER 17th-18th YEAR 1

 Troy and his remaining three comrades were already assimilating into our society. Their meager belongings sat by their new bunks in the main cabin until we could come up with more housing. Sunny and Bubba began the crew on survival training with partners as soon as they passed the Q&A session. The corpse of the fifth man was unceremoniously dumped in the burning field for disposal with the contents of our outhouses.

 It was easy to see why the men had followed Troy without question: he was the only one with any actual skills in fighting, hunting, or escaping fleshies. I'd fully recovered from my 'illness' within a day and a half after the interrogation. Chase, Sunny, and Cal had already assessed Troy's abilities, insisting I put him into regular shifts while the other three newcomers were brought up to par.

 Cal recommended we try to add a few crossbows to our arsenal as well, given how much simpler they are to become proficient with than the bows. I agreed; the amount of practice time we had to spend with the bows could be used for many other ventures. Only a handful of us were decent shots at any distance beyond twenty yards anyhow, even with the compound bows.

Each meal with our freshmen residents yielded new information about the state of things beyond our solitary domain. Amongst tales of ravaged and pillaged strongholds of humans, they reported stories of half-starved vampires keeping humans alive in jail cells or chained together like cattle in the slaughterhouse. Troy spoke quietly about witnessing a couple of skirmishes between small bands of survivors and the Undead they crossed. I could tell he was choosing his words carefully.

"They felt it was the human race against the world. This scraggly group just kept roaming from place to place, foraging for whatever they may be able to use; hiding from the Dead at night, and killing off the vampires during the day. It was like they thought all they had to do was kill everyone who wasn't human anymore, and the world would go back to the way it was.

Fast food would reappear and they wouldn't struggle and everyone would get along fine." He sighed and looked down. "Those guys were full of hope to the point of delusion. They didn't even consider that the ammo might run out if they kept shooting."

The crossbowman shook his head as he finished. Our lunch of roasting possum crackled and burned, forgotten for a moment as we all processed what we heard. Silently, I wondered how this would affect the interactions we maintained with Caelinus and Daemon. I searched each face for any signs that the Pact could be weakening but found only blank expressions.

Seth's story changed those faces entirely. After the cooking meat was remembered and tended, the accountant-turned-spearman set down his bowl. He wiped his glasses on the hem of his shirt and cleared his throat.

"Troy found me last winter after I ran away from my subdivision. I was barely conscious, having done nothing but run from my neighbors and those cursed souls who'd been turned by the infection. All I'd taken was my makeshift spear and a bottle of water. The water ran after an hour or two of running and I didn't eat again until he found me three days later, barricaded against a handful of zombies in a hair salon. I nearly died to avoid what my neighbors were turning to."

While Seth paused to wipe his eyes, I found myself leaning closer. As Chase's hand grazed past mine, I realized I wasn't the only one who'd done so.

"None of us were prepared for the outbreak or the mess that followed. Our suburb was pretty close, so a handful of us pooled our supplies and decided to band together until this whole ordeal blew over. We even had a little party like it was another hurricane come to wash over us; board the windows, get out the emergency kits, drink some booze, and wait."

He started to rock gently as his eyes glossed over with the wisps of memories.

"It was a quick thing to line up the cars and suvs as a wall a few houses past our cul-de-sac entrance. Garden tools and household objects became weapons thanks to duct tape or whatever else we could find. That first month, all we did was keep saying we'd be rescued soon and do our best to destroy those corpses that came up to the vehicles or the brick wall protecting our families."

I looked at the others and recognized the same woeful look on their faces, while Seth cleared his throat and wiped at his nose. A tiny yellow bubble swelled and receded in his nostril as he spoke.

"It was fine for a little while, but soon enough we went from rationing food and drinks to trying to catch bugs and strays. One of the guys said we should send out a party to loot the area for supplies.

'The worst has to be over by now. The Army or the Red Cross or the CDC is probably just a mile or two away putting everything right again. You'll see.'

There were about two-dozen adults and seven or eight kids holed up there. Five of the men went out to search; two came back. They carried a couple of bags of canned food and juice boxes and were covered in blood. Their faces looked decades older.

They just dropped the bags and sat on top of the improvised wall with some guns they'd picked up. Not a word about the other three even when the families cried and begged for an explanation. They just shrugged and stared down the street; those guys wore that vacant expression every minute since. We never learned what happened to the other three."

A couple of people slowly rose and excused themselves back to chores or rest. It was a too familiar story for many.

"As the weeks went on, those two led others out to gather supplies more often, leaving the rest of us to fend off the zombies each day and for a short time, a vampire by night."

Seth paused. His mind seemed to come back to him as he awkwardly realized we were friends with two vampires.

"Not to say all vampires are bad, just the one that kept attacking us. She would swoop down and grab us from the wall or sneak into one of the houses and take one of our folks while they slept."

I patted him on the forearm and gave a weak smile.

This is the first time anyone here has said so much about the past. It's bringing up so much pain; has it really been almost a year?

"Anyways," he continued "she didn't kill anyone; she just drank from them and set them back in the cul-de-sac. Sometimes, some food would be sitting on the asphalt next to the victim. Scared the Hell out of everyone though. One day one of the ladies got a good look at her and recognized our attacker. The next morning, we burned her house down a couple of blocks away; never had another incident with the thing.

The food stopped getting left behind after the fire. Our searches yielded less and less. Soon winter came and we had nothing left. The gardens and emergency kits were bare. Even the pets had 'gone missing' — thankfully, the children never knew the truth. The direness of our circumstances began to sink in. There was no rescue. No supplies. Just an endless stream of zombies and a small pile of bullets and kitchen utensils."

I sharpened my sword as the spearman spoke; I didn't think I was going to be able to look at him and keep my composure for the next part.

"One of the recently widowed had been pregnant when the outbreak came. The baby came early and seemed fine. The lady bled too much and passed away a few minutes after her son cried out. Poor boy didn't even get a name or to see her smile. That's when it began. One of the guys took the woman's body close to the fire and stopped. Instead of burning the corpse like we'd been doing, he pulled out a knife.

The rest of us rushed to stop him, but he just kept ranting about wasting our only chance to live and starving to death. One by one, people took their hands off him. The decision had been made."

Seth wept openly, his hands cupping his face as the tears and snot drizzled through his shaking fingers and onto the ground.

"We ate her. God help me, we cooked that poor woman and devoured every bit of her. No one told the children that we were eating their neighbor, the nice lady who gave out caramel apples every Halloween and babysat them growing up. And two days later, when her innocent and nameless son died, we made him into stew."

Bubba puked into the cooking fire, creating a cloud of stench and sparks. A couple of other residents ran for the outhouse, likely for the same reason as the storyteller fell to his knees in the sand. It seemed Seth spoke to someone or something far away instead of us; it was a plea from a man condemned to his memories.

"I couldn't stay. I couldn't eat the baby, or whoever would die next. The whole group talked about hunting other survivors for their rations and their flesh. I just couldn't live like that. I'm sorry. I'm so, so very sorry..."

His words of remorse trailed off as the guilt overwhelmed the man. Chase and I helped Seth to his feet; the Nurse followed as we laid him down on his cot and took his weapons, belt, and shoelaces away.

We'd all seen the breakdowns before; the past could kill a person in the present easier than any gun. The Nurse stayed with Seth and by dinner, he said the spearman could return to his chores, but to watch him train for a day or two. I thought about the man's tale and wondered if this was the same group of attackers pillaging the area.

I guess it's best not to find out.

***

I hurried from my training with Seth towards my raid-planning meeting. The guy was becoming really good with the spear we gave him in place of his duct-taped weapon; he seemed to delight in learning the nuances of wielding it. I think just being able to provide food and protection gave Seth confidence. Watching him practice and hunt animals was like watching a drowning man figure out how to swim.

During a lesson on spear-fishing, he confided in me that it was his desire to find a way to atone that drove him to become as useful as possible in Nova Nocte.

"It's my only opportunity to make my life count for something. If I can just keep these people safe and free of that kind of depraved existence, then maybe it will absolve a tiny bit of the guilt I feel. If not, then at least I'll be too damned tired from all the hard work to think about it."

I watched him continue to practice his swordsmanship with Randolph; I would need to focus for the raid, it was going much further into town this time. And we had to bring back an extra vehicle.

When I entered the Coffin Cabin, I found a whole lotta crazy gushing out of everyone. Cal and Daemon were arguing over who was going with me on the raid, both clearly watching their words with Troy in the room. Forrest was grumbling about not wanting "that damned cannibal" in the party. Sunny and Chase were holding a very quiet but fervent debate in a corner of the room while the Nurse and Sindbad listened and occasionally seemed to take the smiling husband's side. The other two volunteers for the excursion sat on a bed trying to be invisible.

Over the din, Sunny shouted,

"Dammit, Chase you aren't going on this raid; you will stay here with me. I'm pregnant and I'll be damned if you aren't going to be here to help me defend this fort! Squirrel and the others can pick up those supplies just fine without you."

Silence.

Simultaneously, all heads turned to view the furious woman at the center of attention. Other topics lay forgotten and book-marked as the words sank in.

"Yes Dear."

Chase's smile spread almost beyond his ears at the announcement. He reached out and pushed an escaped strand of hair from her face before kissing his wife.

"Uh, guys, we're going to need to arrange for another volunteer. My wife needs me in camp to help out until you guys get back. If that won't work for anyone here, you can address the issue with my sweetheart."

I shook my head abruptly.

Arguing with Sunny on a good day was iffy at best, I doubt there's anyone insane enough to do so now that she's pregnant and chock full of hormones. Oh and armed with her favorite spear... um, no thanks.

Satisfied with the resulting acceptance of his withdrawal from the raid, Sunny nodded and sat down at the small table.

"Okay, let's work out a shopping list and get a location in mind. Does someone want to go get another volunteer in here so we can get a plan in motion before lunchtime? Daemon, you're staying here and Cal will go with Squirrel and the others."

Hands were raised and mouths opened.

"No Troy, your other two friends need to stay in the fort, they aren't capable enough for this yet. Troy and Seth are going, deal with it Bubba or deal with me. Any other issues?"

After a pause and a toothy grin, Forrest muttered "No ma'am. I'll wrangle up another volunteer."

Seeing a break in the meeting, I hugged Sunny and soon she was engulfed in an outpouring of congratulations on the baby. Chase received pats on the back and a promise to keep an eye out for cigars. Bubba returned a few minutes later with Jake and a small bundle. The older man held out the tied square of cloth to Sunny and Chase.

"Go ahead and open it. Just a little something I want ya'll to have for the baby."

Sunny looked puzzled as she untied the corners of the light blue swatch, revealing a fuzzy stuffed frog with a tiny bow around its neck.

"It was my daughter's and eventually my grandson's favorite dolly. I just thought it'd be nice for someone to be able to play with it again. I kept it clean, but it's durable if ya'll want to wash it."

Forrest smiled gently as a single drop of grief leaked down his face and disappeared into his gray beard.

Daemon put a hand on his shoulder. Sunny burst into tears and almost knocked the poor man over hugging him.

"This is the sweetest thing. Thank you so much Bubba."

After a couple of minutes, emotions were muffled. We gathered at the table and our scheme unfolded. We'd venture beyond the suburbs and vacation rentals and raid just inside town. Although we needed little in way of food or water, there was a great deal we still had to search for. The list was debated for twenty minutes, shrinking and growing like Alice in Wonderland.

Finally we narrowed it down: linens, a basic tool set, coolers, storage bags or food containers, hunting knives, crossbows, arrows, medicines, books on delivering and caring for babies, axes, wind-up flashlights, rucksacks, another vehicle capable of holding a significant number of people, fuel, laundry soap, matches or lighters, a shovel, toilet paper, and canned foods that hadn't expired.

Our plan was basically to go to town, get fuel and another vehicle, load the SUV or truck with as much of the stuff on our list as possible, and come back with all of our people unharmed. If we could get two vehicles and enough fuel, that would be even better. No matter what, we didn't want to interact with any others we found; we had to avoid any of the other bands of survivors who might harm or destroy our community. The group would stay together. There could be no heroics.

Our camp had one real mechanic and three others who knew enough about cars to help him. They'd been maintaining our transportation in the event we had to use Plan B. Plan B was simply to load up the camp into vehicles and become nomads until we could rebuild a home should our current village become unlivable. We'd created the backup plan after hearing how many groups had been destroyed in the area.

Our business concluded and everyone rose to continue his or her day. As the meeting broke, I brought up the topic that had been in the back of my mind.

"There's one other thing. Tomorrow is the anniversary. We don't leave for town until the day after. Should we do anything to acknowledge the day?"

I was staring at a trail of statues as they froze. Cal had already reclined on his bed, Daemon was actually mid-air as he'd been flying himself towards his bunk — he claims it was to practice control of his powers, and the others were in a staggered line for the door.

"Any opinions? I just thought, maybe we should do a small memorial for all we've lost.

Or look towards the progress we've made so far. It just feels like we should do something to, you know, mark the occasion."

I wiped my sweaty hands on my jeans as confused stares burned through me. Chase spoke first.

"We celebrate. We should have a small feast like we do for the holidays or the kids' birthdays. We need to kick up our heels over the fact that we're still here. This community hasn't gone nearly as bad as most of the others. We aren't harboring rapists, or pedophiles, or murdering others for their stuff.

We've found a way to work together and live to see these kids grow a year older and in another six or seven months, we'll even get to see a new life born. It may not be an ideal world for this child to enter, but it could be worse. I say we have a brief time of remembrance and grieving, then we push it aside to focus on all the good."

Smiles and nods answered his speech.

"Okay then. Let's tell everyone at dinner when we have our chill time. Until then, back to work all of us."

I joked as I prepared to do the least popular chore in camp: tote the large tubs from under the outhouses to the burning field for disposal with the day's crop of fleshies. Sunny handed me her work gloves and wished me luck as I prepared to drag the first bin full of waste and vomit out the gate to be dumped and over the bodies and lit. I prayed we found some small chemical toilets on the raid as I opened the outhouse door.

CHAPTER 19 SEPTEMBER 19th – OUTBREAK ANNIVERSARY

Our remembrance time was somber and left me feeling hollow. We announced our plans at dinner and found that the majority of the village preferred to do the memorial immediately and start the celebration in the morning. It was like trying to leave the past losses behind us. The news that Sunny and Chase were expectant parents lifted everyone's spirits.

There was a good half hour of congratulations and hugs and baby advice. Chase couldn't stop smiling while his wife worried about doing her part for the community. It took me all through dinner to convince her that, although she wouldn't be scheduled on raids or latrine disposal, she would still be contributing plenty to the group.

The night breezes blew out some of the candles and even a lantern as we dispersed to bed or to guard duty. Hopeful smiles and grieving frowns flickered as the shadows led everyone to their dreams. I fell asleep hearing sobbing from Marley Guy to my left and a recitation of stories to tell the baby from Bubba on my right.

The morning brought a hearty breakfast, a quick bustle of essential chores, decorations made by the kids, clearing four fleshies and what looked like half a woman from the traps, packing for the raid, and a noontime feast. We played card games, had piggyback races with the children, wheelbarrow races, an archery contest, showing off with weapons, an art contest, sing-a-longs, and Sindbad displayed his tricks for a tin of treats the Nurse found on the last raid. As the sunlight tapered away, Daemon and Caelinus joined the fun with a display of sleight of hand, flying stunts, and stories from ages past — Daemon started to tell jokes, but was roundly popped by Jordy's Mom after she heard the one about a box turtle and a pimp.

Laughing and stretching our way to our beds, I realized the only thing that could make the day better would've been lying down with Daemon at the end of it. He gave me a peck on the cheek before taking off for his patrol; Cal glared at each of us before storming off to his cabin.

Maybe Troy or Sunny could lead and we could be free to be together.

I checked my gear before falling into a restless sleep. My sword and knife were sharp and ready. Canteens were full. My quiver carried a dozen arrows and a crowbar.

I'd eaten my fill in case the next few days would be scarce. I stowed a pen and small notepad in the bag in case I needed to get info to someone. We'd grab our rations of food before leaving. Something was forgotten, unplanned. I dozed off racking my mind for the answer.

I dreamt about running through the dark, hitting a cement and stucco wall. Standing along the wall, feeling for a gap or a way over, holes appeared as shards erupted outwards. Each hole echoed by the sound of gunshots; each tiny cavern in the wall coming closer to me. Laughter grew from the obscurity as the bullets taunted me. The laughter became voices. They hung in the air beckoning me to feed them.

I woke drenched in sweat and on the floor tangled in my blanket.

Of course!

I shook Forrest awake.

"Bubba, Bubba wake up."

"Hummhhuh? What's goin on?"

"Forrest, the guns. Are the guns okay to fire? You've been keeping them in working order, right?"

He sat up and wiped the crust from his weary eyes.

"Yup, they work fine. Why the Hell are ya waking me up fer that? Are we in trouble?"

Bubba pulled on his hunting jacket and reached for his machete. I laid a hand on his arm to stop him as a low chorus of "shhhs" rumbled from the rest of the cabin. I lowered my voice.

"It's fine. I just forgot to make sure. If we're all gone and ransackers attack the camp, they'll need real firepower; whether zombies are in the area or not. Sorry, go back to sleep."

His camouflage jacket half-off, Bubba slumped back onto his cot. By the time I got back in bed, he was snoring like a rusty chainsaw.

CHAPTER 20 SEPTEMBER 20TH YEAR 2

We trudged up to the clearing and loaded the trucks in good time. While Bubba and our mechanic double-checked the vehicles, the rest of us drank some water and stretched. Cal landed smoothly and immediately did a quick inventory of the arms we carried; there would be no other chances to go back for them. Satisfied that all preparations were complete, our team clamored into the truck beds and readied ourselves for the journey into the city outright.

As we drove at a snail's pace, I found myself thinking of how everything had looked just over a year ago. Disney gift shops, timeshares, Lynx buses, and tourists had dominated the scenery. Now there was stalled or overturned cars, scattered Dead, feral dogs, busted windows, and forgotten cartoon faces gathering dust in the stores. Stolen shopping carts laden with spoiled food sat alongside a pile of bones at the on ramp. I wondered if they were the remains of humans or fleshies.

A skeletal form dragged itself towards us. Its leathery skin was pulled taut over its frame and half the teeth were missing or broken. Troy signaled the driver to stop and leapt out of the truck bed. I drew my bow and watched for others as he stomped on the creature's head one time, sending a loud crack and dried up scalp fragments into the dim moonlight. As he climbed back in, I gave the man a nod and lowered my weapon. He looked puzzled and whispered to me.

"That thing looked almost starved to death. Wonder if we could just wait for these corpses to rot to nothing."

"Doubt it, but maybe. It can take years for a body to rot away to dust, depending on the environment. Dude, that one was practically a mummy from sitting out here in the sun, but if it was still here during a hurricane, who knows? For all we know, some of them could get stuck somewhere and rooted up in a decade and start things all over again."

I shook my head and continued as we wove between abandoned vehicles.

"I don't think we can ever be sure they're all gone."

"But there are fewer of them each day; you have to admit that. We've only seen a few dozen this whole drive and most of them have been so decrepit that we could put them down just as easily as that last one."

We stopped to check a Pathfinder to see if we could get it running. A brief look told us to ignore it and press on. Having gathered plenty of gas from it and the surrounding cars, we mounted back up.

"Fair enough, Troy. But until we know for sure if these things can starve out, anyone who wants to survive will have to keep alert and prepared to fight them off."

He smirked.

"Well then, I guess I'll have to settle for trashing zombies and flirting with you. Could be worse."

I did a double take that popped my neck while Jake snorted in laughter. Troy kept smiling and looked around for any hazards. Blushing, I turned away and did the same. While we slowly wound through the graveyard of traffic, I wondered if he was serious. As we got out to check the sixth vehicle (thankfully an acceptable one), Cal chimed in his two cents.

"If you are curious, yes, Troy is quite taken with you. I recommend you consider that. He seems to be a good man. More importantly, he is a human; not a vampire."

As the Roman finished speaking he pulled a gooey corpse from under a Buick and popped its head off like a defective Barbie doll. It's gnawed tongue lolled around in the open mouth a moment before I drove my sword through the left eye socket. I watched the primitive need to consume fade out of the remaining eye. Wiping the tip of my blade on a nearby corpse in a McDonald's uniform, I ignored the comment and searched for more wandering Dead to dispose of.

As the SUV turned over, extra fuel was stored in the back and we split our party between our three vehicles. After another hour of picking our way down the highway, we found the remnants of an outlet mall. I remembered it being mostly deserted even before the outbreak. Except for the drivers, we got out and armed ourselves to explore the camping shop. I was hopeful that we'd be able to find most of our list items here; I just prayed that was all we'd find with such a small team.

Within the first three steps, the fleshies took notice of our arrival and massed in a wobbly assault. Over twenty were in view by the time our swords and axes were drawn. Cal drew his own blade and charged into the sea of dismembered torsos and rotted faces. Seth drove his spear through a rancid woman, whose arms swung from shreds of skin and sinew, withdrew the point and spun to kill the crawling teenager riddled with bullet holes. A pocketknife was still embedded in the things neck, dripping thick black muck down the handle. My blade stuck in the temple of the ashen boy, forcing me to stand on his shoulder to pull the sword out.

Turning in circles to destroy each new approaching Dead, revealed each member of our party fighting but unharmed. Cal stood surrounded by mounds of shattered remains one moment and the next he was by Bubba driving his fingers through the eyes and into the brain of a movie usher. Jake kept near the trucks, swinging his crowbar and cursing the bloated top half of a cop; grass and roadkill was tangled in its loose innards. Jake retched as the scent hit him. With shaking hands he caved in the thing's skull, popping out a clouded eye and ripping off half the scalp in the process.

Troy shot his arrows through lifeless faces and reclaimed them to be fired again. He wiped out the zombies without a sound or hesitation until our party stood alone in the parking lot. The ground was littered with vomit and bodies in various states of decay. Shuffling sounds grew closer as we moved the vehicles next to the outdoor sports store. Our weapons hastily cleaned, the eight of us took a silent moment before we'd take the next step.

Jake, Forrest, Cal, Troy, and myself left the trucks and pried open the door. Seth and the other two drove slowly through the lot to lead away or run down any fleshies outside. I wound my flashlight and shone its beam across the near empty shelves. It appeared the shop had been untouched in months after a frantic rush during the initial outbreak. We spread out slowly in search of supplies and vigilant against the risen deceased.

The cones of light helped me track the progress of all but the vampire; Cal saw fine without the aid of the electric torches. We only came across two corpses in the store. There was a shotgun between them and only fragments of their heads to keep their bones company. Troy gave a low hiss to signal us and the streaks of radiance converged. Most of the guns and ammunition had been taken from the counter, but nine crossbows and around a hundred arrows had been left behind.

Smiling, we loaded ourselves and continued through the shop, gradually acquiring almost the entire list. We flashed our lights out the door three times. The trucks pulled up and we hurriedly unburdened ourselves. Cal flew up above us, assessing our situation. As the Roman touched down he frowned.

"We should go. There are still many more on the way and the night is half spent."

Our team moved quickly into the vehicles in search of shelter for the day, far away from the outlet. Seth eyed the haul and nodded at Bubba and me.

"Not bad. Is there anything we still need from there or are we moving on altogether?"

"Place is about done cleared out fer now, but we should keep it in mind next trip."

Our convoy backtracked towards the edge of town as we scanned each passing home for livability. The tides of Dead seemed much fewer than they had been in months previous as we unloaded and examined three different places.

Finally, coming upon an old cinderblock house, we set up to bed down for the day.

The house sat back from the road and on a decent patch of land apart from its neighbors. There were even some of the items from our list inside and — best of all — it was free of carcasses. Cal made one last sweep of the area before we locked the door and retired.

We paired off for shifts on watch, ate a simple dinner, and arranged our sleeping spots. The other female volunteer laid her sleeping bag next to my blankets although she continued locking eyes with Jake.

I swear to God if they try to hook up right next to me, I'm going to beat them both senseless. And if she tries to start girl talk like this is a slumber party, I'll kill myself.

Troy and Cal took the first watch, whispering as they checked the windows and looked for items of use that may have been missed. I drifted to sleep thinking of my night with Daemon and the look in Troy's eyes.

CHAPTER 21 SEPTEMBER 21st–22nd YEAR 2

The past two days had been uneventful, making the evening's search almost pleasant. Our party had already located everything on the list including baby books and supplies by 4AM. Driving into an upscale neighborhood, we'd only run down a few dozen fleshies.

My heart began to let in a glimmer of hope as I realized how few of the corpses remained and that most of those seemed utterly beyond concern; we may be able to resettle in town one day. The thought of being able to reconnect the pathways to other cities and find more survivors like us was intoxicating.

After moving the wreckage of a Hummer and a Cadillac, the convoy pushed further into the gated suburb in our quest for daytime shelter. Scorch marks, bleached bones, and torn clothing stood testament to previous looting. Ahead of us were scattered bodies on formerly manicured lawns.

I noted the crushed or fragmented skulls; these corpses wouldn't be stalking us. Troy stared at the bullet hole in a small cranium at the stop sign. There was a bit of skin holding the jaw to the rest of the head, the arm of another carcass still within the mouth. He and I locked eyes and nodded to other to move on. Seth pulled into a driveway and cut the engine. The other two vehicles followed and we geared up to assess the location.

I realized his reason for deciding on the house when I saw the garage. It could have easily held five or six cars. Inside we found an Infiniti SUV, a Harley motorcycle, tools, camping equipment, sporting items, and fishing rods for the ocean. Our vehicles were brought inside for the day and we moved into formation to clear the mansion itself.

Silently, we checked each room on the first floor. Nancy pointed emphatically at the open cans on the kitchen counter; someone had eaten here very recently. I gripped my sword more tightly and felt a bead of sweat run down my neck. Everyone froze as the reality sunk in: we have no idea how many people are in here or what arms they may be carrying. The ground floor was empty. No Dead or living lurched at us as we swept for hazards.

As I stood at the foot of the hardwood stairs, Cal grabbed my elbow. He whispered as he held me in place.

"Someone is snoring up there. I only hear one heartbeat and no other movement. Perhaps we should remain here and await our host's arrival."

I lowered my foot from the step and glanced at each of my companions. Seth kept looking at Troy for direction, while Troy just watched me patiently. Forrest and the others had already lowered their weapons and waited for a choice to be made so they could get some rest. I spoke as low as possible.

"Fair enough. We'll stay down here for now. We won't touch anything inside, it's already spoken for, but we will leave a note at this guy's door explaining our presence and that we're not a danger.

Sleep is in shifts as usual. Whoever is on shift will sit here at the base of the stairs; when they hear whoever is up there stirring, quietly wake everyone in the other room."

Cal, Troy, and I sat down for first watch as the others trailed into the living room to unpack. The old vampire smiled as we watched Troy stand back up and follow them. I'd tugged the Roman's sleeve to keep him from rising when Troy had given him a tilted nod. As soon as he was out of sight, Cal chuckled.

"Why so uninterested in the gentleman's company, I wonder." He teased. "Could it be that you worry you'll be tempted?"

I blurted out a hushed "No." and pulled my bag of fruit and meat from my bag.

"Ah, the lady protests far too quickly to be true. Are you concerned for Daemon's feelings?"

I winced at the thought of him being hurt by me before realizing I hadn't done anything. I hadn't even intended to consider doing anything that would hurt Daemon's feelings. I glanced at the elder vampire and saw him grinning.

"Squirrel, the boy will have to accept not having you, just as you will have to move on from him. Although it may pain you, it is the only option. For now, there is a young man who is a nice alternative. Daemon will carry on just fine; he has centuries to find another woman. You've tested your luck too much already; let the lad go."

He gave me a gentle pat on the arm and began to scribble out a note for our unknown patron. Soundlessly, Cal floated up to the door and slid the paper underneath. The next two hours we sat in silence, the conversation echoed in our minds but had concluded with his words. I couldn't argue with Cal; he was right. But just because we both knew he was right, didn't mean I had to acknowledge it.

As Troy and Seth relieved us from our post, footsteps were heard overhead. Seth hurriedly woke the others and our bags were packed and hoisted again. At my urging, weapons were ready but not drawn. In a tense huddle, we waited at the bottom of the elegant stairs like nervous prom dates. The carved maple cherub at the end of the banister laughed as the shuffling upstairs stopped by the door. There was a flurry of movement behind the door and all around that room for the next full minute. We stood like statues, muscles taut with anticipation.

Finally the doorknob turned and there was a crack of light on the wall.

"Hello?"

I cleared my throat.

"Hi. It's okay, we don't want any trouble and we didn't touch any of your stuff. We just needed a place to stay until tonight."

"How many is 'we' exactly?"

I did a quick head count.

"Eight including myself. Are you coming down?"

The light disappeared and we heard footsteps circling for a moment.

"Why did you people come after me if you don't intend to kill me? Are you with that big guy who has those tourist kids?"

Puzzled faces looked at me; my confused face looked right back.

"We didn't know anyone was here until we heard you snoring. What guy with the tourists? Can you come down, or can we come up please?"

"No. No, don't come up. I'll come down, but I'm bringing my weapons. Don't shoot me or those zombies will start marching towards us."

I relaxed a little.

"Not a problem, we don't have any guns on us and we don't care much for fleshies either."

Slowly, the door opened and a graying man in his forties eased his way down the stairs. He held a pistol with a silencer in front of him and a military saber hung on his hip. The man stopped halfway down and holstered his gun.

"Forrest? Bubba is that you?"

Stunned I looked behind me for Bubba, but he had pushed past and was climbing the stairs two at a time.

"Vincent!"

The two men hugged tightly while we watched the tearful reunion. All the fear and worry dissipated as we witnessed that hope we all secretly carried: finding a loved one safe. The embrace was marked with mutterings of 'I thought you'd died' and 'Can't believe I found you'.

And then they kissed. It was passionate, to the point that the forgotten crowd at the base of the stairs became simultaneously entranced with staring at the floor or wallpaper. I think Jake was the one who mumbled 'get a room' causing the couple to break their prolonged embrace.

"Sorry, ya'll. It's just that, well, I done forgot y'all was here. Folks, this is Vincent. Vincent these are some of the people I been living with outta town a ways."

I stepped forward to shake Vincent's hand, followed by each of my companions – Jake needed an elbow to the ribs to bring his manners to him. After Cal did a brief glamoured Q&A, it was agreed that Vincent would gather his stuff and join us. Both he and Bubba appeared overjoyed and inseparable. Pleasantries exchanged, we sat and had a nice breakfast as a group and got to know Forrest's boyfriend.

Vincent was a former Army Captain, hence his dress sword and sidearm. He'd figured out the Dead followed gunshots, and had acquired several silencers on a raid of his own. During the outbreak, he and Forrest had been separated and their townhome destroyed.

Vincent managed to survive by living off of the land and scavenging empty homes. He'd been alone all year, having opted to observe strangers before approaching; the few bands of survivors he'd seen had been vicious or stupid enough to keep infected with them. The group he'd spoken about earlier were cannibals.

***

Our enlarged crew rested through the day. Forrest and his boyfriend caught up and reminisced on the second floor while we slept peacefully on the first. I woke in the afternoon to the smell of Spam in baked beans and corn cooking on the Sterno burners. The party gathered around the glory of warm food and we mentally prepared ourselves for the night's journey home.

Vincent had seen the cannibals the day before. From his descriptions, Seth confirmed they were his neighbors from before the outbreak. The big guy had been the Neighborhood Watch Captain and a rep for the HOA. His recon also established what I'd been worried about; they were somewhere between our current location and our home camp. With a roughly sketched map, we debated possible alternative routes home until the meal was finished. During a lull in the search for options, a scream fractured the air outside the house.

I rushed to the foyer window, moving the thick curtain the barest amount to peek outside. The sight on the opposite yard made my stomach quake and my heart drop. I couldn't breathe when I found the source of the scream. Cal stood next to me, with his eye at the peephole. Crowded behind us, the others began to push for a view. Troy took one look and shoved them away.

"Trust me, you don't want to see." He mumbled. His tan face paled and toned arms shook.

Worried expressions and fidgeting hands waited for an explanation, a plan, and some assurance. I turned to them and gestured to the stairs. Wordlessly, we trailed up the elegant staircase and into Vincent's bedroom. Cal took up a post watching and listening out of a tiny corner of the window. I tried to find the words.

"The murderers we're trying to avoid, um, they're across the street. It looks like those Brazilians, Maria and Fernando, are being tortured and eaten on the front lawn. I can only guess about the rest of their friends."

I stared at the carpet, each thick fiber catching the light differently as I stared at them for an idea. We couldn't leave and we couldn't stay.

We're boned.

Several minutes passed, the hush punctuated sporadically by weaker and more desperate screams from the teenage girl. I barely heard the boy as they cooked him alive over a small fire. Both of the tourists were naked and beaten; Maria was covered in blood between her legs and on her chest. I struggled to grasp the right answer for the situation. Caelinus spoke softly telling us what was happening so that we wouldn't have to see it ourselves.

"They are cutting off strips of the boy's skin and eating him alive. One man just cut a thin strip along the lad's ribs and up near his armpit and yanked it free. They've already raped both of them in turns. Their leader is questioning them in Spanish; he wants to know about the fortress with all the people. The one with the two flying blood-drinkers and the women and food."

I don't know if he was listening or reading lips, but he kept translating and updating us.

"He keeps asking how to get to our camp. The man in charge is cutting her fingers off by the joints and burning the nubs to keep her alive longer. His men are chewing on the fingertips and sucking out the marrow while they laugh about the 'fun' they had today."

He faced us momentarily.

"Apparently, they consumed her toes and nipples this morning during their parade of violations. The girl is pleading with him; she can't remember where the place was. The boy has stopped begging and is now praying in between his coughs."

He turned away from the scene again and took a slow breath.

"We cannot help either of them. They will die and it will be slow and wrought with agony."

He shut the door Troy and I had been walking towards.

"We may be able to protect our people, but not by a frontal assault in the daytime. Those men have you outgunned and evenly numbered. This is one time, where our pact may be your only chance to survive. And I will likely need your blood to heal. For this to work, night has to come."

I rocked slightly with frustration. I couldn't get the sight of his hair singed to the scalp out of my head; I couldn't block out his skin being severed from his muscles for the enjoyment of those savage men. My ears rang with her cries and his prayers. I could hear Fernando dying far from home, praying in a foreign tongue, and I recognized the familiar lilt and timber to his prayer. I quietly prayed along with him even as his voice grew weaker.

"Hail Mary, full of grace…"

Tears rolled down my cheek as we sat on the bed and floor. We huddled in the noiseless gaps between their painful words and the raucous laughter outside. I crept to the window and watched one of the bastards slice off a portion of the boy's butt cheek and bite into it while staring into his eyes. The cannibal grinned widely as a trickle of meat juice wove a path down his chin. The man spit a small piece into Fernando's mouth and burst into renewed humor. They took pleasure in their misery.

Troy draped his arm over my shoulders as I wept at the fate that could await our friends back home; the torment echoed through the empty streets and the peals of joy from its creators mocked the suffering we all pitied. Cal had long since stopped detailing the causes of the noises, but stood witness to the atrocities until the girl's voice became hoarse and the boy's went mercifully silent.

I felt the air beginning to chill as the sun crept towards its bed. The tears halted as I stood and stretched. The others followed suit gradually; they were dominoes following blindly.

"We need to prepare. I refuse to let those people commit those heinous acts on our people. As soon as night falls, we have to be ready to act."

Jake twitched while he spoke.

"What exactly are we going to do? Those Brazilians are way past saving and those assholes have more guns than a Tarantino film. We should just stay here and bail when they've gone; we can rush home and beef up defenses. Besides, they don't know where camp is."

Nancy and the other guy stood by Jake in agreement.

"Won't work. That crew is raiding for gear, just like us. Odds are, they'll be staying a day or two and eating the rest of the Brazilians and eventually they'll probably search this house."

Jake's face fell; he'd aged years in the last few hours.

"Maybe we can outrun them. Just peel out in the trucks and lose them on the way home. I didn't see a car, maybe they're on foot."

Vincent stepped forward and began to stretch to touch his toes.

"They had a couple of motorcycles and a car last time I saw them; they can follow or track us. I only have a couple of guns, but I'm a good shot and I know Forrest is, too."

"And of course, there is a vampire here who has centuries of experience in stealthily hunting and killing humans."

Cal had said the words so quietly it reminded us all of the level of our own voices.

"Here's the plan," I took control of the conversation again " Jake, Nancy, and uh, other guy get into two vehicles and be ready to drive as soon as we're in position. Forrest and Vincent will gather and prep all the guns we have and load the ammo we got in the sport shop.

Cal will head out the back and do his best to discreetly kill some of the cannibals and fly back any weapons he gets off his victims. Troy, Seth, and I will load the supplies into the trucks and position ourselves to fire as soon as we roll out of the garage."

I took a breath and looked to Vincent and Cal for guidance as our military men.

"Any tips guys?"

"I'd say we should have Cal focus on killing off the handful of guys in the house, so that we can run over and shoot down the ones in the yard. We can't risk an enemy getting away and coming back later with a grudge and a larger force."

"Precisely my thoughts. After we've eliminated the threat, we must gather items from that property and return to camp quickly as the gunfire will attract unwanted attention from the Dead."

Cal stood with a bearing that was ingrained over years of Roman training as he doled out his advice and carried his belongings to the SUV. A muted chorus of nods set the plan in action.

Vincent's guns turned out to be not just his 9mm Beretta sidearm but also an M16 rifle, a Colt 45, and two revolvers. He had silencers on each of the pistols and a bayonet for the M16. Properly armed, we waited in the garage for the return of our Undead ally. It was nearly ten minutes we sat in the dark room before the kitchen door opened.

"Sorry, there were three of them inside and I thought it best if I took my dinner before the shooting starts."

Cal held a duffel bag out to us. It held almost a dozen more firearms and various clips loaded with munitions.

"Let's get this over with and return home."

I grabbed one of the rifles to add to my silenced handgun and turned off the safety. Our team mounted the truck beds and entered the SUV, readied our weapons, and gave a thumbs-up to Cal. The vampire threw open the garage door as the engines roared to life. He flitted to the other yard and plunged his fangs into the nearest man's jugular, shaking the startled man like a wolf devouring a steak. We drove at the four remaining adversaries firing rounds as they clamored for their weapons.

Our drive-by netted us two wounded rivals before the battle began. Their leader made it to his rifle and began returning fire; a stream of holes went up the side of the F150 wounding Troy in the arm. Seth took Troy's gun and fired at the assailant. Another of the enemy men fired into our driver's side, killing the guy Jake and I rode with.

Jake turned off the engine and wrenched the steering wheel under his control. Before coming to a stop, we spun out and hit the curb, plowing down one of his men and sending the lead cannibal into the night with his remaining two comrades.

Cal continued the hunt briefly as we took aim at the fleeing brutes. As the trio rounded the corner of a house, one shadow slumped to the earth and we gave chase. We found the man crippled in a heap on the sidewalk; his blood gushed from the center of his back accompanied by his wails for mercy. In the distance I heard bursts of gunshots and the low groans of fleshies. Vincent turned his head and decapitated the dying man.

"More mercy than he deserved." I commented with a smirk as we rushed towards the sounds of a firefight.

"Maybe, but I'd like to think we're better people than to take joy in another's suffering; deserved or not."

As we ran we watched Cal plummet to the ground with a loud "umph" and the familiar sound of cracking bones. Checking on our friend, we noted dozens of gunshot wounds in various states of healing.

"Their leader managed to elude me, but I just drained his last henchman. His car didn't start, so perhaps he will end up stranded and eaten. The Dead aren't far off. We should retreat to our camp, now."

We helped the injured vamp to his feet and returned to the vehicles. Our party reconvened, I turned to the teenage tourists. Fernando had died earlier, but Maria lingered. I raised one of the silenced pistols to her forehead and looked into the girl's eyes.

Through her anguish, I saw a glimmer of recognition and distrust. I remembered our last meeting, my fury at her attempt to kill Daemon, the hours of listening to her torture, and Vincent's words. I drew a steady breath and discharged a single round through her brain. Her ordeal ended, she was thrown in the fire with the boy. It was as close as we could come to a funeral for the last of the Brazilian tour group.

We suffered only one casualty and a few injuries. Troy's arm bore a flesh wound wrapped in gauze. Quickly, we moved our deceased into the back of the Dodge, loaded all items of use, and drove towards the main road. This time the vampire rode shotgun to recuperate; he spent the entire night intently staring out the window for signs of our escaped opposition.

We traveled away from the city engulfed in bereavement. Although the guy had been in our community for almost three months, none of us knew the poor man's name. I scolded myself for not remembering the name I'd written on schedules for months. The only comfort was that he would at least have a proper burial.

Our funeral procession moved far beyond the wreckage of the living world, into the wilderness, and back to our reality. Our convoy drove without stopping for anything but fuel and to relieve our bladders. Cal rode inside the SUV trunk, with blankets lodged in the windows and hung across the backseat as protection from the sun. After what seemed ages, we arrived at the clearing and walked to the gates laden with our goods and a corpse.

CHAPTER 22 SEPTEMBER 23rd-25th YEAR 2

After we entered the gate of our fort, we laid Ezra to rest with a small service under a blanket of stars. We sent the children to the coffin cabin to listen to "Uncle Cal" telling them about Icarus flying too close to the Sun while we told the rest of our community about the raid's events. There was a murmur suggesting we track the lone cannibal and his remaining campmates. Chase ended that conversation within seconds.

"No. We're not going to start the first post-apocalyptic war. For all we know, that bastard is already dead and the others in that suburb may already have died without supplies. We'll keep our defenses up, work towards survival, and do our best to forget the things those pricks did. If anyone wants to argue the point, take the floor and state your case; I intend to focus on our lives rather than on the deaths of those murdering thieves."

Sunny stood by her husband, looking around for any signs of dispute. None arrived. The topic changed to the storage and disbursement of our haul. A small cache of baby jumpers and pacifiers materialized out of Forrest's bag, joined by some books and bottles I'd found in the cupboards on our mission. The funeral became a war meeting became a baby shower.

    The night carried additional questions about the dwindling number and condition of the Dead. Their deteriorated status was an unexpected turn of events that brought several conflicting ideas about what our future should be and whether the Pact held a place there. Each meal the next day felt uneasy as the conversations ended or shifted topic whenever I sat down. At dinner I sat apart, sure I'd somehow offended the group, until Troy and Seth planted themselves firmly next to me.

    "Hello beautiful, why so glum?"

    I smiled at the confident man with the crossbow on his shoulder. Seth just waved a brief "Hi" and dove into his meal.

    "I'm fine, just trying to figure out why everyone is acting like I'm a pariah."

    He chuckled and lifted his spoon.

    "It's not you, it's Daemon and Cal. Everyone knows how close you and the fangy guys are. They're just sorting out how they feel about things and how they think you'll react if they propose ending the arrangement with the vamps."

Troy took a large bite of his pigeon stew while I experienced an explosion in my brain.

"What? Why would anyone think we should end the Pact; it's one of the reasons we're all sitting here alive. And why would they think I am closer to the vampires than anyone else in particular? I thought they blamed me for Ezra's death."

Seth accidentally sloshed his bowl, tipping a bit of his food into the sand.

"Really? It's pretty obvious you and Daemon are an item; besides, the old Roman acts like you're his daughter one minute and his general the next."

"That's right, although I'd prefer if you were that close with me instead of the eternal teenager, it's clear you two have a thing; it's more obvious since you're both visibly trying to avoid being alone together."

He took a bite while I looked away.

Guess I'm not as low-key and subtle as I thought.

"All the info we brought back about conditions in town changed the game. If the Dead can be managed without the help of the Pact and we're capable of providing our own food, what is really keeping us from dusting them one morning and retaking the city? Or having them back us up while we clear the city of foes and then parting ways amicably?"

Troy spoke without any malice in his tone. Seth merely shrugged.

They honestly don't care either way.

I felt my jaw drop and watched both men for a moment. Troy flashed his smile in response.

"We go with you, whatever you decide, but a good number of the others are suddenly wanting to start over inside the city limits and several want to go it with only humans. Pretty sure Chase, Sunny, Bubba, and his boyfriend are with you too. The folks with kids will probably follow wherever the Nurse and his pup go; too scared to risk losing the healthcare and zombie-sniffer. Not to certain beyond that, though."

I felt a whirlwind of panic coated with acid rising in my stomach.

"Do you think anyone would try to kill Daemon or Cal?"

"No." "Not a chance." They chorused. Seth elaborated for me.

"They may leave or eventually bring around the possibility with you one afternoon away from the cabins, but no one would do anything in camp without approval. I'm fairly certain they all believe you'd take such a thing personal and things would end badly."

The spearman shrank into his dinner as his words trailed off. My community feared my reaction so much that they were trying to get a consensus together before even recommending any course of action. I'd somehow been forced into the role of leader and had now been cast as a dictator.

Can't we ever just have a mellow day anymore?

CHAPTER 23 SEPTEMBER 26TH- OCTOBER 9TH YEAR 2

For two weeks, I'd made a point of speaking one on one with every person in camp; I needed to assess what he or she thought about Cal and Daemon. As soon as Troy and Seth filled me in on the whispers and concerns within the community, I had them go to the coffin cabin with me. Under the pretense of surveying the housing situation in the fort, the five of us discussed the information.

"Well it sucks to be us." Daemon commented as he sat up on his bunk.

I noticed he kept looking beside me at Troy. I was almost certain I saw him flex his muscles as he crossed his arms in front of his bare chest. Cal darted his eyes over the pair of them and shook his head before settling his gaze on me.

"Eloquently put. So, Squirrel, how should we proceed?"

"Well for now, I think we need to gauge where everyone stands on the issues: the Pact, moving back into the city, and handling the cannibal raiders. We should rearrange the sleeping quarters; it's getting crowded in the main cabin anyways, so it ought to be easy to convince everyone."

I checked each man's eyes for signs of agreement or dissension. Satisfied that we wore the same uniform, I elaborated on the rest of my improvised concept.

"We need to move the bunks and belongings to even out the residents between all three cabins. I want to put Chase and Sunny in the second cabin; it's mostly couples and families anyhow. Forrest and Vincent stay in the main cabin but I'd like to get the Nurse, myself, Troy, Seth, and a couple of others that are against the Pact moved in here."

"Seriously? You want to put guys in here who want to stake us on purpose?"

Cal set his palm on his protégé's shoulder to prevent him jumping up in his excitement.

"It is the wisest move; if they stay with us, we may be able to sway their views over time - by erecting bonds of camaraderie and friendship. If not, we'll have our enemies where they can be monitored and their attempts at causing unrest negated swiftly."

"Exactly. However, I don't want either of you to use glamour to change their minds, they have the right to leave and think whatever they want. The line is at trying to harm any of our people and – despite what some of them think — you are both our people, too. I'm hoping these changes will remind them."

I made a quick mental prayer while trying to think of how to phrase the rest of the discussion. The words were practically a whisper when I managed to force them out of my tightening throat.

"We need to decide a course of action… in case, well in case the group is divided on the Pact too severely."

I didn't look up. The sensation of eyes burrowing through my head said they'd heard me. When I finally raised my eyes from the worn out New Balances on the floor where I'd been staring, I noticed the only surprised face belonged to Daemon. Troy and Seth just looked at me with an indifferent but determined expressions. Cal had zoned out facing the doorway.

"I feared this would happen eventually. This is why we kept our kind a myth for so many centuries; kept living in the shadows, anonymous and forgotten."

The elder vampire drew a deep breath and let it out slowly, his jaw resolute.

"As it stands, Sunny is no longer an acceptable donor and Ezra is dead. We are already close to the limit of a healthy donation schedule. If we lose more than four or five adults, the continued vigor of either the two of us or the rest of you will be significantly lessened.

We must to impress upon the community that continuation of the Pact is a matter of our mutual best interest; it is essential for both our species to survive and maintain a semblance of civilization."

He turned to face us; Seth began pacing between the beds. I rubbed my temples and tried to find the right words.

"I know. As far as clearing the city of fleshies and moving back in, I think it's a ton of risk with no real perks, but I can agree if we have a game plan and do it gradually. The cannibals are a different kind of issue."

Daemon leapt to his feet, causing Seth to stumble in surprise and flip over someone's trunk. Troy flinched, bringing his hand to his knife for an instant. Troy pulled his startled friend back to his feet and we stared at the fledgling vampire.

"What if me and Cal took out the people-munchers?"

I smiled.

"That could help. Besides, maybe the folks who stay in their camp are unaware of the things those guys do on their raids. Some of those people could be allies. Even if not, getting rid of the threat that big guy and his team of brutes pose is important: they keep destroying other settlements full of other survivors who could join our camp. We should consider getting a crew together to deal with it."

"No. You wouldn't go, just us vamps."

Troy smirked at the comment.

"No humans on the hunt, huh? Yeah that won't raise any eyebrows or distrust. Don't be stupid, we're going with you if this goes down."

"But alone, we vamps can fly out, waste the bad guys – supplying us with sustenance for the trip – sort out the rest of Seth's old subdivision, and pop back here easier than a drunk stripper on Valentine's Day. With a bunch of you folks in tow, the journey takes longer and the shuffling corpses become an issue; also the food and bathroom stuff."

The two men stood less than an arm-length apart, Daemon's eyes gleamed bright emerald while Troy's pearly teeth shone through his half-smile.

"If we're supposed to make everyone here trust you guys, we need to be able to believe it's not just you two hunting up extra cattle for the winter. One of you has to stay and the other one goes as part of a team."

I watched the argument like a tennis match.

"Gentlemen, it's a matter for discussion with the community as a whole, not just us. Calm yourselves and sit down."

They stood inches from each other; eyes locked and noses flaring.

"Okay guys, time to focus." I stepped closer and set my hand on Daemon's forearm, leading him unblinking to his cot. "Let the macho out of the room and we'll figure up what options we should present to the group and when."

Troy still stood between the beds watching me with a confused look. After a good thirty seconds of tense silence, he sat down next to Seth. Caelinus rubbed his eyes and stood in the center of the cabin.

"Squirrel, perhaps we should just agree to adjust the lodging within the fort. After that we can touch base with our known allies about the pact and decipher who is a danger. Once we know who stands where, you can arrange a town council to address our external foes and pose the question of resettlement within the city limits. The majority will have to resolve these matters, not this small contingent."

"Sounds good to me."

I rose to leave and fill in Sunny, Chase, and the others on the plan. Daemon rose also, stood at attention, and saluted the Roman. Jokingly he heralded,

"So orders the great Caelinus Gaius, Under Commander of the First File of the Roman Empire."

With a light chuckle, he waved the three of us goodbye and returned to his bed.

"Sorry, been waiting to do that for months; just needed an excuse."

The Roman waved us out of the room and approached his protégé.

"It's going to be a long eternity…"

***

That evening the entire camp agreed to the reassignment of quarters; although some of those assigned to live with the vampires were visibly displeased. One guy mumbled about sleeping in a scarf and turtleneck. Although the relocation only took an hour, the council meeting barely dealt with the possibility of retaking the city and didn't address the cannibal situation at all.

Chase had pointed out the need to ease everyone into each topic week by week. It felt like the best option only because it gave our small group the chance to work out all the alternatives we faced. We were playing chess, trying to see five moves ahead and get into the minds of our adversaries. Our small group of planners spoke at length while we worked on our chores, practicing retorts for each potential dissension.

The division in our tiny group kept waylaying our meetings over the cannibals: everyone agreed a search and destroy mission was needed, but the personnel and plan remained the point of contention. Troy and Daemon usually ended up squaring off verbally while the rest of us sat on the other side of the room trying to sort out how beneficial it would be to remain in our encampment versus moving our community into the urban areas.

"Look, Fang Boy, when we chase down those cannibals, it won't be just you and Grandpa Dracula; I'm going too."

Cal shrugged at this latest nickname in their debate.

"Children, is this really helping? The rest of us have already decided to present both choices for the journey to the assembly at the next council. Can't you two please sit down and be useful?"

Neither moved or said anything. I shook my head.

"Fine. Troy, please check on the sentries." With a frown, he strode out of the cabin, the door slamming behind him. I turned to his beaming opponent, "Daemon, I think it's time to patrol the perimeter." The wide smile slid off his face as he followed the bowman's path outside.

"Better?" I asked the others.

All nods and agreements, we pressed on with the discussion and drew up two more backup plans for emergencies before joining the camp at supper.

CHAPTER 24 OCTOBER 10TH YEAR 2

    Our day was busy. I heard the yells from the spike pits; Nancy had gone with Ellen's Father to gather oranges and guava at dawn. It was a good distance from the safety of the wall, and at midday, only humans would be able to help. My partner Troy and I ran towards the orchard. I clutched my spear as we sprinted down the worn path. I knew others were with us by the pounding of feet echoing behind me.

    As we made it to the fields, the frantic shouts trailed off. I looked around me for a sign of where they might be and watched Troy, Jake, and the Nurse doing the same. The Nurse's dog found the answer and led us to the western edge of the grove. We arrived out of breath. Droplets of sweat burned my eyes, while my denim jacket clung to my skin like a leotard on fire.

    Ellen's Father lay at an odd angle and his skin was pale. There was no sign of Nancy or the cause of her yells. The Nurse examined the unresponsive man; the rest of us searched nearby for signs of our missing resident.

    "He's not breathing."

    The Nurse began CPR.

"Were they attacked? Does it look like fleshies or humans did this to him?" I asked while checking for signs of a struggle or blood on the ground.

"Looks like he was bitten by a snake."

I hopped back about a mile and clenched my weapon tightly.

"SNAKE! Where?"

The others watched me lose my cool with bemused expressions and tilted heads. I forced a confident posture and regrouped my wits.

"I mean, uh, okay. Everyone watch for snakes."

"Don't worry, sweetness, I'll keep the bad serpent away from you." Troy laughed as he brought himself to my side and threw me a wink. "Unless you really want one."

"Nancy probably had the same reaction as you and ran." Jake offered while I ignored the advance and inspected the ground for a scaly nightmare.

We began calling her name while the Nurse continued his attempts to save Ellen's Father. Troy and I glanced back at the man's dedication; we had no way of fighting snakebites. Finally, we heard a response back toward the path.

"Over here! Hurry!"

Troy and I followed the voice. Jake stayed to keep the Nurse and Sindbad company. We found her at the edge of the woods sitting in a pine tree. I thought out loud as we approached.

"Why would she climb a tree after running from a snake?"

"Kill it!" Nancy yelled as we reached the trunk.

"Honey, I don't think she's trying to escape a snake. That stinky fellow looks like the culprit."

I saw it moving through the grass. The top half of a zombie was pulling itself by bony fingertips; the nails had been ripped off sometime prior. I assumed it had once been a woman from the exposed breast implant hanging from the torso.

Gray skin clung to the silicon and patches of blond hair with brown roots persisted on its scalp. The eyes were clouded except for the sky blue contact lenses. The left one was crooked on the eyeball revealing the milky pupil like an eclipsed moon. The creature inched closer to the scared woman. I grew calm, realizing I wouldn't be facing a snake.

In a blink, my spear tip protruded at an odd angle through the woman's forehead. Its snail-like progression towards Nancy halted abruptly and it found a final end. While she climbed down, I reclaimed my weapon and took note of the tribal butterfly tattoo on her assailant's lower back.

Nice ink. It really held up well.

"Let's get back. No telling if there's others. Just kick the cadaver into the path, and we can carry it to the burning grounds on the trip home."

I led the pair back to our companions. We found Jake standing over the body; his windbreaker lay over Ellen's Father. The Nurse was cursing and kicking a tree repeatedly. Troy set his hand on the frustrated man's shoulder. Without any words, we carried both sets of remains to the camp. We left the fleshie to be torched and sent Nancy ahead with the Nurse to notify his family.

We entered the gate to the sounds of his wife bawling and his daughter sobbing gently. The community was lined up at the entrance to pay their respects to our fallen member. Jordy hugged his mother while Michael and Bobbi held tightly to Randolph. I felt ashamed that I hadn't been able to prevent such an unnecessary death.

Memories played through my mind. I thought of the five people who died over the last winter of illness and the three others who'd been killed by random accidents.

The Reaper still likes to do things the mundane way sometimes. Pointless losses. Each person we lose is another generation that won't be seen later.

The night was doleful and we postponed our discussion on retaking the city. I lay awake until midnight. Giving up on rest, I went outside to chat with Daemon about anything but death.

After ten minutes, I found him sitting on the center tower with the sentry. Randolph tilted his head when I climbed over the top of the ladder.

"I thought Marley Guy was relieving me in an hour?"

"Oh, sorry. Couldn't sleep and thought I'd come be social for a bit."

Daemon sat on the edge looking into distant obscurity, swinging his legs and humming. Randolph chuckled quietly.

"Uh huh. Well, I think maybe I'll hit the outhouse real quick and you two can be social and keep a lookout."

I held out my hand for the night vision binoculars to cover him.

"No problem."

As Randolph descended, I heard him mumbling indistinctly to himself.

"Heard that, Randolph." Daemon called after him. "We have a room, but Cal's bunk is between us."

I blushed at the truth of it, even though we laughed it off. The Roman had insisted on the arrangement.

Our eyes met and the full moon shone on his eyelashes, creating a halo of illumination. The weight of the binoculars reminded me to check the tree line. The fledgling rose to stand beside me.

"How come you couldn't sleep?"

"Dunno. Just too much in my brain to get any rest. Why are you hanging out on the platform?"

He shrugged.

"Because I thought you'd be sleeping and I didn't feel like taking lessons on being a proper Undead citizen with Cal."

The breeze shifted, sending a chill up my back and a mild shiver through my weary limbs.

"You cold, Squirrel?"

"You're not?"

"Nope. Vampire."

"Oh. Yeah, guess that makes sense."

I scanned the horizon. I turned away only to feel his hands rubbing my arms gently. I warmed up, but a different shiver came over me. Daemon spoke softly into my ear.

"Better?"

I cleared my suddenly dry throat.

"Yeah, much better. Thanks."

I kept my eyes on the lenses but I was sure he could hear my heart pounding. My thoughts grew foggy as I tried to think of how to look him in the eyes without feeling that desire. The steady thuds below announced Randolph's return. Daemon stopped his caresses and kissed where my cheek met my ear.

"For what it's worth, my heart races when I'm next to you, too. Sweet dreams." he whispered before taking flight. "I think I'll go work on my control with Cal after all."

When the guard reached the top, I handed him the binoculars and moved towards the ladder. In total silence, Randolph reclaimed his post and I returned to bed. Lying there, I listened to the snores and breathing of my roommates and replayed our one night together in my head. My sleep was a pleasant escape from the day's loss and doubts.

I dreamed of flying and laughing and all the things I never let myself wish for. I dreamt of Daemon and peace and fearlessness. I lost myself in hope and forgetting the last year had been real. I rode roller coasters and ate ice cream, watched movies, and played cards with my family. There was funnel cakes and friends and fireworks. It was the last time I remember having such repose.

CHAPTER 25 OCTOBER 16TH YEAR 2

The vote was clear and we decided to stay in our current fort — at least until after the rampaging cannibals were handled. Although there had been only five hands for retaking the town immediately, over half of the remaining twenty-one other adults said they wanted to revisit the option later. It seemed like we would either be moving or splitting the camp in the future, possibly both.

Everyone with children, as well as Sunny and Chase, debated enthusiastically for remaining where we'd built a secure life. One of Troy's men stood and argued that the town was ours for the taking; he fumed when the raised hands revealed he'd only swayed four others. Neither Troy nor Seth was part of that group. The guy spit on the ground and stormed off talking about loyalty and priorities; he didn't bother to return for the discussion of Seth's old neighbors.

For the entire portion of the council regarding our foes, Seth sat cross-legged and watched the dust settle on his shoes. I began the topic as I'd rehearsed with the others from the raid.

"Alright everyone, we won't worry about going back into Orlando for now. That's a matter for a later date, and we'll consider it strongly at that time. With that said, it's time to get down to the reason we're staying here: there's a group of people raping, killing, and eating other survivors. We all know that this last raid put us in direct conflict with them. Several of us witnessed the level of cruelty and sadism they inflict on others. It'd be crazy to expect them to treat us any differently if they find us."

"What exactly did you guys see them doing?"

I calmly looked at the man who'd asked.

"I won't discuss it now; there are children present. Find one of us later and we can tell you. None of us want to relive those events. I'll say that those people may be human, but there is no humanity or decency left in them. The things they did are barbaric and unforgivable. Those weren't actions of survival, they took pleasure in the things they did."

"So we should take your word that it's worth staying here and running back and forth when we could just kill off the last few zombies and get the world back in order?"

"No, you have to use your best judgment. But that world is long gone. If you want to go try, go ahead. But you haven't volunteered for a raid in over six months and you've got no idea what it's like; the world isn't that simple. Let it go."

"But…"

"Shut your mouth or leave!"

Sunny glared at me; I'd lost focus out of frustration. I heard Daemon whistling Let It Be and breathed deeply.

"I'm sorry for that outburst. You have a right to your say, but please let me finish first. Alright?"

I tried to plaster a polite smile on my face like I used to do when dealing with rude guests at work. His alarmed expression hardened and he nodded before crossing his arms. I tried not to stare at how much his fingers shook on his elbows or the red of his face.

"Thank you. The issue is, we have several ways to manage this problem and we need to decide how to proceed as a community. The first is what we've been doing since we first heard about pillagers: increase our defenses and training, while limiting our travels from the fort. They're getting closer and actively seeking us out — not a great long-term solution."

I hesitated. All of my years of sales came to mind as I presented the real choices.

"The second is a team of volunteers and one vamp locate their home location and eradicate them. That includes any other survivors who reside there. This option would mean killing people who may not have even know about many of the atrocities that gained them supplies; it would also be extremely dangerous since we don't know how many or how well armed our enemy is."

I purposely paused to drink some water to let these choices sink in. Cal said fear sinks in best with time. Time gives a person time to think of everything that could go wrong.

Here goes nothing, convince them and everything will be fine.

"Third alternative is we let Cal and Daemon go on this task alone."

Already heads were shaking and eyes flicked over to our non-human residents. Little Bobbi sat drawing in the sand with Ellen, both completely unaware of what was happening. Her brother just watched the grown-ups and pursed his eyebrows; I suddenly knew how uncomfortable it must be for a parent to realize the jokes in a Mel Brooks film no longer went over their child's head. My palms sweating, I elaborated.

"One trip to survey and evaluate how they're set up. Another trip to make the final decision on whether or not we're even capable of taking these dudes down. They'd be risking everything to keep us safe; but we would have to trust their judgment."

This was the moment we'd prepared for, the opportunity we hoped would be selected. I waited and watched the assembly for signs of a favored path. I doubted anyone would opt for the first. The second meant extra danger for all of us except Cal and Daemon, but it also meant that the distrust of the pair had grown to where the risk was considered acceptable.

There was a low rumble of conversation.

I prayed our community wasn't already that concerned about the Pact. The third was the safest and most logical. It left all humans in camp and able to defend against attack, as well as able to acquire more food for winter. The third choice also meant the relationship between the humans and vampires was stable and the camp wouldn't be divided easily.

The chatter and banter made my head buzz. Only a handful of people seemed emphatic in their motions and tone. I sat down and looked in all directions as the fate of every person I knew hung in the balance. I'd cast my line and it was time to wait for a fish to bite.

My chest was bursting with every slow minute that dragged by without a resolution. I reminded myself that I had to remain patient and mellow so that the crowd would decide without feeling influenced. Chase, Troy, and Sunny had all agreed that it was a matter of trusting in our companions to make the right choice — even if we were trying to nudge them towards the third option.

After thirty-seven anxious minutes, it was agreed that we should vote. This time everyone wanted to vote by paper ballot. I cringed inside at why so many wanted to vote anonymously, but consented with a smile at Cal's urging.

"Of course, I'll get the supplies."

The meal table was transformed into a polling place. I placed torn squares of notebook paper under a rock and six or seven pens beside them. An unused pot was laid in the center of the table with its lid. As each adult walked up, I handed him or her a scrap of paper and they wrote their choice, folded the paper, and dropped it inside.

"One vote per adult, write one, two, or three. No one may abstain and the first couple to vote, please cover the sentries so they can voice their opinion as well."

I watched as a line formed; some fought to join the end in an attempt to gauge how the vote was leaning before casting their lots. As the end of the line reached me, I jotted down a shaky three and steadied myself to see the results. Each of my conspirators had placed themselves in the line at intervals in the hopes that they might subtly influence their neighbors that the third choice was optimal. It was a coordinated effort and I felt guilty until I began tallying the votes on the ground.

It hadn't worked.

"Only one vote left and we stand at: first option has three votes, second and third options are tied at eleven apiece."

The crowd leaned forward and my chest hammered as I unfolded the tiny piece of hope. I showed the number to the group and composed myself to announce the decision.

"The second alternative is our course of action."

CHAPTER 26 OCTOBER 17TH-19th YEAR 2

The planning process sucked. We spent two days deciding who was going on the hunt and whether or not the cannibal we'd seen was the only ones we'd execute. Very quickly it became apparent that the camp was once again divided; half wanted to destroy every person that lived in the hostile encampment while half wanted to just assassinate the leader and negotiate a truce with the remainder.

"Everybody shut the hell up!"

I rubbed my temples in an endeavor to make their bickering stop reverberating in my mind. The volunteers all froze and gawked at me.

"We aren't going to risk the lives of every person in this fort to kill one guy who might already be deceased. If we're going to search out and exterminate another living person to protect ourselves, we are going to completely eliminate the danger. If we enter their camp, none of them walk out."

I raised my head to peer into each of their eyes.

What did they think this would be? They voted to do it this way, did they think it was an easy decision to kill people?

Jake walked towards the door.

"I can't do this; I'm not volunteering anymore. Not for a slaughter."

Marley Guy and two others started to follow him.

"Marley Guy, you're staying."

"Wha? Why you think I'm gonna stay and go do this? I can leave just like them three."

Cal stepped closer, his concern as visible. I took my hands from my head and waved him off.

"Because, you kept ranting about how important it was the whole populace vote for this choice and not the third option. You personally swayed several people to choose this path. It's only right that you see it through."

I turned to face each of my accomplices.

"I know I don't have any formal authority to force him to stay and do this, but if he gets to walk away from the burden he helped create, I'll refuse to take any part in this. We all know that the third option was wisest and I only agreed to participate in this to keep our people safe."

I pointed at the forty-something Jamaican man.

"Either Marley Guy pulls his weight in this venture, or the entire village does another vote; I'm not ending lives with my own hands when he chose to put me there and gets to sit here without a care."

The lull in the cabin grew longer as each volunteer glanced at each other. Their faces spoke volumes about how much they wanted to completely rethink this mission. I doubt many of them actually believed we'd be taking human lives; they'd grown accustomed to putting down the Dead, but this was different. I was surprised when Seth broke the quiet reflection.

"They know what's happening. All of us knew, even in the beginning. Anyone who didn't leave is a part of those actions. I knew these people before the outbreak. The big guy is their leader, but taking him down won't do anything but make them target us more. That suburb was full of followers, the next guy to step up will do the same."

A tear ran down his cheek.

"I voted to let the vampires do our dirty work. I knew the only way to stop them was to massacre all of my neighbors. I have to live with what I've done to survive but I never found joy in it. Those people do."

His fists clenched, as he seemed to gain some determination.

"Maybe the kids can be saved, but I'm not even sure they won't just try to kill us in our sleep. It's a shitty thing to have to consider, but these are the actions we settled on with the vote."

Seth and Troy blocked the doorway. Chase and Daemon joined them and soon the Jamaican stood alone in the center of the room.

"Should we call for a new vote?" I asked. "A vote by hand, after you've told the community that you'd rather let Daemon and Cal brave the hazards and the possible guilt of this errand."

I honestly hoped they'd call for the vote and we could just allow the food chain to be put to use. I didn't want to think about shooting or stabbing people who may be innocent.

"You be right." Marley Guy spoke so low I almost didn't hear him. "I'll go on the journey and what must be is what will be happening. Jah forgive me, that is what I gonna do."

I wanted to hurl. Instead I tightened my jaw and nodded. Everyone returned to their seats and waited for the meeting to resume. I choked back the rising bile and pressed on with the meeting.

"We should leave day after tomorrow at the latest. I'd like to get underway tomorrow so that we can get this over with before those pricks have time to track us down."

"How would they find us? We're miles away from where they last saw us." Troy asked.

"All they need is to come across one of the dozens of people who've passed through here."

Vincent quickly added his thoughts to mine.

"Or to follow your tracks as best they could and look for signs of a running vehicle in the brush. Once they made it to the clearing where the vehicles are stored, they'll have found us."

Several eyes widened around the room. Daemon tossed cards into a hat at the end of the bed and Cal shrugged. I suppose they'd been expecting this possibility.

At least I'm not the only one who worries about this crap.

"So, back to the plan. We are one team split into three details: detail one is Daemon and Caelinus, detail two is Troy, Seth, and the Nurse, and detail three is Forrest, Vincent, Marley Guy, and myself."

"You forgot me, Squirrel." Chase raised his hand a little.

I sighed.

"No I didn't. You need to stay here."

"I volunteered and can carry my own weight. If it's the arm..."

"It's not the arm, Chase. We need you to keep everyone here at home safe. Besides, with Sunny getting sick every hour from the pregnancy, you should be nearby. And I'm not about to argue with her about you being away."

"Sunny will understand." He bristled.

"Really, I'll understand?"

Sunny stood in the door with her hands firmly on her hips and a Mom Glare fixed on the two of us.

"Uh, sweetie I thought you were resting."

"Is that why you sneaked over here to volunteer to run off to battle?"

The smile disappeared at the same instant Chase turned a bright scarlet. Everyone looked away; none of us was brave enough to face a pregnant Sunny while she dressed down her husband. We'd face cannibals or zombies no problem, but that was a risk we'd never take.

"And Squirrel, what makes you think I need Chase here to take care of me. I'm pregnant, not comatose. I can protect myself and I can do my part to keep this fort secure."

"So...so I can go?" Chase offered skittishly despite his size.

Cal placed his palm over his eyes and Daemon dropped his cards to watch. I couldn't tear my eyes away from such an epic failure of common sense.

"Are you freaking kidding me? No! Chase, you need to stay here and help me keep things running smoothly. We also need the Nurse here in case anything goes wrong. I'm growing our baby." She rubbed her growing stomach; the circular motion was hypnotic.

The Nurse immediately grabbed his knapsack and left the cabin in compliance.

Smart man. Can't fault Sunny's logic anyways.

"Um, I'll see if I can round up a few more volunteers for you guys." Chase said as he shuffled towards the door.

We waved goodbye as the couple left the meeting. I could hear them talking beyond the walls of the cabin for a distance.

"Okay new plan. I think we'll be fine with just us eight. We can split into two details instead of three, though, if anyone feels more comfortable that way."

Troy smiled. "I like the idea of us being in two details; easier on sleep shifts while traveling and I'd get to see your pretty face."

I blushed a little and was fairly certain I heard Daemon growl. The vampire's eyes had gold flecks in the midst of emerald.

"Alright. Detail one is going to fly ahead of us and scope out our target, while detail two travels at our best pace, sleeping in shifts to prevent ambushes. When the vamps return with info on the enemy setup, we can sort out a plan and attack that night."

I studied their reactions.

So far everyone's in agreement.

"Any other thoughts before we move on to what gear we need?"

Blank stares again.

"Fair enough."

After another hour of discussion, each of us had a list of chores and equipment to prepare. This would be one of the few times we'd be carrying firearms. Vincent and Forrest gave us a basic lesson in cleaning and fixing our designated weapons while Cal and Daemon looked on. Afterward, Cal took me aside.

"Thank you, Squirrel, for the vote of confidence."

"I trust you both, and so does everyone in camp. Some of them just forget occasionally."

We shared a smile and he patted me on the back.

"You are doing well. Don't let the pressure of commanding a populace harm you. If it were easy, you'd be doing it wrong."

***

We sat around the fire pit for dinner with the rest of the residents. Somehow we'd managed to sit to one side, naturally excluding the expedition members; our bags and weapons sat behind our chairs. The meal was quiet except for Michael's admonitions that he could go on the raid and help fight. I marveled at his innocence. Despite the horrible things the little boy had seen and the loss of his own family, Michael was still a child who saw adventure in a task we adults dreaded.

"Michael, I need you here to keep an eye on things for us. Cal and Daemon will be with us, so more grown-ups will be keeping guard during the night. I'm depending on you to help them out during the day and to keep your sister and Ellen safe. Can you and Jordy do that?"

He stood at attention and saluted.

"Yes ma'am."

Turning on his heel, he ran off to check on his sister and help the older boy load the arrows into quivers. A chorus of laughs rang out around the table and the stagnant air felt alive again. Cal stood up from his storytelling with the small princesses to see what the commotion was. A paper crown tumbled off his head and Ellen scolded him for losing his royal hat. He shook his head, bowed to both girls, and resumed the tale.

An hour later, he flew off with Daemon to begin our morbid errand. Bubba led us to the clearing and we filed into the two trucks. Although we'd wiped the interior down last run, a brown streak of dried blood remained as a grim reminder of our recent loss. Troy hastily jumped into the one he hadn't been shot in; he mumbled something about jinxes.

We listened to CDs as we drove in the direction Seth said he'd lived before the world had died. I'd nearly forgotten what it was like to push a button and have something turn on; hearing music flow from the speakers was a miracle I'd missed. All night we moved towards our goal: a subdivision a couple of miles from our foes anticipated location. Around 4:30AM, the first detail landed at our side as we impaled a couple of zombies.

"Would you folks like a hand?" Daemon joked as he grabbed an ambling corpse through the eyes and popped its head off. He tossed the impromptu bowling ball into a street sign and wiped his hands on a golf towel he'd clipped to the bottom of his leather jacket. "Strike!"

Cal smacked him, messing up his long hair. "What?"

The Roman soldier ignored his protégé and stomped the skull of crawling zombie.

"We found the area Seth told us about; it isn't what we're looking for."

Seth looked frantic.

"They aren't there? Are you sure?"

With a momentary look of disgust, Cal retorted.

"Of course I'm sure. I'm a vampire, not a blind man. And it is not just that the murderers aren't in that place. That place is full of nothing but bones, primarily human."

Cal focused on the stars and sighed.

"There is no sign of any children having been in that place for quite some time, but… there are small bones in the piles of trash. They all have teeth marks."

"No. No no no, they wouldn't do that. They couldn't." Seth fell to his knees. "Those kids belonged to some of those men, they wouldn't have allowed it. Their moms would've fought to protect them. You must be wrong."

Marley Guy lowered his weapon and breathed in short gasps.

Seth wept as Caelinus walked over and placed a comforting hand on his shoulder.

"I'm sorry, Seth. There were bones of many men, women, and children; there were no signs of life. None of the craniums had been destroyed. They were not made zombies. Perhaps they died of illness or hunger, but there is no one to save or spare from harm. They are all lost."

The sobbing drew a handful of moans from the distant shadows. Weapons were raised in alarm.

"Fleshies are coming. Let's get to a safe place for the day and regroup."

I put the rifle strap over my shoulder and lent a hand carrying the overwhelmed spearman into the cab of the Ford. We loaded up and drove six blocks back the way we came. Finding an adequate house with a brick wall, we forced the iron gate and got comfortable for the day. We eased the grieving man on the bed and did our best to ignore the sound of him crying himself to sleep.

Without any proper leads, our team had two options to fall back on: return home and wait for the escaped cannibal to maybe find us one day or go back to the site of our last skirmish and attempt to track him that way.

"He could've been killed already. He was alone and maybe wounded. The guy might have died of infection, gotten bitten by one of the Dead, starved, or any number of things."

Vincent sounded hopeful.

"He coulda been killed by 'nuther group they already messed with."

Forrest leaned his rifle against the wall as he spoke. "And so far as we know, the bastard is runnin by hiself, not much of a hazard to us."

The muffled whimpering eased up from the other room. I thought about it for a minute. Marley Guy interrupted my contemplation.

"We should go back to de camp. If is just one guy, is not bein a real threat. All likeliness, he is dead. You folks think we can leave in the morning?"

"No." Daemon's expression was as serious as a bill collector. "We should make sure he's gone. I'd like to go back to track him at sunset. You guys could head back, but I want to be certain he hasn't got another posse somewhere plotting to make our friends a buffet."

"I think the boy is correct. It should only take the two of us a day or so to ascertain the man's whereabouts."

I looked at the other four humans for input. Seth had finally grown quiet in the backroom. The house was silent. For a minute I missed the noises of a vibrant city. Or even the low hum of a dull town.

"Okay, how about we go to the cul-de-sac and search for clues about what happened during the afternoon and you two investigate the head people-eater as soon as dusk hits. We can meet up here tomorrow just before dawn. If anyone isn't here by then, we wait another twenty-four hours before returning to camp."

Five sets of wide eyes and raised eyebrows surrounded me.

"Not a good idea?" I asked.

Daemon cleared his throat.

"Well it's a good idea, but I'd prefer if you six went back and just let us manage this search. Personally, I kind of hoped you wouldn't have to see that place. And if Troy's sidekick sees it, he'll probably have a nervous breakdown."

"Can you really blame him?" Troy tensed his jaw as he rotated an arrow between his fingers. "He already feels awful for what happened when they were all starving, imagine how he feels after learning what became of those people he'd been friends with for years?"

"Look, let's just lighten up on Seth and focus on what we're doing now." I placed myself between the two men. "Are you guys okay with this plan?"

I waited for answers while Cal just strolled through the living room, glancing at the photos of the family who had lived there.

"It is agreeable to me." He announced softly.

"Hell, y'all know I'm up for exploring a bit. Ought to do this one thorough anyhow; no telling if this fella will drop in on us one day."

Vincent just nodded and held his boyfriend's hand. The Jamaican looked everywhere but at me. His mouth kept moving but no distinguishable words fell out.

Troy stood.

"Well I guess we should get some rest if we're heading out in a few hours. I'll check on Seth real quick before bed. Wake me for my watch."

Watching him walk down the hall, I volunteered for a two-hour shift. To my surprise, the Roman offered to sit with me until it was time to wake the lovebirds. Daemon said goodnight and shuffled upstairs for the day, tossing us a frown. Soon, Cal and I were alone in the living room.

I walked to the window to sneak a glance outside.

"I take it Daemon wanted to team up with me for watch; I recall you prefer to sleep early and he likes to wait to rest."

"Of course. I wanted to speak to you privately. Eliminating possible temptation for the two of you was merely a happy perk."

"I don't need a babysitter. I hope that's not the only thing you wanted to talk about, because

I really do enjoy chatting with you about everything else."

"It was a good decision to double-check what Daemon and I told you."

I stopped peeking out the curtains.

"What?" I faced him, letting the fabric fall from my hands. "That's not why…"

"Yes it is. You want to make a run to that suburb so that when we return you can honestly tell the entire camp what was found. I don't harbor any sense of insult over it; I'm more impressed that you controlled your emotions so well."

I willed my face and body to appear as neutral as possible. The vampire grinned widely.

"Exactly like that, Squirrel. I suppose Daemon isn't the only one who has been practicing their control lately."

"Well, our situation didn't give us much of a choice, did it?"

"No, it did not. But things could be worse; being unable to follow your romantic desires is far better than to suffer killing your lover."

Rummaging through my bag for a snack, I shrugged.

"We haven't done anything else, so you can forget the lesson."

I set some dried meat and veggies out. I tried to keep my hands steady and my voice level.

Just like playing poker.

"So I see. I'm sorry you and the boy have to step away from your feelings, but it's for the best. At least it has assisted your growth as a leader."

The Undead Roman crossed the darkened room to the stack of bags. I ignored the buzz of retorts flitting around in my head as he opened the nearest one.

"Here, you'll want some water with that."

I accepted the canteen and pushed my anger down.

"How does not being with someone I love make me a better leader?" My words came out more snidely than I'd intended. Taking slow breaths, I looked Cal in the eyes.

Get your breathing level and maintain normalcy. Just go blank like you did at work when it got too busy during the summer. No personal feelings, just focus.

"It's not avoiding love, but controlling your heart that is helping you. Every great general or politician must learn to make difficult decisions with a mask of non-expression. I can hear you working to regulate your heart rate as we speak; it has become instinct."

I sensed the truth of his words and hated him for it.

"You've been forced to make tough decisions for the greater good of our society, despite your feelings of empathy and remorse." He looked away with a grin, dusted off a table, and sifted through the stack of magazines underneath. "The Jamaican tested you and you passed, albeit with a more visible reaction than I'd recommend. When Daemon and I told you about the ruined neighborhood, you again made the correct choice in resolving to verify our story. I am equally proud of you and sad for you."

I ripped off a chunk of the smoked meat with my teeth. Chewing furiously, I heard my snarkiness before realizing I'd said the words aloud.

"Glad you're pleased with my progress, but I didn't do any of this to please you. I'm just trying to keep everyone alive. And I'm not going to stop talking to Daemon; I can survive not being with him, but I refuse to live without him in my life."

I cleared my throat to keep back the tears I felt welling upwards.

Cal slowly came to my side and bent to give me a gentle hug.

"I'm not cruel enough to suggest you two cease your friendship; not that either of you would ever comply." He forced a chuckle. "I just want you both to be safe. I wish you a long life and him a life free of the torment I already endure. Neither of you know what it is to destroy your lover, and I pray to Jupiter that it remains that way."

I felt the drops weaving their way down my cheeks. I thought of my own loneliness and tried to imagine Daemon spending eons beaten down by guilt and sorrow. The weight of my heartache and sympathy for Cal broke my strength. I let myself cry at the sadness while the vampire held me and stroked my back. When I finally looked up, I saw the lines carved into his face by centuries of anguish.

"Are you alright?" He asked as he leaned away.

"Yeah. Thanks, I'll be fine. I'm sorry Cal. I didn't mean to take it out on you, I know you're just looking out for us."

"Everything is well, Squirrel." He stood and placed a blanket on the dusty couch. "Our shift is nearly done. I'll wake the next pair; you get to bed. It will be a lengthy day."

I put away my food and made myself comfortable. He tucked me in and kissed my forehead before exiting the room. I thought briefly of my parents. My eyes ached and my head pounded as I closed my eyes, wishing I'd wake to find this world a dream.

CHAPTER 27 OCTOBER 20th YEAR 2

The day was a waste. Seth's former home was exactly as the vamps had described it. On seeing the inglorious heaps of human remains, the spearman climbed out of the F150 and walked into one of the cookie-cutter houses. Seth walked past the refuse and bone shards to the barren flower garden, retrieved a key from a false rock, and opened the beige door. I watched as he wiped both feet on the gore-laden welcome mat.

Vincent, Marley Guy, and Bubba stayed with the vehicles, providing coverage in case of attack. Troy and I followed the former accountant inside. Cautiously we peered around the rooms in search of our companion. Pictures and clothing were strewn over the floor. I tripped over a bowling trophy and fell into a bookcase. Tomes on bookkeeping and investing toppled onto me, blanketing me with a layer of dust.

Troy helped me to my feet, kicking the useless books to the side. We continued our exploration of the house. The kitchen cupboards were bare and a trail of footprints was revealed.

Sunlight streamed in the cracked windows and onto the take-out menus covering the counter. Troy called out.

"Seth. Seth where are you?"

Reaching the master bedroom, we found him. The former accountant sat on the closet floor mumbling gibberish. In his hands was an open shoebox of various items.

"Mom's earrings, Dad's favorite fishing lure, Granddad's medals from the war..."

Troy brushed past me.

"Seth, hey man, whatcha doing there?"

I watched as he knelt and reached for the cardboard box. Seth's head snapped up and he glared at his friend.

"Don't touch. Just...just leave me alone."

He moved a foot away and went back to rifling through the memento package. I noticed the photos on the nightstand; they all showed a smiling man surrounded by loved ones. The same man sat in the dust on the cold floor, a good thirty pounds lighter and aged ten years by misery.

"Troy, give him a minute. It's his house."

Troy glanced around and relaxed his stance.

"Alright, Seth, we'll be right outside the room. Let us know if you want anything."

Gradually, the bowman stood and made his way to the doorway. As though stung by a bee, he straightened, turned, and picked up his friend's gun. As he passed me he whispered.

"Don't take your eyes off him. I'm going to look around for a few minutes and then we need to go."

I nodded and watched Seth nervously.

After ten minutes, the accountant closed the little box and rose to his feet. I looked away while he wiped his eyes and nose. I smiled weakly at him and realized a lot of the spark had left his eyes.

"Thanks, I'm just going to grab a couple of things and we can go."

Without another word, the three of us carried our belongings out of the lifeless abode and rejoined our detail. The others surveyed the broken man and avoided asking questions. Our detail clamored into our gas-guzzling chariots and advanced to the main road. We'd be in the familiar clearing by sunset, detail one arriving within an hour past. It was expected to be a mellow return to Nova Nocte. We should have known life doesn't conform to such plans.

CHAPTER 28 OCTOBER 21st YEAR 2

We heard the rat-a-tat-tat of gunfire before our vehicles reached the clearing. The sun was still lingering above the horizon as we pulled into the field. Vincent and Bubba jumped into the third vehicle, the soldier readying his weapon in the passenger seat. We did the same while our convoy plowed through the brush and grasses to our encampment.

Marley Guy kept muttering as he drove and I found myself praying that we made it in time. I heard a variety of blasts; there was the boom of a shotgun in the midst of the quick bursts from an automatic weapon, the regular bang of rifles, and several handgun pops. I wrapped the rifle sling around my wrist and locked it into my shoulder as we neared our home. I looked ahead and saw Troy already leaning out his window with a sawed-off shotgun in his right hand and a pistol in his left.

Coming over the last hill, the situation became clear: the big guy had rounded up the rest of his headhunter pals and tracked down our place. There were nine or ten men unloading round after round into the steel wall and wooden platforms. Sparks and splinters flew on each impact. We were behind the assailants; their thundering barrage of bullets masked our arrival.

We opened fire as we neared. I saw two men fall, one shooting his comrade in the leg as his torso spewed blood onto the parked Hummer. The besiegers rounded on us. We kept driving past the attackers, firing on them in uneven volleys while our sentries inside camp rained down cover fire from the towers. Soon, only five men were standing and we stopped the vehicles to face them. From the wooded area behind our fort we saw the smoke.

One of the ravagers had sneaked around the wall before we'd turned up; he'd tossed several Molotov cocktails inside. There was screaming from inside the camp as the smoke thickened and grew black against the multi-colored dusk sky. I spotted the firebug running back to his decimated militia, flinging another bottle of flame against the nearby tower as he ran. I saw the sentry jump from the blazing platform; it looked like Jake.

Seth emerged from the truck and heaved his spear. It drove through the arsonist's stomach and through his back. The spearman howled with rage as he charged at the man, firing his revolver with each step.

"How could you do those things, Aaron? How could you! You were a doctor."

Holes exploded from the deceased man's torso, leg, and chin as the projectiles found their marks. I yelled to the others.

"Get the vehicles to the gate and deal with the fire. Go to Plan B!"

Vincent, Marley, and Bubba hauled off to rescue our people. Troy and I took refuge behind our lumber stack and continued picking off the cannibals. Soon, there were only two men left and the gunshots tapered off. Hearing the click of an empty magazine, we both charged with our swords drawn; we'd run out of ammo minutes before, but someone in camp had upheld protective fire for us.

I plunged my blade into the nearest man's ribcage while Troy beheaded the other in one quick swing. He took three more swings, severing the remains into chunks of gushing red and gurgles of air escaping its human cage. I pulled my blade free and felt a sharp pain in my lower leg as my victim stabbed me with a pocketknife. Furious, I brained him with the pommel of my sword and proceeded to hack at him until I was drenched in sweat and sanguine fluid.

I wiped his blood out of my eyes and surveyed the situation. The camp was engulfed in flames and everyone was now being loaded into the vehicles with any supplies we could carry. I ran to help, stepping on the leader of this rampage; he'd died of a single gunshot through the back of his skull. The vamps had landed as soon as the evening had begun and rescued most of our residents.

Ignoring the pain in my leg, I followed Chase back in for whatever items could be salvaged. The supply building had been emptied, but the burning cabins had been untouched. As I ran to retrieve my possessions, I felt an arm wrap around me. Turning, I found a bloody Daemon pulling me away.

"It's too late, the cabins are too far gone. Leave it."

"No, I can…"

He shook his head and flew me over the wall to the others.

"We have to go. The noise and flames have drawn every zombie for miles; we need to get everyone far from here before dawn."

The fledgling lifted me into one of the truck beds and loaded his back with four large duffels.

"Cal and I already took out the other force of marauders to the east. You guys drive towards the base in Winter Haven. Cal and I will fly this gear and help clear the way. Stop each hour so we can meet up and rest a minute."

He took to the air and our society began our nomadic life. The Nurse bandaged my leg, double-checked the health of the kids, and monitored Sunny's vitals as we rode. When we stopped and hour later, the damage was assessed fully.

Nancy and two others had been killed in the assault, one woman had died on the drive from smoke inhalation, and four others had been wounded. None of the wounds appeared life threatening, but we had no medicines to fight infection. Thankfully, Randolph had gotten all of the kids to the SUV safely. Jordy's Mother had been shot shielding him. The preteen had resorted to throwing burning sticks and angry words at the gunman when she slumped over.

We fought grief and Dead throughout the night before making camp inside a large house. We were miles short of our intended destination. I'd watched the fire illuminate the nighttime clouds while my community mourned around me. My mind wandered numbly to the vibrant paintings I'd seen during the numerous art shows in town; the same colors of this destruction shone in my memory as beautiful.

I ignored the looks and questions bombarding me. I thought of my journal turned to ash and thought of my printed calendar folded neatly in my pack. Time still existed; so would we. I inhaled the cool air and scanned the air above us for our Undead entourage. Seeing the twin silhouettes just ahead, I closed my eyes and waited for the blood on my skin to dry into flakes.

CHAPTER 29 OCTOBER 24TH-25TH YEAR 2

Found a new notebook to use as a journal in this house today. It's just a simple green spiral, but it comforts me to know that my words can continue. I just spent the last day and a half recording all I could remember of my last journal – the few notes from my calendar help me estimate the dates. We've been trapped in this house during the day, only getting out tonight after Cal and Daemon were able to help us put down the swarm of fleshies who'd followed us.

One of our wounded died yesterday after he was bitten by one of the Dead; I hesitated before putting Jake down. Cal glamoured the poor kid into believing he was reliving his happiest moment; he wasn't aware of any fear or pain. We buried him near the swing in the backyard. Sunny's baby still has a strong heartbeat according to Daemon and Cal; we remaining wounded are healing fine.

We now have a traveling pack of two vampires, nineteen human adults, and four children. We have enough food and water with us to last around one month, but not an entire winter. Our only concern is getting to a place we can make habitable again before our rations give out. Especially the water and medicine.

Tonight our caravan rolled to the outskirts of the National Guard base. The kids stayed in the SUV with Ellen's Mom and Randolph. The trucks protected them from ahead and behind. We carry a mix of weapons now: the firearms to guard us from humans and the silent arms to save us from the zombies. The vamps met up with us each hour all night, quietly cutting a path through the masses of decayed Dead surrounding our troop.

Myself and the other adults rotated walking briskly beside the vehicles and riding. Keeping the children and supplies loaded meant a severe lack of space. After only two hours of tonight's journey, we'd had to replace the F150 with a Chevy in desperate need of a tune up. I was thankful our mechanic hadn't been killed when the beast of a truck was resurrected in a blast of milky blue smoke and knocking pistons.

Switching the gear had taken ten minutes. Sunny and I stood watch with Troy while Seth and Chase led the rest on a potty run into a nearby house. They sprinted out seconds after entering. Running to help destroy whoever or whatever they fled, I burst through the crooked door with my arrow ready to fire.

Looking into the dim foyer for a figure of a person, I eased my bow around the corner to view the living room. Seeing no people and no fleshies, I began to lower my weapon, confused about the reason for evacuating the building so abruptly. Then I felt it wrap around my ankle.

Looking down, I expected one of the zombies but found instead a writhing snake tangling itself on my leg.

"Holy shit!"

I screamed like a baby and shook the scaly monster off my leg while fleeing. I dropped my bow in the process.

"Snake, snake, kill it! Someone get the snake away from me!"

I flailed as I sped towards my friends. The thin black creature held fast to me and I drew my sword to pry the thing away. I heard laughter over my screams as Troy strolled over and grabbed the snake behind the head. He freed me from my passenger and held it up.

"Just a little rat snake, darling. It won't hurt you." He drew his knife and cut off the head. "Makes a good meal though."

I looked at the rest of our camp clinging to the autos and realized my hands were shaking. Remembering my bow, I quickly picked it up and composed myself.

"Thanks Troy." Facing the group, I rambled. "I don't like snakes. They're all creepy and snake-like. They just really freak me out. Sorry."

Distant moans carried on the light breeze.

Smooth move leader lady. Way to announce dinner for the fleshies.

"Fuck. Sorry guys, our potty party needs to relocate to an elsewhere. The departed are arriving so let's bail."

Loading up, we trekked down the road until we found a place to crash for the day. During our march, we managed to hunt up a raccoon and two possums to eat. Using pool chlorine, a bucket of water was slowly made drinkable.

Seeing the faded brick and concrete house, our community came to a halt. Waking the kids, the vehicles were backed up to the front porch and we disembarked. This time, I stayed back while the building was cleared of enemies and pests.

***

As daybreak drew close, I finished my road kill stew and settled in to wait for my watch. I sat on the front porch with both my bow and rifle to watch the sunrise; being on second watch, I saw no point in getting two hours of sleep beforehand. I thought about the people I was responsible for.

The four children snuggled up in the first bedroom with their caregivers lying just outside the door. The two vampires resting in the crawlspace, hiding from the beams of light that cascaded so gently on my face. And of course the eighteen other adults who were either snoring on the floor or sitting awake for a turn as sentry. There was almost no chatter.

What are we going to do?

The front door creaked open and I turned to greet my visitor.

"Morning Troy. What brings you out here?"

He displayed his sly smile.

"Well, I always like to sit alone on a porch with a pretty lady. Besides, who's going to keep all the bad snakes away if I'm not here?"

Playfully hitting his arm, I pulled him into the chair next to me.

"Not funny. It was scary and on me and it wouldn't let go. Even Indiana Jones doesn't like snakes. Would you tease him?"

He shook his head with a little chuckle and looked out into the distance.

Tendrils of clouds floated along the Technicolor skyscape casting shadows over the ruins of humanity below. I remembered a similar morning from my youth, listening to Bryan Adams on the radio and scribbling little nothings in a notebook. I felt the sides of my mouth crawl upwards at the peace of it.

"Thinking something good over there, Squirrel?" he teased and laid his crossbow against the wall.

"Just observing."

"And?"

"Nothing much. Just enjoying the little moments of harmony and dazzling magnificence that occur in the middle of all this hideousness." I watched a flock of water birds flying over the treetops, then looked at his raised eyebrow. "The world has gone to shit, but it occasionally doesn't stink."

He rocked on the back two legs of the chair. For a minute, we sat in comfortable silence watching the debut of a new day.

"That sounds about right. And a little less fancy."

I stretched my arms overhead and was rewarded with a series of pops from my back. Rolling my head to each side, I stood to extend my legs after a weary night. Turning to ask Troy what he thought, I found his lips against mine and his calloused hands perched on my hips. Startled by the kiss, I stepped back. Troy held the kiss, stepping with me and encircling his arms around my waist.

As I let my lips part, he gently massaged my tongue with his. My hands found their way around his neck as he did something wavy with his tongue I thought impossible. I ran my fingers up the back of his neck and into his short hair; the soft tips tickled the back of my hand. As my lust for him grew, a thought Daemon flashed through my mind.

I slid my hands onto Troy's strong chest and gave a little pressure, breaking our embrace.

My body screamed at me for its disappointed lust and my brain for my failure to think logically; my heart calmly debated with both.

Heart wants what heart wants.

I thought of Daemon lying under the floor of the house hearing my heart race like this with Troy and felt a pang of guilt.

"I'm sorry, Troy. I like you, but I just can't."

Without letting our eyes meet again, I stooped to grab my weaponry and strode to the door. I went to open it and was stopped by a gentle hand on mine.

"It's okay. I get it. I've got plenty of time to wait; if fang boy is my only competition, it reasons that eventually this will work out."

With the grin of a high school kid after his first date, Troy pulled the door open for me. Dumbfounded, I stood planted beside him.

"Don't worry, I won't go bragging about our moment."

I felt the blush and fought it down as I gave a tiny nod and stepped through.

"Thanks."

"My pleasure. It's always nice to be able to watch the morning greet the world and just bask in her rays awhile, isn't it?" he prodded jokingly.

***

The day went quickly. Only two Dead came near the house. Both were so decrepit that the first was put down by hand. The second one was eliminated by bow mid-afternoon after several failed shots from the porch. Both guards decided to keep firing and gathering the arrows for practice.

I opted to split the first's skull rather than risk wasting an arrow; I couldn't even tell if had been male or female in life. The thing had lost everything below the upper ribs and had peeled most of its skin off dragging along the pavement. I looked at the thin trail the rotted cadaver had left behind on the driveway and wondered how long it had been trying to get here.

As night blanketed our hideaway, the community was wakened for the evening's travel. The vehicles were given an once-over and fueled up while the group ate. While we barricaded the children into the SUV and packed our belongings, we discussed our plans.

"We're going to break a big rule and go towards the National Guard base in Winter Haven; most likely it has a good number of fleshies roaming around it, but they're probably manageable if we work together as a team with Cal and Daemon."

I gestured to our resident vamps as reassurance of their zombie-fighting prowess. Daemon struck a Charlie's Angels pose. Both His mentor and I did our best to ignore it, but I still felt the smile creeping on my cheeks.

"We aren't going to try to clear the whole area, we just want to get near enough to see if the place is worth raiding or securing. Not being in Orlando outright, I'm hoping it wasn't overrun too badly."

Everyone kept arming himself or herself and mobilizing for the trek; occasionally my words would be met with a nod or a weak smile. Aside from some snickering at Daemon's goofiness, there was nothing. I sighed. Noting my frustration, Chase cleared his throat.

"Guys, Squirrel is trying to get some input here; anyone got a comment?"

It felt like watching an entire herd of deer stunned in headlights. I watched the blank stares for a minute before the truth of it hit me: they aren't thinking about it.

"Are you guys seriously just following no matter what the plan is at this point?" I blurted as fast as the realization could be formed into words.

"Of course."

Several nods and shrugs followed the answer from Marley Guy. I turned my head thinking I'd see someone shake their head or something. I looked to Cal for guidance only to observe him rubbing his temples in circles. Our eldest member spoke coolly.

"You people make me fucking sad."

People stopped prepping to leave.

"She may be leading you, but you aren't supposed to follow blindly. Squirrel is trying to keep everyone involved so that if something happens, you may be able to use something gleaned from the experience to survive. And you dumbfucks have chosen instead to become lemmings. Sheep follow directions unless it's against their best interest, whereas lemmings will follow unto their own demise for lack of thought."

Nothing.

"Does anyone have an opinion at least about this attempt to keep the group alive? Or a reason to agree or dissent? Anything to say, really?" He stared each person down, eyes beginning to shine with his fervor.

"Yes, I do." Sunny piped up as she climbed out of the truck and placed her hands on her hips. "I'm agreeing to go, because I don't see another option that's worth a damn. Chase and I are responsible for our own well-being but we aren't dumb enough to think a group effort wouldn't be simpler.

If anyone wants to split up or try to go back and rebuild, I'll go along if it's a better choice. But I'm not going to run around the state forever hoping to find a perfect place; we have to make one. I'd prefer to just trust Squirrel and you to guide us."

It seemed like thunder rolling as a dozen people spoke simultaneously.

"We can't go back, the place was burnt down."

"I want to just keep moving until we find a better plan."

"Did Cal just call us dumbfucks?"

"What about those gunmen; there could be more. Why shouldn't we keep running?"

"I thought we were going to the base for the winter and rebuild the old place in spring?"

"Anyone seen my revolver, I could've sworn I had it in my pocket a minute ago."

I held my hands up in a plea for quiet.

"Guys, c'mon we can sort this out fast, but not if everyone's talking at the same time."

Troy let out a loud whistle.

"Shut up. Let's work and talk. We've made too much noise to stay tonight either way, so shut up."

"Thanks, Troy." The herd watched me intently now. "We're going to the base because it is one of the only things I could come up with. There may be items we desperately need to make it through the winter. I don't think there are any others from that pack of marauders, but who knows for sure."

I shouldered my faded green duffel before checking my rifle was loaded and had the safety on. Closing the gate of the Chevy, I set my bow and quiver in the back since it wouldn't fit.

"I haven't even considered if this base would be permanent or if we'd become the Bedouins of the Southeast or if we'd return to our old camp and rebuild. Those are all things we need to think about and decide as a whole. Think about that and we'll hold a proper council after we've settled in at the base."

With a hand signal, we began to take our places in the low speed procession. The hours were passed in discussion of our future. Each hour we stopped to switch walkers and riders while the vamps checked in. Sunny took a turn walking beside her hubby — with her weapons and canteen only — after the Nurse admitted it wouldn't cause her baby any harm.

By 4AM it was time to find a new hideout for the day. I made a mental note that Cal hadn't needed a donor since the battle and Daemon had needed only a little tonight. It had been more than a little awkward being his donor when twelve hours prior I'd been kissing Troy. Before the sun had set, I'd managed to clean up with a tin of water and some baby wipes; I didn't want Troy's scent on me in case Daemon could smell it.

As we began our search of the first building we came upon, it was deemed unlivable. Apparently, someone had gone out with a blast; the decayed remains of at least forty people were strewn about the living room in various states of undress. A table laden with empty liquor bottles, drugs, and poisons sat in the center of the room. It was an altar to their final spree of excess.

The front door was shut as abruptly as the stench reached our noses. Our lead group skipped the next two houses in case of contamination or infestation from the earlier scene. The fourth place was a nice town home with a large garage and screened pool. Finding the place cleared out and mostly raided of supplies; we set up camp for the day. Taking turns bathing in the pool lifted everyone's spirits. Thankfully no one had taken the pool cleaning equipment.

With an hour left until dawn, I met with several others to raid the neighboring house for any usable goods or vehicles. As soon as Seth got the door open, I could see the place was trashed.

"Doesn't look promising." I commented.

A scraping sound came from the rear of the building, drawing my sword out of its scabbard with a metallic ring. Cautiously, we moved towards the noise in the obscured rooms. Each room was clear until the kitchen. Up against the open fridge was the long dead body of a woman. She had gaping holes where bites had been taken and her tattered dress clung to the exposed ribs. Her neck and cheeks bore scratch marks and the small indents from children's teeth.

Nearing the putrid corpse, the head tilted towards my footsteps and the withered eyes fixated on me.

I know that stare.

I gasped as I remembered Lonnie and Amber's mother and father leading them away from camp on Daemon's first night.

"I'm so sorry."

I closed my eyes as my blade cut through the side of her skull. I opened them as I jiggled the wedged sword out of the wound, shaking off the bits of cranium and hair onto the linoleum. The cadaver slumped sideways to the floor, finally deceased. I heard Chase whispering a farewell to our former ally and a prayer for her family. His words halted as the scraping continued to our right.

Please don't be them. Please whatever God or Goddess or higher power or spirits can hear me, just please don't let it be them.

I prayed to myself with each step. Turning the knob on the back bedroom, I eased the door open. With each inch the room's contents were revealed: a stained sock monkey, some clothes, used bandages, a katana, empty food cans, and a child's Sponge Bob backpack. Across the room Lonnie and Amber were scratching the metal closet door.

Dried streaks of tar-like blood embedded with skin and fingernails coated the door - signs of the extended attempts. At the sound of the door creaking wide, they both turned. Lifeless eyes stared at me from cherub faces. Tripping over her broken leg, Amber lunged for us, making that guttural moan that echoes in my nightmares. Lonnie followed with disjointed steps, his only arm reaching with bone-tipped fingers.

From the closet I began to hear sobbing as our party backed up to fight. Amber drew close to me, her open mouth missing half her teeth; I fought the rising bile in my throat and thrust my broadsword at her.

No Tooth Fairy for you, Sweet-pea.
"Dammit."

Missing her head, I'd clipped her neck and let her get too close. I took a large step back and put my hips into a diagonal swing. The sensation of steel driving through bone and flesh ricocheted up my arm as the little zombie was split from her ear through her chin; the blade continued the arc taking a chunk off Amber's left shoulder and rebounding off the door frame.

Lonnie was right behind his sister grasping for flesh. An upward slash tore through his torso releasing fetid organs and splitting the jaw. It wasn't high enough, and the Dead boy stumbled nearer, the once vital pieces all swaying and hanging as gravity called the organs to the ground.

Backing into the kitchen, I was able to move to the side. Lonnie paused and groaned as he was confronted with multiple people to eat. Chase lifted his axe and stepped towards the fleshie. Lonnie immediately charged him and slipped in the pool of infected blood. Chase's swing missed the falling zombie and put a large crack in the checkered linoleum instead.

"Ugghh." He exclaimed as he tried to pry the weapon out of the floor.

Lonnie started to crawl towards him and Seth pulled Chase back from the axe.

"Watch out, I got it."

Seth's spear point erupted from the back of the boy's head, spraying the wall with gray matter.

I helped Chase retrieve his weapon from the pulverized floor, trying to think of something to say.

"So Chase, I'm afraid you almost lost the duel of the one-handed. We may have to reconsider the axe as your primary arsenal in the future." I joked to keep from vomiting at the ordeal.

He grinned, but it was clear it was forced. Hefting the axe onto his shoulder, he tilted his head towards the bedroom.

"Should we go check that out or get reinforcements? Someone's in there, but we don't know with what."

I took a deep breath.

"I'll go in first, Seth stay to my right and Chase move to my left. I'll pull the closet door and we'll wing it from there. Okay?"

My partners nodded and we got in place.

I tugged at the door. It wouldn't budge. The crying had stopped and now a whisper escaped.

"H-hello?"

"Look, we took out the three zombies; open the door and come out slowly. We don't want to hurt you."

"Squirrel? Is that you?"

It's him.

"Yeah, Paul, it' me. I've got Chase and another guy named Seth here, too. It's safe."

I put away my sword and took a step back. The door came loose and revealed the same mild man I used to know. Paul was now gray-haired, twenty pounds lighter, and a wreck of his former self. He was sitting in a mess of his own filth and empty boxes of supplies surrounded him.

He must've been in here for weeks.

My composure wavered and I propelled my rational mind to take control of my body. The acid from my stomach subsided and my pulse leveled out. I took a moment to focus on keeping my voice calm and even and my words simple.

"Seth, please go get us some help. Chase and I are going to talk to Paul for a minute."

The spearman departed without a response and I knelt down to look the traumatized man in the eyes.

"Paul, I'm sorry about your family. I know that you must have been in this closet for a long time and that this has been very difficult for you. We're here to help. Do you think you can stand up?"

Paul just looked through me and wept.

"Everything was fine; for a long time it was fine. We raided and trapped and kept moving and the four of us were fine."

"I know, Paul. You did a good job. I know you loved them and you did your best; life is just really tough right now. We'll give them a proper goodbye later, but right now I need you to look at me. Do you think you can stand up?"

Chase squirmed uncomfortably for a moment before leaving the room. I heard him retching into the sink.

"The winter was really hard but we did okay. Lonnie got really good at setting traps for meat and Amber helped Pamela with the gardening and gathering. She used to sing songs for us. 'Tweet tweet little birdie hopping on the car, tweet tweet little birdie flying far'"

The puking stopped and Chase returned. Together we listened to the broken man sing the little song.

"I covered the bodies with some curtains. Can he walk or should we pick him up?"

"Chase, I don't think he can get his mind around what's happened. Let's wait for backup and go from there. Just talk to him for now."

"Hey Paul. How long have you been here?"

I elbowed Chase and shook my head.

Too serious a question for him right now.

He seemed to catch my hint; The broken man just kept singing his daughter's tunes as though he hadn't heard the question.

"Here little raindrops, make my veggies grow. Careful little raindrops, no storms though."

Hearing footsteps, we turned to find Seth returned with Daemon, Sunny, the Nurse, and Sindbad.

"I got some help. How is he?"

I pointed out the door to the other room.

"Paul, we're going to leave you in here for a second, but I'll be right back. We're going to help you out of there and get you cleaned up."

"Big dog plays with little pup, all dogs are winners. Nice dog helps us all, mean dogs for dinner. Play little pup pup, roll in the grass…"

I met with the others in the kitchen.

"Guys, he's had it bad. Paul's really screwed up right now, I think we should just try to keep him mellow, get him next door, clean him up, and have a simple funeral for his family. That's all I've got, so I defer to the medic among us."

"I think this man is in shock. Sindbad didn't signal infected, but he's probably malnourished, a bit delusional, and possibly injured. I agree with your plan, but we should keep him away from weapons and the kids for now."

"Agreed. Here Seth." I handed him my arms. "Chase, he knows you, can you help me with Paul?"

Both of us disarmed, we slowly walked into the room and knelt at the closet.

"Paul, I'm going to come in and get you to your feet. If you can, please stand up when I lift; if not, Chase will come in and help okay?"

I waited for any sign of acceptance or resistance before moving. I rose and took a step into the narrow room, pushing debris out of my path with each step.

"Can you kill me now?"

I stopped.

"No, Paul. We're not here to hurt you. I just want to get you cleaned up and somewhere safe. I promise, we'll have a service later today for Pam and the kids. I'm sorry Paul, but we're here to help."

"No." His eyes became focused as laser beams. "Kill me. I can't do it myself."

I forced the memories away as he pleaded through tears.

"Please, end it."

"No, Paul, don't ask me that. Please."

I found myself shaking and crying as I retreated little by little out of the shrinking room.

"Please Squirrel. I want to be with them. If I do it, I can't be with them in Heaven. Please kill me."

I felt a hand softly pulling me back from the closet.

"Squirrel, I'll help. You go back to check the others." Daemon rubbed my shoulder as he spoke.

"Amber got bit first. Pam and I couldn't do it, not to our sweet angel. And then when she turned, we kept her locked in the other room. Kill me please. I can't forget; the memories won't stop. Please."

Owen crying on the floor. Rocking back and forth, each sway punctuated by blood drizzling down his bandaged calf. "Rhia, please don't let me become like them. I don't want to suffer like Mom and Dad.

"Squirrel, let me get you out of here." The vampire eased me closer to the exit as I began to hear those memories come to life again; Hell in surround sound.

Dropping my looted supplies and reinforcing the barricaded bedroom door. Ignoring the scrapes and moans from within while I change Owen's dressings. "I can't do it little man. I'm your big sis, it's my job to look after you. Take this medicine, I'll be back soon with some more food." Wiping the tears from his face and the feverish sweat from his forehead, before going out to check the traps.

"Lonnie heard a loud noise and tried to check on her, she ate part of his arm. I tried to get Pam to leave but she wouldn't. Please end it; kill me. Pam tried to save Lonnie, but he'd already bled out. I wanted to run away when the kids started to eat Pam, but I couldn't. Please, Squirrel. Please kill me."

"Stop it! I can't do it. Please, don't ask..." I dropped to my knees as those words overtook me. The past overwhelmed me as I felt myself rocking.

I have to force it away. It's over, I need to get in control. Don't listen, just try not to listen.

Powerful arms lifted me and I felt myself slipping from the moment and cascading through my recollections. I closed my eyes and fought to keep a hold of the present moment.

"Why is she rocking? What's happening to her?"

"She'll be fine Sunny. It's her past. Take care of that guy, I'm taking her next door."

"I'll be there in a minute to check her vitals."

Coming back to find that stranger hovering over Owen's crushed body with a baseball bat. The door open and my parents destroyed. The man's face when he turned around. Blood painting my childhood home as I lashed out. Jabbing my blade into him repeatedly and slashing off his limbs. Kicking and crying until my muscles ached and all I heard was my own shattered laughter and the coming rain. Passing out from exhaustion, ready for the Reaper to take me.

The next thing I knew, I was lying on the pull out couch with Daemon stroking my hair. He was whispering in my ear.

Waking up drenched in blood and scraps of skin. The sensation of walking into rain to wash the death away. Packing a bag full of the remaining supplies, pouring the rubbing alcohol over the corpses, starting the warm fire, and jogging to the library around the corner. What day is it?

"Squirrel, come back to me. It's over. Your family is already gone; they aren't asking anymore. Come back to us. I'm here for you, just follow my voice."

Sunny's voice cut through the tension.

"How do you know what she's freaking out about?"

"Because, we talked about it a few times. We talk about everything."

I was vaguely aware of other voices floating around the room. A flashlight shone in my eyes, and I heard the Nurse's familiar lilt.

"She's healthy, just give her a little more time to come around. I think she'll be okay."

"I'm here." The caressing stopped as I sat upright. "Sorry, just had a moment."

I looked around at the worried faces of my conspirators and the Nurse. With a weak smile I tried to regain my footing in the current moment. "Where is Paul, did you get him cleaned up?"

Cal sat beside me and patted my hand.

"He is being buried beside his family right now. We had a small memorial ten minutes ago. Vincent said some nice words. If you would like to, someone can take you out to say farewell."

I knew what had occurred without needing to ask; someone had granted Paul's request. I mumbled a weak "sure" and let Randolph guide me out to the graves in the yard. I noticed my shoelaces had been removed as well as my weapons. Bowing my head I said a few prayers for the souls of the family I'd sacrificed for Daemon's admission to the group.

I remembered my parent's begging me, in turn, to end their suffering after they'd been infected and Owen weeping in pain. I prayed for all of them to a deity I struggled to have faith in. Hoping for everyone who'd passed to find peace. I neglected to pray for my own soul; it felt a lost cause.

"I'm better now. Let's go inside."

Randolph stayed close as I trudged up the porch stairs and into the crowded abode. He watched me with concern as though I may pass out at any instant.

"I'm fine Randolph. Thanks, though."

"Just wanted to be sure you wasn't going to drop."

Left on my own, I sat down on the now empty couch. Chase popped his head around the corner and knocked lightly on the door frame.

"Knock knock. Feel up for some company?"

"Of course. Is your wife trailing you?"

He laughed as he joined me. He took off his sunglasses; the pale ovals surrounded by pink skin revealed his most recent sunburn.

"Nope, Sunny is in the back having a snack. And a lunch. And possibly dessert."

The tips of his mouth reached the far sides of his face as he beamed.

"It's good she's eating enough. We all want the baby to be born healthy."

"I just wish we had a way to find out the due date and the sex of the baby. It'd be nice to know what to name the kid."

"Really? I thought you'd be worried about getting surprised with triplets or something." I teased.

"That would be nice, but I think that's plenty of small talk for now. I know you've had a bad day, and that's fine. We all have those moments, yours just had witnesses. Thing is though, we need to know what you want to do when we get to Winter Haven tomorrow."

My body stiffened.

"I guess we'll evaluate the National Guard Armory and raid what we can if possible. If it looks like a place we can make a new life at, we may give it a shot for a long-term home."

"What if it's overrun or barren? What if we can't survive there?"

I shrugged with more nonchalance than I felt.

"Then we choose a new place and move on until we either find a new residence or maybe go back northeast and rebuild our old camp. That's all we can do for now."

Chase stroked his chin as he sat. I recognized it as a sign of weighing decisions; I'd seen the gesture a million times working in sales.

"What are you thinking?"

I made a point of sitting so that I appeared relaxed. I tried to watch his reaction with my peripheral vision; I wanted Chase to feel comfortable enough to speak freely.

"I'm just wondering if we should just go back and rebuild before the winter makes gathering food too difficult." He said as though the words tumbled out. Sitting a bit straighter, he pressed on. "There can't be anything in this place we can't find where we already lived. Our attackers are dead and we know the land. We built a home once, we could do it again."

"I agree."

Chase perked up.

"But we have to check if there are items we need. We're dangerously low on medical supplies and ammunition. We need more food that will last without refrigeration; not to mention vehicles with large gas cans for spare fuel, and tools to make a new camp happen. A military installation could have all of this. If it was overrun or abandoned, most of those things could still be sitting there for the taking. We have to try."

He smiled.

"Good deal. I'll spread the word." He rose to rejoin the others, pausing in the doorway. "What if there's nothing?"

"Then we go to the next idea; probably return to where we started and hope we can make it through another winter and get the gardens going again."

He tapped the door frame with his knuckles twice and faded away. I laid back and fell into a restless slumber.

CHAPTER 30 OCTOBER 26TH YEAR 2

The armory was a bust. We had to put down fleshies for nearly an hour and we only found a handful of ammo and eight MREs. The vehicles had long since gone with the usable arms. The only things worthwhile were the dozen folding shovels with sharpened edges; they made great weapons and tools and came with nice carry cases.

Disheartened by the lack of success, we started to look nearby for an acceptable place to pass the day. Wandering up the street a bit, we found a trail of cardboard signs. Each one bore an arrow directing 'any living soul of honorable intentions' to a safe residence.

"Probably been posted for the last year; those people are likely gone already." Someone exclaimed as Daemon pointed out the placards during an hourly check-in.

I scrutinized the nearest sign. The marker wasn't runny and the cardboard was stiff to the touch.

"We're following them." I announced, pulling out a baggie of gator jerky. Glancing around I saw confusion and amusement.

"Someone has clearly made this sign recently. It rained a few days ago and this is just a box with marker; no way it would've survived the downpour. Someone around here has left us an open invitation. We're in no position not to accept. We're going to follow the signs. Cautiously, of course."

"Coolies. I like scavenger hunts." Daemon sat on the roof of the Infiniti. Cal examined the token of hospitality.

"Squirrel is correct. This is recently placed."

Sunny and Chase started putting up the bags of rations. Soon the entire community took the hint and prepared to investigate the opportunity before us.

"Alright then; let's stay alert in case it's a trap and hope for the best."

Following the trail of multi-colored arrows for an hour, we found a sign made of painted wood. Instead of an arrow and the usual message, it read: 'Stay here & wait. Deadly traps ahead. Back every day at dawn'. Below was another cardboard sign: 'blue house across street safe. Stay there if needed'.

"Looks like we gonna bed down o'er there for the rest of the night. What about Cal and Daemon; sign says we meet in the morning?"

I pondered Bubba's question, thankful that the fledgling Undead answered first.

"You guys can go ahead and come get us at dusk. If you aren't sure about these people, just meet them and ask to wait until we get up to follow them."

Seeing the logic in the idea, I nodded.

"Sounds like a plan. Okay by you Cal?"

Caelinus gave a slight bow of assent and we piled into the designated waiting area without any debate.

The blue house was free of bodies or bloodstains. There were blankets and pillows in the rooms and a portable chemical toilet sat beside the porcelain one in the restroom. In the pantry we found: a massive stack of tissue paper, first aid kits, a can opener, four cans of soup, and a gallon of drinking water. There was a stack of sign materials sitting on the dining room table. A small bookshelf in the living room held a variety of books and puzzles; the box of crayons and stack of Disney coloring books were pounced upon by the kids as soon as we walked in.

I whistled, "Nice digs. I already like our hosts."

We parked the SUV and Dodge in the garage and left the Chevy in the driveway. Our essential gear was massed near the door and we explored the pristine house. I felt like I had just entered a hotel on vacation. Wary smiles found their way onto everybody's face.

For the first time in a week, we rested for the second half of the night. The vampires took the centermost room and used some of the cardboard to block out the window for their daytime protection. After the donations were made, the group sat at the table and around the kitchen area to unwind and relax. The adults played with an old poker set while the kids played chutes and ladders. Taking up a spot on the floor in the master bedroom, I fell asleep with hope in mind.

CHAPTER 31 OCTOBER 27TH YEAR 2

At dawn, ten of us waited at the sign to meet our generous host. We carried a couple of rifles, but mostly wore our usual arms. I worried that the person may see the guns and avoid us out of fear, but I refused to be caught in an ambush unprepared.

A few minutes after the first rays of light bathed us in warmth, a voice came out from the bushes.

"Um, hi. Did you guys see the signs?"

We looked around for the source of the voice.

"Yes, we did." I answered. "Where are you?"

"Why do you all have so many guns? Are you soldiers or something?"

Facing the tree the voice seemed to emanate from, I set my bow back over my shoulder and took a step forward, holding my open palms up.

"No, we aren't soldiers. We have the weapons partly for hunting and partly for defense. We don't mean any harm, we just couldn't be sure if this was a trick. Could you please come out here so we know who has been kind enough to lead us to the safehouse?"

After a long silence, a scrawny boy around fourteen years old walked out. He had a crowbar in hand and a Gryffindor Satchel on his shoulder. Adjusting his glasses, he eyed the assembly of relatively clean people carrying swords and came closer.

"Hello." He held his right hand out to me. "My name is Liam."

I shook the outstretched hand with relief mingled with awe.

"Hi, Liam. You can call me Squirrel."
"Seriously?"
I heard muffled giggling from behind me.
"Yes, seriously. So who else is with you?"
"Oh, it's just me and my Gammy. She's back at our place. We haven't had anyone come by before, so she's going to be pretty surprised when I walk in with company." He turned to pet Sindbad. The dog sniffed the teen and let him scratch behind his ears. "You guys seem to be pretty decent. It'll be nice to have someone around to hang out with; just follow me and I'll lead you past the traps."

Liam stood and began to retreat into the shrubbery.

"Wait, Liam."

"Oh, sorry. I forgot to wait for you." He said as he smiled and put his hands in his pockets. "No rush."

I shook my head in bewilderment.
Is this kid for real?

"It's not that; we have others waiting for us. Some of them won't be able to travel for a few more hours. Could we just meet you again with the entire group at dusk?"

He hesitated before speaking.

"That shouldn't be a problem; you could even go with me and help if you wanted. But how many are there total?"

"Total, we are twenty-five: twenty-one adults, four children. We'd be happy to introduce you at the other house and help you with whatever you're doing until then."

"Twenty-five! Wow, I can't believe there are that many of you still alive out here."

Liam started rushing towards the blue building, words pouring out of him faster than beer at a frat party.

"I can't wait to meet everybody. Are any of the kids my age? Where have you all been this year; I thought everyone got infected? I only started doing the signs three months ago, I can't believe that many others found them."

We hurried behind the energized teen.

"Hold on, boy. Wait for us!" Troy yelled as the group laughed and followed.

On reaching the porch, we found Sunny with her spear blocking Liam from entering. The kid turned into a bunny as she demanded to know who he was to come charging up towards her with a crowbar.

"No, Sunny, it's okay. He's the guy we're here to meet." I put my hand on the shaft of the spear, guiding her to put it away. "This is Liam. Liam this is Sunny. Sorry, she's on guard duty, so you kinda freaked her out."

I raised my eyebrows at her while our host cleared his throat and offered a shaky hand.

"Pleasure to meet you ma'am."

Sunny finally moved her weapon from the boy's face and made the greeting. She remained firmly planted in the doorway.

"You too. Sorry, pregnancy hormones. So who's with you out here?"

"Oh, I already told Squirrel and the others; it's just me and my Gammy. Can I go in and meet everyone, please? I haven't seen any other survivors in person for a long time. Squirrel said there were kids, too. It would be nice to have a friend to play with again." He rambled as he kept bobbing his head to each side, trying to see inside.

"Um, sure kid. Go ahead." She moved and waved the eager teen inside before turning to me. "Is this child serious? Just him and his grandmother and he's running around out here alone; do you believe him?"

"Actually, yeah. He's either telling the truth or the best actor I've ever seen."

"Weird."

She walked inside to wake her husband. Liam stood in the living room talking rapidly to each person he saw.

"Does anyone here like games? I have board games and cards at our place; it will be nice to play with more than two people for a change."

Jordy and Michael took to Liam instantly, while the girls just asked him if he had more coloring books. The general expression worn by the adults was one of pleasant amazement. After thirty minutes of small talk – during which I spoke with Daemon and Cal – I interrupted the animated conversation.

"Alright everyone, settle down. Liam said he'll show us up to his place at sunset, but first I agreed to help him with his errand."

"Oh yeah. I'm supposed to be searching for some more gardening supplies and checking the buildings for stuff. You sure you don't mind keeping me company?"

"I'll be happy to help. We'll throw together a quick raiding party and head out." I picked up an empty bag and tossed on my quiver again. "It's the least we can do."

***

Throughout the raid, our crew encountered nineteen Dead. Thankfully, twelve of them were caught in traps Liam had set and posed no danger. The others were dealt with by the gangly teen with a smash of his crowbar to the head. He simply shook off the steel tool and used it to open the locked doors as though he was just strolling through a supermarket; there was no real fear in the way he moved. It appeared to me that he thought of this an adventure, instead of a hazardous endeavor.

"That one was gooey, ick. Think that was my old soccer coach. So, I noticed you guys seem really tense; remind me to make you folks some tea when we get home tonight."

As the day wore on, it felt more like a game than our usual raids. Liam asked about our previous camp, and we filled him in on what had happened in as PG-13 a way as possible.

"They really burned your place down and shot at you? Did they realize the little kids were in there?"

"They didn't care. You and your Gammy have been fortunate not to meet any people like that; it's been a rough year. The world's changed. How did you two manage to stay so safe all this time?"

"We always kept a greenhouse and a bunch of emergency supplies on hand after Hurricane Charley. As soon as the outbreak started, my Pops set up our traps all over the property and showed me how to do the same. He made me stay with Gammy while he went out to make more traps and always came back with more stuff we might need."

I looked at the writhing rotted zombies in one of the traps; there was no way for them to get out without getting even more stuck, probably destroyed. Liam looked at the gray-skinned corpse in the sundress, before throwing a rock at its head. His aim was good, and the creature slumped into a true death. The boy smiled as he persisted with his answer.

"He used to be an engineer in the Army and he built us a rain-catcher and a water purifier. He ran out and got all the solar panels he could find and hooked them up so we wouldn't need a generator. My Pops left us with all the stuff we'd need for at least a year and taught me everything for when our stock ran low. He was awesome."

He zoned out for a second and took a long breath. The boy's eyes softened.

"May I ask what happened to your father?"

"He died from his cancer. He was diagnosed stage three about a month before the outbreak. One night he went to bed and when I came in to bring him his breakfast…"

I saw the tears welling up and put my arm around his shoulders.

"I understand. You don't have to talk about it if you don't want to. Do you want to take a lunch break?"

He nodded and the five of us had lunch in a church across from the park. Sitting on the wooden pews, we ate our meal in silence. Once finished, we checked the office for first aid kits and left the house of God. The sun was high overhead and we circled back to the blue house.

Returning from the trip near evening, we found the community sitting in the living room or waiting with the cars. Our belongings were ready for transport when we walked in the door.

"Eager to go guys?" Troy teased at the sight.

With nervous grins, the group nodded or chuckled.

Daemon glanced at the crossbowman before rising to greet the stranger in the room.

"Hi, I'm Daemon and this is Cal. We were asleep when you were here before."

Cal joined his protégé and offered his hand to our host.

"It's a pleasure to meet you, Liam. We appreciate you and your grandmother leading us here and allowing us to stay here for the day."

"Not a problem. We haven't seen any other living people in person for nearly a year; it will be nice to have the company. It's just not the same over the internet. Are you all ready to go to the house? I'm not sure we have enough room, but we can always add traps around this one and the one next door for everyone to live here."

I think I heard necks crack as we did double takes and eyes widened.

"Did you say you talk to people online?" I asked with air I'd forgotten to breath.

"Yeah, my Pops set us up with a satellite receiver like the cable companies use so we could maintain service if they lost power. Why?"

I sat on the thick cream carpet and let his words sink in.

"Liam, who do you talk to online? Where are the other survivors?"

He looked at me like I'd just asked him if the sky was blue.

"The people outside of the quarantine zone. No one inside seems to have a connection. Mostly, I video chat with people in Canada and the UK, but sometimes I load a language translator and talk to people in other places."

My world went tilty and exploded for a second.

We're in a fucking quarantine. The world abandoned us in the shithole. This can't be real.

"Squirrel, are you okay? You look like you might puke. Why is everyone so quiet?" Liam said as he watched our community absorb the news he'd just dropped on us like an atomic bomb.

Cal was the first to reclaim the ability to speak.

"Well, it makes sense. Epidemic like this, you just contain and clean up after it dies out. Very prudent. Also horribly inconvenient for those of us trapped inside the net, but prudent nonetheless."

He breathed deeply and looked concerned before continuing.

"Liam, we were unaware that there were other survivors in the world, so this has been a bit of a shock to us. Could you please excuse us for a moment? Perhaps you'd like to freshen up or help yourself to some food in the kitchen."

"Oh. Wow, sorry guys; I really thought you knew. Yeah, I'll just go chill in the other room for five or ten minutes and look through what we gathered today."

The adolescent hustled out of the room with his shoulders hunched and his face scarlet.

"Squirrel, we have a major problem. Did anyone tell the lad about Daemon and myself?"

I shook the stupor off.

"No. I thought it might be best to ease him and his grandmother into that after we'd had a proper chance to meet. Why is that the problem? We just found out the rest of the world locked us up in a zombie playground and they are out there going about their regular days playing on the fucking computer and not dodging cannibal rapists."

Most of the assembly sat in silence. Randolph stood.

"I think I'll take the kids out of here."

"Wait." Cal blocked him. "We need everyone to make sure not to say anything about vampires; including the children. Daemon and I need all of you to help us hide our kind's existence."

Ellen stood up and hugged Cal.

"We won't tell you drink blood Uncle Cal. Promise."

Bobbi and Michael both agreed and went to follow Randolph away from the grown up talk. Jordy nodded but remained seated.

"Me too. I won't say anything if you don't want."

"Fine, no one will say anything about Undead people. Ellen's Mom and me are gonna get the kids in the other room with Liam; someone fill us in on why later. C'mon Jordy."

The boy remained seated.

"No, I'm old enough to stay. I've been through adult stuff, it's time I got treated like one; you aren't my parent."

"He can stay." I realized the voice was mine. "The kid is almost Liam's age and he's right. He may not be old enough for some of the responsibilities, but I think he understands and does enough to sit in on meetings."

"Your call. Alright you three, let's go play a game with the new boy."

The five exited and we sat to hear out the Roman.

~ 345 ~

"Floor is yours Cal. We won't say anything, but I'd like to know why it's so damned important after what we just learned."

Assuming a soldier's posture, he explained.

"If they chat with the rest of the world, anything we tell them could become known by the entire population outside this area. If the remainder of the world is intact, then the laws of our kind are as well. The most important of which is preventing our existence from being known. It is essential to the survival of our people that we remain a secret. Otherwise, things can become strained between both of our species."

"What does that matter if we're here and the other vamps are out there?" Chase snapped. His fist was clenched so tightly, his knuckles were white and a vein protruded in his neck. "If we're stuck here, waiting to die – which would starve you two out as well – why should we care what happens beyond the boundary?"

"Because, if we comply, I may be able to signal others of our kind to assist us in leaving this quarantine. Also, I do have others I care about and I would not like to cause them immense suffering or execution. The added potential for an interspecies war is a factor as well, and should be of concern to you."

Chase leapt to his feet, fury jumping off of him like bolts of electricity.

"I'll keep the secret either way, but if you think you can get us out of here, do it. I don't want to sit here waiting to die and praying my wife and baby make it through labor when they could deliver in a hospital instead.

I shouldn't have had to be stuck in this cesspool of decay, watching people I cared about die and never knowing what happened to my family. I shouldn't have needed to hack off my arm. Do what you have to, but now that I know about the quarantine, I'm getting my wife and myself the hell out of here."

He waved his stump as frustration poured out with his tears. Sunny hugged him and they cried together.

"We'll get out. It's okay, honey. It'll be okay." She repeated as she rubbed his back in wide circles. Others in the group broke down into tears as we all reflected on our losses. The meaninglessness of it all was unbearable.

"Caelinus and I will do whatever we can. We aren't going anywhere without you guys. As soon as we find out where the safe zone is, we can all work our way to it."

I clasped Daemon's hand.

"It's agreed: no one knows anything about vampires. We'll split the group into day and night with a few doing an in-between shift, so these two don't stick out. From now on the donations schedule isn't written down. Keep the donations private and hide any marks. If we can't get help from the vampiric society outside the infected zone, we move to meet them at wherever the border is. The Pact is a secret we keep for the rest of our lives, and one we'll need to maintain until we're out of the quarantine."

Our fate chosen, we composed ourselves and called the others from the room. Troy comforted Seth in the other room while he explained things to Randolph and Ellen's mother.

Seth took the news worse than Chase; he couldn't get over the fact that he'd been starved into eating a woman because of some unknown quarantine line. He refused to go with us. Instead, Seth marched out to the car and picked up his pistol. Troy pursued him and lunged for the gun.

Several of us watched horror-stricken as he put the barrel against his temple and sprayed his brains over the driveway. The blast sounded louder than any I'd ever heard and I could see the wraith of smoke that followed the pink spray of his blood. Troy reached his friend too late to do anything but topple into a heap beside the corpse.

The younger kids were kept from the gruesome view. Jordy stood pale and sniffling as he choked back his dinner; his posture straightened as he walked inside the house. Liam stood in a puddle of his own pigeon-laced bile while he stared at the body from the porch steps.

"What happened? Why would he do that?" He asked no one in particular as he heaved and wept.

No one answered him at first. Troy wailed and cussed over Seth's warm remains. Someone went inside and returned with the military shovels and started the hole three feet from the body. No one spoke except Troy and he only spoke to the spirit of his companion. I did my best not to listen to the grief in his voice as I accepted one of the spades and dug. I found my voice in the din of hard earth being moved and bawling.

"Liam, please go home tonight. We need the night to mourn our friend and wrap our heads around everything. I'm sorry. Please tell your Gammy we appreciate the hospitality you two have offered and we'll be happy to come over tomorrow evening."

The sickened boy wiped his mouth and left at a run. We buried Seth by starlight. Each person took a turn standing at the unmarked grave and saying his or her goodbye. Some mumbled prayers, some cursed him, and others just stood in lamentation.

One by one, we entered the house to push away the sorrow with busywork and planning. Troy insisted on being left alone. As the group split in half to take watch or sleep, I curled up next to Daemon. I needed someone to talk to. We spoke for hours about what the truth meant until I drifted off to sleep against his chest. The night was restless and I frequently stirred; each time I found Daemon's powerful arms wrapping around me, protecting me from my nightmares.

CHAPTER 32 OCTOBER 28TH YEAR 2

The week passed in blur rampant with bewilderment and amusement. We followed Liam through nearly an acre of traps, spike pits, and sections of various fences arranged in labyrinthine style. Our deflated band of twenty-four abandoned souls trailed behind the adolescent guide in twos and threes. Every bunch was laden with belongings and supplies and carrying a dozen different conversations. Even Sindbad had been recruited into carrying medical supplies strapped to his back in two handbags.

The house is a Tudor with three large greenhouses in back, a large garage that's used for storage since the protective measures prevent vehicle traffic, a massive satellite receiver, a dozen fruit trees, solar panels on the roofs as well as platforms, and plenty of space. As we came past the final picket white fence, a figure stood in the front door calling out to us.

"Liam, where are your manners? Bring those people up here and make a proper introduction; they'll want set their belongings down and rest awhile before you start showing them around."

"Yes, Gammy." Liam quickly veered away from the orange tree and led us to the door. "Squirrel, this is my Gammy, Edith Hedburg. Gammy, this is the lady I told you about and her friends."

His part done, the teen stood to the side. The overhead light flicked on, startling and blinding me for a moment. When my vision adjusted I looked at the elderly woman who was already giving me a hug and welcoming us to her home. She was my height – which is to say short – and made me think of Betty White; she looked like a typical sweet old lady, but her eyes and voice betrayed her energy and zest. I liked her instantly.

"Thank you for having us Mrs. Hedburg. We appreciate the hospitality and we'll earn our keep while we're here."

She released me from her grip and stepped back grinning.

"It's no trouble. I'm sorry to hear about what happened last night. Hopefully your friend will be the last to go that way. Please come in and get unpacked, I'm about to start on supper. I'll be doing my video blog in an hour, and I'd love to introduce all of you to my fans."

"Gammy's a worldwide internet sensation. She talks about all sorts of random stuff."

"Oh yes, if anyone would like to use one of the computers, we have a couple of laptops in the family room hooked up and charged. Feel free to make yourselves at home and catch up on current events; Liam says you've been in the dark since the outbreak began. Those damned contaminated Botox shots..."

"Yeah, who'd have thought injecting deadly toxins into your forehead could turn out badly." I grumbled before realizing I was being rude. "I'm sorry about the outburst. I think we'll get settled in and cleaned up a little. Some of us will help with dinner; we brought some food with us. Thank you again for your help."

She smiled and took Cal by the arm.

"That's alright. And you, handsome man, can keep me company while I show you around. You can even sleep in my room. I can think of dozens of ways for you to earn your keep."

She winked at him while her grandson mocked puking before leading us on a brief tour of the rooms. At each stop bags were unloaded and weapons removed. Edith insisted we take the rest of the hour to wash the crust off of us, volunteering to lend the elder vampire a hand with the loofah until he blushed like an altar boy in Vegas. Everybody giggled, stretched, and rubbed their aches as we made it to the bathrooms to clean up.

The miracle of warm showers greeted several of us as we took two-minute turns washing the last year away. The young kids were bathed in a tub first, with poor Jordy hopping in after. Most of the adults shared. The vamps, Troy, Bubba, Vincent, and myself volunteered to take the final turns; even ice cold it was wonderful. Seeing everyone fresh and thoroughly clean by the glow of electric lights amazed me.

Even if we don't get back to civilization, this wouldn't be a bad way to live.

END BOOK ONE OF THE NOVA NOCTE SERIES

Please continue the tale with:

Quarantined in Chaos & Retaking Oblivion

CHAPTER 1 NOVEMBER 25TH - YEAR 2

Tonight's new moon was perfect. After the busy month at Edith Hedburg's place, it was nice to watch Daemon and Cal fly without worrying about getting caught. It wasn't that our group distrusted the sweet – if flirtatious – old gal; it's just that her being an internet sensation put the two vampires in a predicament.

We have to keep the world beyond the zombie quarantine from learning about vamps and Edith has a tendency to tell all in her video blogs. Our Undead allies have taken to walking on patrols for over a mile before being able to hit the skies; watching them has been akin to witnessing a bird after it's feathers have been clipped.

The other two dozen people in our community have become polarized; most want to remain here with Mrs. Hedburg and her grandson Liam, but a handful are pushing to travel. They think if we manage to work our way from Central Florida to Canada, we'll be welcomed out of the quarantine. I can picture the journey: half-rotted fleshies, cannibals, rogue vampires, pillaging humans, and almost no supplies or shelter.

Sounds fun. I can't fault my friends for wanting to try to get back to the normal world, though.

Sunny and Chase are desperate to escape this mess; they don't want their child born into this life. They just want their bundle of joy to arrive in a clean hospital with a real doctor far from the decay that surrounds us here. Cal and I spent hours yesterday convincing them to wait until the elder Undead could hear back from his contacts in the vampire community. Sunny threw herself into potting carrots in the new greenhouse. Her husband slathered sunscreen on his face and stormed out the front door.

"I'm gonna find a buddy and clear some of the Dead from the traps." He yelled to us and grabbed a machete from the porch.

Cal, Daemon, and I have been spending a lot of time at the blue safe-house down the hill from the Hedburgs. With Liam's guidance, the house has been rigged with solar panels and we've added a greenhouse. Our group has settled into the two houses, but a lavender one nearby should be ready soon; we're still searching for more solar panels and materials for traps. The three of us only venture up to the main house when Edith isn't doing her video blogs; we don't want the outside world to be able to recognize us in case we have to cross the border in disguise.

Generally we only go there to check on the rest of our community and use the internet. Poor Cal spends an hour every night emailing coded messages back and forth. I got worried this evening when his brow furrowed and he stopped responding to the contacts. I waited for him, Daemon, and me to be alone in the remote abode before asking about his reaction.

"They may be working out logistics. This endeavor could take days or months; I'm getting little response thus far. No one is permitted past the quarantine line, not even aircraft."

Caelinus rubbed his eyes, gradually working his fingertips out to his temples.

"But these people will help us, right?" I asked.

He turned to me. Daemon avoided my glance and pretended to be absorbed in his Buffy comic book.

"Some of them might assist us, yes. However, I'm unsure how many of our people they will opt to take. Nor do I yet know the penalty Daemon and I will be subject to upon arrival outside of the blockade."

I stiffened as I watched Cal's face drain of the minimal color it contained. Daemon winced and put aside the comic. Neither would look at me.

What could scare these two this much?

***

Thank you for reading my book. If you enjoyed it, please take a moment to leave me a review at your favorite retailer. I look forward to hearing your thoughts on my Facebook and Twitter pages as well. Thank you.

About the Author

Melissa Gibbo has been living and working in the Orlando area for nearly ten years. During this time she has worked at both Walt Disney World and Universal Orlando Resort. She has a large extended family, a loving wife, and three evil but loved cats. Melissa grew up in Columbus, Georgia and visits as often as possible.

Made in the USA
Columbia, SC
12 July 2022